There is no more powerful force on Krynn than a dragon, and Dhamon Grimwulf is a singular one. Transformed by the sorcery of a dying shadow dragon, he is a former dark knight trapped in a dragon's body, a creature both magnificent and cursed. Making the best of things, Dhamon has claimed a part of the overlord Sable's vast swamp as his own, is eluding and slaying her minions—and collecting an impressive horde of treasure.

But as his might and riches grow, so does his emptiness. His mounds of steel pieces cannot ease his loneliness. He misses human society.

Born a man, Dhamon Grimwulf decides to try to regain his humanity. With his stoic draconian companion, he embarks on a search for the necessary magic.

Their quest leads from Dhamon's steamy lair to the forests of the Qualinesti, where he is reunited with a dear friend who agrees to help in his goal. Their path leads to the Lake of Death, which covers the fabled elven city of Qualinost, destroyed and submerged during the War of Souls. But the magic contained in the Lake of Death is elusive, and he must accept the aid of dead elf wizards who may have ulterior motives.

It all ends back home, in the foul swamp, where Dhamon must prove his honor by fighting Sable for a final release from unhappiness and torture.

The former dark knight turned champion of Goldmoon, Dhamon Grimwulf made his initial appearance in *Dawning of a New Age*, the first book in the Fifth Age trilogy. His adventures continued in *Downfall, Betrayal*, and *Redemption*, all written by Jean Rabe, who brings his saga to a sensational conclusion in *The Lake of Death*.

The Age of Mortals

Conundrum
Jeff Crook

The Lioness
Nancy Varian Berberick

Dark Thane
Jeff Crook

Prisoner of Haven
Nancy Varian Berberick

The Lake of Death
Jean Rabe

THE LAKE OF DEATH

JEAN RABE

THE LAKE OF DEATH
©2004 Wizards of the Coast, Inc.

Distributed in the United States by Holtzbrinck Publishing. Distributed in Canada by Fenn Ltd.

Distributed to the hobby, toy, and comic trade in the United States and Canada by regional distributors.

Distributed worldwide by Wizards of the Coast, Inc. and regional distributors.

Cover art by Matt Stawicki
Map by Dennis Kauth
First Printing: October 2004
Library of Congress Catalog Card Number: 2004106769

9 8 7 6 5 4 3 2

US ISBN: 0-7869-3364-X
UK ISBN: 0-7869-3365-8
620-17580-001-EN

U.S., CANADA,
ASIA, PACIFIC, & LATIN AMERICA
Wizards of the Coast, Inc.
P.O. Box 707
Renton, WA 98057-0707
+1-800-324-6496

EUROPEAN HEADQUARTERS
Wizards of the Coast, Belgium
T Hofveld 6d
1702 Groot-Bijgaarden
Belgium
+322 467 3360

Visit our web site at **www.wizards.com**

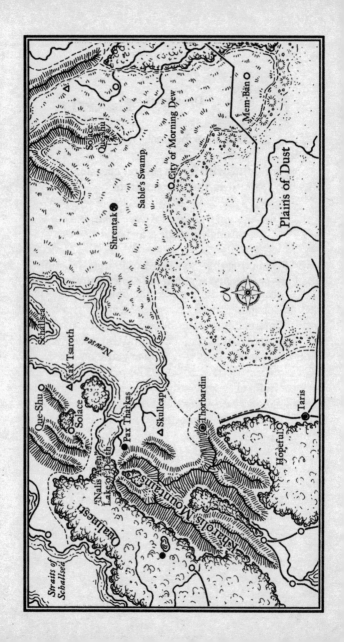

CHAPTER

1

The dragon burst from the lake in a tremendous spray of water, midnight black and brilliant blue scales gleaming like perfect gems in the light of two full moons. It took to the sky and spread its wings, hanging above the steamiest land in Ansalon. The great beast seemed the sum of every dragon on Krynn, of every creature that lived in the primordial swamp. Elegant in form, it was at the same time breathtakingly beautiful and awe-inspiringly terrifying. Demonic and divine, repulsive and majestic—it was all of those things at once.

The creature dipped its head, drew its wings in close and dived. It became a stroke of glistening blue-black that arced down like lightning then rose at the very last instant to unfurl its wings before crashing. Beating them almost imperceptibly to keep itself a breath above the water, it glided forward. Dangling front talons, it brushed across the surface of the lake, heading toward the marshy shore. It settled, half on the bank and half in the shallows, stretching its neck into a row of young cypress trees that grew beyond the lake's edge, its nostrils quivering, jaws opening, tongue snaking out to seek prey.

Suddenly the dragon clamped its teeth on a creature hiding in the small trees, a thing that looked like a cross between a man and a lizard. Called a bakali, the creature was thickly muscled and had the girth of an ogre. It carried a double-bladed poleaxe and boasted a mouthful of jagged teeth that added to its fierce countenance. To the dragon, the bakali scout was a nuisance, certainly not a threat, and was almost beneath its notice.

Almost.

The haft of the creature's poleaxe splintered like a dry twig when the dragon slammed its jaws shut. The creature's bones broke just as easily, and the dragon swallowed it in one gulp. Instantly the undergrowth sprang alive. A force of bakali had been quietly approaching behind the scout, each scaly soldier weighed down with weapons—axes, swords, spears, knives, and javelins. Now they rushed the dragon as one, whooping a long, hideous war cry, panicking parrots and egrets that flew screeching from the trees to add to the hellish cacophony.

The largest of the bakali barked orders over his shoulder as he closed in on the dragon, his commands a series of hisses and clicks. There were well more than a hundred bakali, and as the first wave reached the dragon—with spears and javelins thrusting forward—their war whoops turned to screams.

The dragon surged against the bakali, slamming them into the row of cypresses, snapping the trees and biting at the creatures, tossing its head back lustily as it swallowed bakali after bakali. At the same time it slashed with its front claws, cutting through the soldiers' thick flesh, slicing several in two and causing blood to splatter and rain everywhere. Its huge tail whipped back and forth, batting away the ones who were splashing into the water and trying to come at it from the side, its rear claws pinning the nearest bakali beneath it, drowning them in the shallows. It lowered its head and skewered a few of the berserk creatures on its splendid horns, then with a flick tossed them yards away and began to spear more.

The sounds of the fight were deafening—the war cries from the still-attacking bakali, the death-screams of the closest victims, the cracking of weapon hafts and tree limbs and bakali bones, the ghastly crunching as the dragon continued to devour its foes, and now all of it was topped by a great whoosh of wind created by the dragon's beating wings. The rush of air hurled many of the bakali to the ground. Those still on their feet fell victim to the dragon's powerful jaws, but despite the carnage and their dwindling numbers, the bakali did not retreat.

The bank was slick with blood as the dragon crawled up onto higher ground, crushing a dozen bakali beneath its massive body. More than half the enemy were down, dying, or slaughtered, and the remaining creatures continued to press their hopeless onslaught as the dragon edged deeper into the trees. A barrel-chested bakali directed the soldiers to concentrate on the dragon's front legs and to stay clear of its haunches, where its tail was proving especially lethal. Another ordered those in the second rank to hurl spears and knives at the dragon's head. Seemingly oblivious, the dragon persisted in its wholesale butchering of the bakali until one clever foe stepped in close and shoved a javelin between a narrow gap in the scales on its chest. Black blood spurted from the wound. The valiant bakali hollered excitedly and again swung hard with his cutlass at the spot. This drew more blood and compelled the dragon's attention, briefly giving it pause.

A claw swept in and snatched up the offending bakali, lifting him high while ignoring the frenzied blows of his comrades. The dragon brought the soldier up close, holding him even with its ink-black eyes and studying him intently for a moment before squishing him. Then the dragon dropped the pulpy mass and returned its focus to the bakali that were swarming around and trying to breach its armor-like scales. It growled horribly at them, the first sound it had uttered, then it did a surprising thing—it closed its eyes. Despite the chaos of the battle, the dragon was relaxing, releasing the tight control it had been maintaining over its innate fear aura. Liberated, the magical wave pulsed outward, sweeping over the surviving bakali soldiers and instantly filling them with bone-numbing fright. Most of them dropped their weapons and ran pell-mell, crashing through the foliage with no thought as to where they were going—as long as they got far away from the dragon. Only a mere handful were able to rally against the dragonfear and stand their ground, and these were dealt with swiftly.

In the span of only a few minutes all, of the scaly soldiers were slain or routed. The dragon plucked the javelin still sticking from its chest and tossed it into a bed of ferns as it watched the last few survivors flee deep into the swamp. It could smell their fear and their sweat even after they were lost from view, and something else—the coppery scent of blood—its own, and that of the fallen bakalis. Those acrid smells, coupled with the foul redolence of its own body, overpowered the richer and more pleasant odors of the fen, and therefore angered the dragon.

It roared its displeasure that the land near its precious lake had been sullied and the air tainted. Then it pushed aside a bakali corpse that had fallen too near a red chokeberry bush, a favorite plant of the dragon's. It began to rake aside other bodies, then stopped and raised its head, nostrils quivering, picking up a new odor—the faint trace of sulfur evoking a blacksmith's shop. It spun to face the source.

"That rout was impressive. Truly impressive." The whispered words came from the base of a willow tree that reached high above the young cypresses. "I started running when I heard the commotion, fast as I could, but by the time I got here, it was all over."

The speaker swept aside a veil of leaves and emerged, plodding toward the dragon, making his way around the bakali corpses and stopping to tug free a few coin pouches he spotted. The scent of sulfur grew stronger as he approached.

The newcomer was a sivak draconian, a scaled creature, manlike in form but far more powerful, birthed centuries past by the goddess Takhisis from the corrupted egg of a silver dragon. His kind usually had wings and, like the dragon, could soar above this swamp and any other land, but this particular sivak could not fly. Scarred, knobby patches of hide marked where his wings once were.

"You could have left at least one of those beasts for me. You know I enjoy a good fight now and again."

"You'll have other chances," the dragon growled softly, so that only the faintest tremor rippled through the ground beneath the sivak's feet. "As you know, this wasn't the first force sent against me, and it won't be the last, but yes, next time, I'll try to remember to save a few of the stupid bakali just for you."

"Disgusting beasts they are."

The sivak prodded one of the dead bodies with his foot before stepping over it, and he unsuccessfully tried to conceal a shiver as he paused near an uprooted sapling a few yards from the dragon's snout. The dragon recognized the sivak's discomfort and again suppressed its fear aura.

The sivak quit trembling and nodded his thanks. He pulled a leather satchel off the back of one bakali and put the coin pouches and a few other trinkets inside it. Then he drew closer to the dragon, keeping himself from gagging at the great stench. Though he was large for a draconian and much larger than a man, his broad shoulders barely came up to the dragon's dewclaw. He put the satchel on his own back, looked up into the dragon's monstrous black eyes, and shook his head wearily.

"Dhamon, I well know that won't be the last army to come for a visit. There'll be another and another. Each one has been larger. First, men, a handful, then practically a whole army led by a Knight of Neraka with braids and medals on his chest and a sorcerer in tow. Now bakali, next spawn and abominations I reckon, maybe something worse, and all of them loyal to that demon of a dragon Sable."

"Maybe," the dragon said after a moment. He lowered his head until the barbels that hung from his jaw grazed the ground. A slimy rope of spittle edged over his lower lip. "Maybe, Ragh. Maybe she'll send something to surprise us one of these days . . . something worse."

"Oh, I think you can very definitely count on worse coming our way." The sivak let out a deep breath. "I keep telling you, it's not safe around here, Dhamon."

The dragon cast his gaze about the marshy landscape, taking in the broken bodies of the bakali and the pools of blood that glimmered darkly in the light of the moons Solinari and Lunitari. The air was still, and everything was eerily silent; not even the insects were chirping in the aftermath of the fight.

"Not safe here, Ragh? Not safe for the bakali, don't you mean? Or any spawn. Sable's minions are not welcome in my lands."

"These aren't *your* lands, Dhamon," the sivak muttered under his breath. "Sable certainly doesn't see it that way. She thinks this whole swamp is hers. She created it, after all."

The dragon pretended to ignore him, turned and started west, careful not to trample the sivak in the process or disturb the prized chokeberry. The sivak was quick to follow, pausing only to grab at a few bakali corpses where the moonlight glinted off valuables. Here a well-made halberd, there some matched throwing daggers and another coin pouch, a small bag filled with ivory belt buckles, another pouch filled with pearls—all things the bakali had no doubt taken off hapless victims. After several minutes there was a flutter overhead, the birds finally returning to the trees. From somewhere along the shores of the lake behind them came a series of splashes, likely large alligators and gar getting busy feeding on the bakali remains.

The dragon's course took them through a stand of ancient locusts and water hickories, the canopy so dense that the bright moonlight was reduced to haunting, infrequent beams. The cattails and marsh bulrushes were thick between the trunks, and there was a sizeable patch of pickerel weed stalks and tall switch grass. Salt-marsh fleabane was growing nearby. The camphor scent its purple flowers gave off was heavy in the humid air. Beneath it was the sweet odor of wild azaleas.

In spite of Dhamon's size, he was able to slip through the maze of swampland. Though neither he nor the draconian were attempting to be quiet, the animals that made their homes in this desolate area, mainly snakes and lizards that lounged on the high branches, barely gave the odd pair passing notice. A king snake wrapped around the base of a green ash only half-opened its eyes. The creatures were used to the draconian and the dragon by now and knew they were irrelevant to the pair.

The canopy thinned where the dragon crossed a wide stream, and the moonlight spilled down on a clearing circled predominantly by weeping cedars and black oaks. In the center was a bog patch swarming with craneflies and mosquitoes. The dragon and sivak skirted the bog on their way to a hoary shagbark, one of the giants of the swamp. Dhamon pressed against the trunk as he went, letting the uneven knobs scratch his side. Behind the tree lay an even denser weave of branches. Though a man would be blind here, the dragon could make out a small rise and further a cave opening that was well masked by a cascade of vines. Dhamon exhaled, his breath fluttering the vines and effectively parting before him. He stepped through, then listened for the sivak to follow.

The draconian's claws clicked lightly against the stone floor, which was smooth from the frequent passage of the dragon. One hand brushed against the side of the cave. Here the darkness was so black that neither of them could see, and shortly, the sivak took his hand from the wall and mumbled sing-song words that caused a globe of pale blue light to settle in his open palm. It was one of the small number of modest spells he had learned by studying under sorcerers he'd met and later killed during his centuries on Krynn. It was a spell he found exceedingly useful in this swamp, and in particular, in Dhamon's dark lair.

The magic light revealed moisture-slick walls of gray granite that sparkled with crystals and veins of minerals, surrounding a floor that sloped down at a relatively steep angle. The sivak hurried past the dragon and took the lead, holding the light high, and with a few arcane words, coaxing an even brighter illumination. The wide passage narrowed as it plunged, and Dhamon could barely squeeze through the entrance. Then it opened into a massive chamber, one side of which was filled with mountains of coins, piles of decorative weapons, and mounds of other shiny baubles the dragon had collected during the past several months. The sivak added the halberd and the bag of ivory belt buckles to a pile.

The air in the cave was warm and suffocating, filled with the malodorous scent of the dragon. Ragh fought against the bile he felt rising in his throat and breathed shallowly as he concentrated. After a few minutes he was able to inure himself to the awful smell.

"Sable will find this place eventually and send her force right into our lair," the draconian said. "She's looking for it now. I spent enough years under her claw to know how she thinks, and don't think she won't discover this place, Dhamon. She will. She makes it a point of pride to know about everything in this damnable swamp."

The dragon stretched out on the far side of the chamber and rested his head on a large mound of steel pieces. He snaked a claw forward and with a talon drew a crystal ball toward him. It was a souvenir from a Knight of Neraka sorcerer he'd bested and brutally killed, who had been among the most recent attackers.

"Well, Sable hasn't found out about my lair yet, Ragh, or she'd have sent the bakali here tonight. Why send them to the lake? The advantage was mine out in the open. Here they might have trapped me. No, Sable doesn't have a clue . . . yet."

Dhamon began tapping on the crystal until silvery wisps of fog appeared inside it.

The draconian thought a moment and scratched at his chin. "Maybe she didn't send a force here because you're rarely here, Dhamon. Because . . . because you're usually out prowling around the lowlands. Because you like the marsh that's by the lake, and you spend most of your time there. You're almost peaceful by that marsh; you drop your guard. Maybe that's why the bakali attacked there."

"I don't drop my guard," Dhamon growled softly, an old memory tugging at his mind, "and I don't care much for the water. Even the bakali must know that."

"The water hides your scent, so you were able to surprise them."

"Sable's minions are easy to surprise."

The draconian shrugged. "Dhamon, sooner or later she will send an army here—an army so large that even you won't be able to triumph."

"Maybe because she's waiting for me to accumulate more of a horde so she can swoop in and add it to her own. What little I have thus far . . ."

". . . is considerable, Dhamon, and you gain more treasure with every force she sends against you. I don't see the point of collecting all this stuff. Frankly, if we don't do something with it . . ."

Ragh sat the globe of light at his feet, tugged off the backpack, and upended it. Pouches of coins and pearls spilled out, along with a small sculpture of a nightbird that Ragh suspected was magical, and two exceptional daggers with inlaid handles.

Ragh bent and picked up one of the pouches he remembered was filled with pearls. He hefted it as if to judge their value. Then he picked up his light globe again with his other hand. "This hoard is sure to attract Sable, mark my words."

The dragon shifted his head and several coins rolled from the mound and clinked against the floor. The silver wisps brightened in the crystal ball and something indistinct appeared in the center.

"Let her send more bakali and knights against me, wherever she can find me. Let her send all the minions she has."

"You don't mean that."

Dhamon's eyes narrowed. "I do. Perhaps I want Sable to come herself."

The draconian started pacing, the light globe in his hand causing the shadows to dance as he stepped past alcoves and overhangs. "You can't mean that. You can't possibly mean that. Tell me you don't really mean that."

Dhamon didn't reply. He was studying the indistinct something in the crystal ball, cocking his head as if listening to another voice. "Where?" he asked the crystal. "Where?" His eyes narrowed as he leaned his head closer. "Just what is it?"

Ragh stared at him quizzically.

"You've told me the 'where' of it, crystal. Now tell me the 'what.' Saying what I seek is in a lake is not good enough. I repeat, I do not care for lakes, and I will not search one for a mysterious *something*. I need to know what is so important. What?" The object in the crystal remained indistinct. "Tell me!"

What is "what?" Ragh mouthed. It was all mysterious to the sivak, and he wanted to know what Dhamon was talking about, what Dhamon was searching for in the crystal ball, but he knew now wasn't the time. The dragon's rising irritation was already causing the cave floor to tremble ominously.

"What?" Dhamon repeated with a snarl. "What exactly do I need to find?"

Ragh studied his friend, relaxing finally when Dhamon appeared to give up the searching. The sivak had watched Dhamon use the crystal ball before, but he still couldn't figure out how it worked—and neither could the dragon, Ragh guessed. Perhaps they should have left the sorcerer alive and had him work the crystal's magic. Perhaps they should go find another sorcerer . . .

"I should look at that wound."

Dhamon reluctantly glanced up from the crystal. "It will heal on its own. It's not deep." Dhamon idly stirred some of the steel pieces with a talon and drew back from the crystal ball. The silver wisps disappeared. He grunted irritably.

"We've got enough treasure, that's for sure. Pouches of steel pieces, ivory buckles, pearls. We should get far away from here, take the treasure with us."

"The treasure is meaningless," the dragon said. "These steel pieces—as valuable as these things might be, they're worthless to me, yet I find that I want ever more. More!"

The draconian was startled by this statement, and he nearly dropped the light globe and the pouch of pearls. The light flickered and Ragh had to concentrate to make it brighter again.

"I can't walk into a town with a bulging coin purse and rent a room at an inn or buy a lady's company, can

I, Ragh? I don't need expensive clothes. I certainly don't need to buy fancy food. I can eat my enemies when I'm hungry, though the gods know those bakali tasted horrid. I can't spend a single steel piece, no matter how many thousands upon thousands I hoard."

"The places where I would be welcome to spend them, Dhamon, I no longer care to go either," Ragh whispered plaintively.

"So why do I—why does any dragon hoard this stuff?"

Ragh padded over. "Dhamon, I . . ."

"I want more. Like a man who craves ale, I crave wealth." He shook his great head, the barbels knocking loose steel pieces from the mound. The dragon stretched his neck and caught Ragh's stare. Dhamon's eyes held a great sadness. "Senseless for me to have bothered collecting all this from the men Sable sent against me, senseless for both of us. Whatever possesses me to want all of this?"

"Perhaps, Dhamon . . ."

"Maybe it's a dragon's instinct . . . this collecting. Maybe whatever shred of humanity is left in my soul thinks I will someday need these coins and jewels. The gods know that when I ran with Maldred we were always after treasure—never could get enough in those days either. Maybe that piece of me thinks that one day again I'll be able to stroll into a tavern, drop some steel on the bar, and order a tankard of dwarf spirits." He settled his head back down on the coins.

"Yes, maybe someday you'll be human again," the sivak offered consolingly. "There's magic in the world again. You've been consulting the crystal ball about the possibility. I've seen you try it many times. Dhamon . . ."

Dhamon let out a chuckle, the harsh sound bouncing off the walls and causing the stone floor to shudder. A row of spears that had been propped against a wall shifted and a few of them toppled over.

"Ragh, my friend, I stopped being human almost a year ago, remember? You were there when it happened in the mountains, and you followed me here—you, my only friend."

The draconian nudged some spilled coins with a foot. The light caught an old gold one and made it softly gleam. "Of all the places to settle, Dhamon," he scolded. "You could've picked someplace far from an overlord's land. There's nothing special about this damnable swamp—except the constant danger."

"Sable claims it. That's special to me, and I'm claiming some of it as my own—more and more and more of it."

"Stop raging against her, Dhamon. You can't win."

"At least I trouble her."

"Dhamon . . ."

The dragon raised what amounted to a large, scaly eyebrow.

"Dhamon, this swamp isn't safe anymore, if it ever was. Isn't there someplace you'd rather be? Let's leave this place. Let Sable have her damned swamp."

"As I said, I didn't force you to follow me here."

The draconian dropped the pouch of pearls and shifted the light globe to his other hand. "I've no friends either, save you. Where else was I to go?"

Dhamon wrapped his tail around his side, the gesture oddly catlike. After a moment, the sivak tried again.

"You've got wings, Dhamon. You can go anywhere. Don't you want to explore the world? We could go to the Dragon Isles, visit places I haven't seen in decades, places you have never seen—maybe places where even a dragon and a draconian can spend some of this wealth."

"Places that are safe?"

"Places that are safer than this."

The dragon's expression made it clear he was tiring of the discussion. "I have no intention of leaving because of Sable. In fact, I think I'll start expanding my territory some more tomorrow."

"Fine!" The draconian tossed the light globe up and let it hover just below the ceiling. Its glow paled just a bit, and Ragh knew that away from his hand it would go out within minutes. "Fine. Fine. Fine." He ground the ball of his foot against the stone. "Let's go exploring tomorrow—maybe find ways to expand your territory, add to your hoard, whatever you want. Fight all of Sable's armies. Why not . . .?"

A rumble raced through the cavern floor and sent everything to jangling.

"Aw, Dhamon, there must be some place that interests you . . ."

The dragon stared at the crystal ball. "Some place? No. But there is someone."

CHAPTER

2

She wore tattoos on her face not terribly long ago—a lightning bolt and a jay feather, the latter symbolic of her favorite bird, the former declaring that she once claimed a pack of wolves as her family. Fast as lightning the pack used to race along Southern Ergoth's sea cliffs—sometimes in pursuit of prey, but most often just for the sheer exhilaration. It was, perhaps, the best time in her life. There was beauty in the simplicity of those wild days. Now when she thought of that blissful time, she swore she could once again feel the soft, thick-bladed grass beneath her feet and the cool of the woods' afternoon shadows. She could still imagine the sweet, salt-tinged breeze blowing east from the Sirrion Sea and the pleasing sounds of the gulls and blue herons. All of that was several years ago and many, many miles from here.

She hadn't run with wolves since the overlords arrived. The white dragon Frost had descended on the island continent of the Kagonesti elves and turned nearly all of it into a frigid wasteland. Not many of the wolves survived the dragon's coming. Not many of the Kagonesti chose to stay and struggle against the harsh conditions. They left for other lands. Feril left too, though not with any of the nomadic bands of her kinsmen. She struck out on her own, roaming, backtracking, circling, never staying in one spot for more than a few days . . . until she crossed paths with Dhamon Grimwulf and his rag-tag crew—all champions of the legendary mystic healer Goldmoon. For a reason still unknown to her, Feril defied her solitary nature and joined them. She fought at their side, grew close to them, to Dhamon in particular. She gave every ounce of her nature-magic and physical strength at the Window to the Stars, an ancient portal where the dragon overlords gathered one night. She and her companions couldn't best even a single dragon there, but they experienced some measure of victory and gained hope that mortals might someday triumph.

After the Window they had parted company.

The leaving was hard for her, but fated to be, she thought at the time. *Necessary*, she told Dhamon, when he tried to persuade her to stay. She then went to the isle of Cristyne and aided refugees who had fled there from her homeland and elsewhere. The work was hard and rewarding and distracting—she rarely thought of Dhamon. After a year she moved on again—to Witdel, then Portsmith, Gwyntarr, and Caergoth, where at a shop near the docks she paid an old sailor to remove the tattoos that so easily branded her as a Kagonesti. She wasn't trying to hide her elven heritage, as she still wore the fringed leather clothing favored by her people and made no effort to conceal her pointed ears, but she was trying to put distance between herself and her past, and the tattoos were a symbol of the past.

She cut her hair a month ago. Once it had been a gorgeous, unruly mass of curls that cascaded past her shoulders like a lion's mane. Now she was keeping it cropped short, too short to festoon with hawk and jay feathers and painted wooden beads like she used to do. She told herself it was a practical measure, as she was living in the forest now, and long tresses would only become tangled in the lowest branches. In truth, it was one more step in creating a new identity.

Another new start, another new home—this time the Qualinesti forest of Wayreth. There were wolves here— she'd seen their tracks and spoor several times—and right now she was watching one that sat a dozen yards away, across the creek she was bending over to slake her thirst. The gray was a young female, large and well fed, and her eyes met the Kagonesti's, making Feril remember those days of racing along the sea cliffs.

Run with me, the wolf teased with her eyes. There was no misreading the invitation, as Feril understood animals far better than people. *Run with me along this stream. Discover where the water takes us. Run with me, sister.*

A part of Feril wanted to shout yes. *Let's fly like lightning!* This new identity came with new responsibilities, albeit self-imposed ones. She sadly shook her head. *Later, my wolf-sister,* her eyes replied.

"There are men I must find this day," she said aloud. "I have serious work to do."

The wolf tipped her muzzle back and howled softly. Other wolves concealed in the trees to the north answered the cry. A last look at Feril, and she ran toward a copse of river birch to join the hidden pack.

Feril dipped her hands in the creek and splashed water on her face and the back of her neck, cutting the heat of this late summer day. She drank her fill and stood, looking to the trees for some last sign of the wolf, then reluctantly turned in the opposite direction. Keeping after the tracks she'd been so diligently following for the past day and a half, she loped through the high grass and cherry laurel.

There were four or five men, she thought, though she couldn't be entirely certain. It had rained briefly last night, which, though making the forest smell fresh and wonderful, made following the tracks challenging. Fortunately the men were armored and were wearing hard-soled boots. There were other signs she relied on, too—fallen twigs that had been snapped by heavy footsteps, crushed beetles, broken branches on a crowberry shrub, a scraped piece of bark. The men hadn't been building a fire at night, though she could tell where they camped yesterday because of the tamped-down grass and a few discarded apple cores.

"How far ahead are you?" she mused. She knelt beneath a gnarled, striped maple and thrust her fingers into the moist earth. Closing her eyes, she reached out with her senses, her mind touching the husks of long-dead insects, brushing up against the tree's spreading roots. She envisioned herself as the earth, felt low-spreading evergreens and chamomile herbs growing, worms and earwigs gently and tenaciously burrowing. She sensed a doe treading lightly a mile or so away, a rabbit near the doe, two ground squirrels cavorting, a young wolf running. At the edge of her senses was a wild boar in rut. There was no trace of the men. She wasn't near enough yet.

"I will find you," she vowed. "I must." Her new life, in this new place, her self-imposed responsibilities, her pledge to keep the people in these woods safe all depended upon it.

For the better part of the day she continued to track them, stopping from time to time to converse with animals—a family of woodpeckers making its home in a yellow walnut tree, a large starling paralleling her path, and an elderly fox that proved most helpful. The fox had watched the men come this way after dawn. He couldn't tell Feril how many there were, as numbers were unknown to him. *As many or more than the woodpeckers in that tree*, he tried after she persisted.

Four or five, Feril translated, which was already her guess.

The trail led her through an idyllic glade—weeping birch and thin, graceful larches, the bases of which were ringed by hostas, creeping dogwood, and spreading ferns. She slowed her pace for a few minutes so she could better appreciate her surroundings, then, when she passed through the glade and the foliage drastically changed, she started to run.

Abruptly the forest turned repulsive, the trees for the most part dead, the scant living ones scrawny and twisted, looking thoroughly corrupted. The devastation went on as far as she could see—it was a much larger section of scarred woods than what she had passed through a few days ago. Dark magic was in large part to blame, Feril realized, as she noted the scorched perfect circles on the ground and the trunks completely stripped of bark. She'd traveled with the great sorcerer Palin Majere long enough to recognize the remnants of certain spells. But other forces were also responsible; she spotted patches of burned bark and places where hatchets had slashed deeply into maples and elms. To the west she saw the charred remains of a few cabins. To the south of the cabins were large earthen and rock mounds marked by carved, weathered staves. She suspected these were mass graves gone months untended, most likely holding remains of numerous Qualinesti elves. She considered stopping to pay her respects to the fallen, but she did not want to tarry in this unpleasant place. The sooner she was back in a vibrant part of the forest, the better she would feel.

By late afternoon she had passed beyond the bleak woods and was running along a game trail. The section of forest she traveled through now was very old. The giant pines stretched more than two hundred feet into the cloudy sky, and there were oaks with the circumference of a small cottage. Feril had been to the Qualinesti woods some years ago with Palin, when the great overlord Beryl held sway. She had seen with her own eyes how the dragon had used magic to age the trees and cover every bit of earth with something growing. The distorted lushness was a perversion of nature, Feril knew, but she had to admit—then and now—that it was somewhat to her liking. Though the dragon overlord was dead, Feril was pleased the gargantuan trees remained. If only men and creatures left the dragon's woods alone, she thought. If only they didn't have to destroy things . . .

She stopped suddenly, hearing some noise beyond a tight row of poplars.

Feril dropped to her stomach and crawled forward, the aroma from the grass and the rich earth beneath it heady. She found herself distracted by the scents, and it took some effort to force her senses to flow through the ground and past the poplars, down a small rise and across a clearing that was cut by a branch of the White Rage River. The men she sought must be there, on the far side of the river. Looking small because of the distance, they were standing in the growing shadows of a thick stand of maples and sycamores. The setting sun was making their dark armor shine, flickering amidst the tall grass and the river, making the muddy water that churned against the banks sparkle like bits of gold.

There were fourteen Knights of Neraka, the ones she'd been tracking having met up with others. A small force as far as the Knights were concerned, and only some of them were wearing the traditional heavy black plate mail of the Order. As she edged through the poplars and to the crest of a rise, she could make out more details. There were raised lilies on the pauldrons and breastplates and on shields that had been propped against tree trunks. Half wore coats of plates, leather jerkins with pieces of black metal riveted on them—not warriors, these, perhaps scouts or agents of the knights, perhaps assassins or trackers. As she watched, another knight joined the group, hinting that there might be yet more camped beyond the trees.

"Fifteen now," she whispered. "Quite a nest of vipers I've found."

The newcomer was larger than the rest, wearing blued armor—fine black metal that had been heated to give it a blue sheen. There were skulls on his plate mail instead of lilies, so Feril decided he was a priest, no doubt their commander; the others were clearly deferring to him. All of them wore gauntlets and either hard leather boots or sabbatons, boots covered by plate segments. They had flowing black capes and visored helmets, some of which were sitting on the ground near the shields. Their faces were glistening with sweat.

Among Goldmoon's champions had been the Solamnic Knight Fiona. Feril marveled at how the woman could wear fifty or more pounds of plate armor under the warmest of conditions. Why anyone would want to wear so much armor was still a puzzlement to her. While it afforded protection, it also most certainly made its wearer thoroughly miserable, especially in today's considerable heat.

Feril could have heard what the Knights were saying if she wanted to; she could have spread her senses and put enough energy into a spell. Perhaps she should, she thought for a moment, as their conversation might provide useful information. She was weary from tracking them for so long, and she wanted to act swiftly before any more joined the group here beneath the trees and presented a force too large for her to deal with. She directed all of her energy into a different enchantment, letting the magic begin to flow outward from her fingertips.

Like an artist spreading paint with a palette knife, Feril smoothed the magic onto the ground and pointed it toward the knights, stretching it away from her, and then beyond them to the trees that towered above and behind them. She instantly felt cooled by the shadows those trees cast, and by the river that ran nearby. Rejuvenated, she felt even stronger and her spell grew more powerful.

"Help me," she entreated the trees. "Help me stop the defilers of these woods and the slayers of my elf cousins. Bend."

She cast her energy into the roots of the great maples. It pulsed into the trunks in time with the beating of her heart. Feril closed her eyes and guided the energy up and up, high into the treetops, outward to the very ends of branches. A silent prayer sent to Habbakuk, whom she revered most among Krynn's gods, then she felt the branches begin to rustle.

"Commander!" one of the Lily Knights shouted loud enough for her to hear. "The trees are alive!"

First the branches became limp and hung like ribbons, then a heartbeat later they whipped up to curl around the arms and legs of the surprised knights. Under Feril's command the branches stiffened and recoiled, lifting the knights off the ground and bringing them close to the trunks.

"Help me," Feril urged. "Help me slay the defilers!"

The trees complied with her command, their limbs constricting, the smallest of the branches finding their way beneath the pauldrons on the knights' breastplates, inside the cuisse plates on their legs, into the gaps on the gorgets about the men's necks—and tightening like nooses.

Feril continued to concentrate on the enchantment, speaking to the trees as she stood and bounded down the rise and to the river, no longer concealing her presence.

"Kill them!" she called to the trees. "Twist the life from them as they have bled the life from this priceless forest!"

In the back of her mind she saw the devastation clearly: the mass-grave mounds of the Qualinesti elves and the scorched remains of village after village she had passed through on the trail.

She paused and watched the Knights of Neraka struggle. They were only fifty yards in front of her, their eyes bulging and filled with fury, the one in the blued armor red-faced with rage while frantically working his fingers to begin his own spell. Skull Knights were priests, Feril reminded herself, therefore capable of magic. With a gesture from her, fingerlike branches swept down and tangled the priest's hands, another wrapped across his mouth in order to keep him from uttering any arcane words. His frustration grew and he struggled harder.

Feril waded into the river, all the men watching her fearfully. It was relatively shallow, but after a few steps she could no longer touch bottom and she felt herself being tugged by a strong undertow. Feril swam quickly across to keep from being pulled to the bottom. The trees continued to strangle the men, and most of the knights were dead by the time Feril climbed out of the water near them.

"Despoilers and ravagers, all of you!" she called to the few still clinging to life as she approached. "Murderers! You'll kill no more!"

The few remaining knights looked piteously at this slight female Kagonesti who had so easily caused their downfall.

Why? one mouthed.

"The last village you attacked," she explained as she drew closer, surprising herself by answering the knight. "The last village you burned, the last elf families you slew. I tracked you from there. You'll kill no more, I say. This I swear!"

The branches tightened, sapping more energy from Feril. Her eyes locked onto the Skull Knight's florid face. He was gasping and thrashing feebly now.

Then without warning came a commotion, loud noises emanating from somewhere to the east—well beyond the knights and the old maples and sycamores. More Knights of Neraka? Feril wondered. How many more? Perhaps an entire talon of them was lurking deep in the woods. She could handle a few more, she knew, maybe a dozen, as she was surrounded by eager trees and branches and she still had some magical energy left. What if they were too many? She was tired from the journey, from casting this difficult enchantment. Her strength was ebbing, and she was going to be vulnerable all too soon.

Feril took a few steps back toward the river and watched as the rest of the knights gradually stopped struggling, hanging limp from the trees as if they'd been tried and sentenced by a jury and hanged for their crimes on a scaffold.

The approaching noise was growing louder, and after long moments Feril saw shapes thrashing amid the trees. More Knights of Neraka were arriving and they, too, were being scooped up by the deadly tree branches—charged, sentenced, and hanged according to Feril's swift justice. She focused on the ground, on the arcane energy she was continuing to feed and that was animating the trees.

"So tired." The more she put into this powerful spell, the more it disoriented her. Feril's arms felt wooden, her head so heavy she could hardly hold it up.

"Everything," she whispered, feeling as though she was giving the last measure of her arcane strength. The magical force pulsed into the roots fast and unfalteringly, and the branches grabbed at the new foes. There must be at least fifty knights arriving, Feril estimated, and some of the knights were breaking through the entangling branches despite the intensity of her spell. A small group was now racing toward her.

Swords drawn, eyes wide, and spittle flying from their open mouths, they charged. A few were shouting, all were spreading out to surround her—her senses were so acute that she felt their heavy steps like painful thunder rumbling through the ground. The summer heat and their heavy armor did not seem to impede them. She slammed her eyes shut and waited for the end to come, knowing she was too weak to flee and that she had no weapons to defend herself. Then the pounding swept past her, and she opened her eyes to discover that the knights were not running *toward* her—they were running *away* from something still cloaked by the trees.

A thrashing noise coming from the trees grew deafening, and then she spied a much larger shape. It was easily brushing aside the lashing, entangling limbs and bending the smallest trees completely over, snapping most of them.

"In Habbakuk's name, please give me more strength." The magical pulse she had used to enchant the trees was dimming to nothing. She had no energy left.

It was some great shadowy beast, she realized faintly. She heard it utter a harsh, ear-splitting snarl, heard the splashes of the Knights of Neraka who had plunged into the river in order to escape its clutches. She hadn't been able to touch bottom in the river where she had crossed, nor could they. Without looking, she pictured their heavy plate metal dragging them down, the strong undertow sealing their doom. Only a few wisely avoided the river, running southeast parallel to its banks, dropping their swords and shields as they went.

The howl of the creature shook the ground. Feril's spell was finally dissipated. The Knights of Neraka she'd hung in the maples and sycamores fell like discarded dolls amidst their shields and helmets.

"By Habbakuk's fist," she said in a hushed voice, when she realized what the monstrous shape really was. "A black dragon."

A wave of fear struck her, as palpable a blow as if she had been struck over the head with a club. She lost all focus, shivered uncontrollably, and her legs gave out.

The dragon emerging from the trees was singular in that most of its scales looked like black mirrors, a few shimmering silver, a scattering of blue ones glimmering here and there. Its shadowy-black horns resembled those of a red, the wings looking scalloped like a blue's. The claws were webbed like a white's.

"Black, but not a black dragon," Feril murmured, as she tried to struggle to her knees and crawl away. "What is it?"

The dragon spat out a Lily Knight and brushed away the body of the Knight Commander that had fallen on the ground in front of it. Blood dripped from the dragon's mouth, and Feril could see where a black tabard was caught on a tooth.

"Tired," she said. "So tired. I'm finished." She wouldn't surrender so easily to one of Krynn's damnable dragons, she vowed, gritting her teeth. She spread her fingers wide against the ground. "Habbakuk, guide me. I beseech you to give me one last . . . there!" Somehow she managed to send a feeble stroke of energy toward the trees, virtually begging them to aid her a final time. She fed some of her essence into the spell and was rewarded by faint feeling, a small wave of energy moving up the thick trunk of a maple, edging toward the top branches.

She watched the dragon step close to her; half of the huge creature was clear of the trees, but its haunches still rested under her enchanted maple. The dragonfear nauseated her. Closer, the dragon looked at once elegant and grotesque. Blood dripped from its jaws, a slimy rope of spittle edging over its lower lip. Its stink was overpowering. The dragon smelled like rotting wood, moldy leaves, and a dozen, disquieting worse things she couldn't put a name to. When it opened its maw wide, she nearly swooned with disgust.

"Habbakuk, guide me." She watched as the animated branches dipped lower, snaking out to try to ensnare the dragon. Then she stared in horror as the dragon effortlessly ripped away those branches and headed straight toward her. She watched the beast's eyes, its massive black eyes that reflected . . . something.

Something familiar.

The dragonfear wavered a little, and she pulled herself closer, forward, trying to fathom what she recognized in the eyes.

There was a man's face reflected there.

"Not possible," she said aloud, her voice barely audible.

A face all angles and planes, once handsome, and with a rare, flashing smile.

"By all the gods, it's not possible."

Then the last of her stamina vanished and she slumped, the shadows that stretched from the trees to the dragon to the dark parts of her mind, claiming her.

CHAPTER

3

Feril opened her eyes and saw her own reflection—smooth, unmarked face, short hair, bewildered expression. She gasped when she realized she wasn't looking into any mirror but into the eye of the dragon. That eye was just inches away, the dragon's head tucked into its neck at an odd angle to be able to scrutinize her closely. This near, the scent of the beast was overwhelming, and she felt weak. She rolled on her side, retching until there was nothing left in her stomach.

She told herself to be brave and accept her fate as, fighting dizziness, she struggled to her knees. Her teeth chattered. The Kagonesti couldn't run away from the creature, she knew, and she certainly couldn't stand and fight. She must still be alive because the creature wanted information. She knew some dragons were curious, so this one might mean her no harm at all, or it might mean to swallow her quickly after it gleaned whatever tidbit of knowledge it sought.

"Feril." The word softly rumbled, shaking the ground. The dragon repeated her name, certain she hadn't heard him the first time.

She wiped at her face, squared her shoulders. She thrust her chin out and adopted a proud, defiant look. She managed to keep the look of surprise off her face that the dragon somehow knew her name.

"Feril, I was wrong to come here. I should have let the past stay buried. I should have stayed in my swamp."

There was something reassuringly familiar about the sonorous voice, and also about the dragon's eyes, where not a touch of menace appeared to lurk. Feril searched them for a hint of the man she thought she detected earlier, but all she could see was her own reflection. She continued to tremble from the dragonfear, though not as much as before—less and less, it seemed, with each passing moment.

"How do you know my name? How can . . ."

Feril rose with a start when she saw a sivak draconian step into view from behind the dragon. She glanced back and forth between the two creatures, inhaled sharply, then almost retched again from the combination of horrible smells.

"It's all right," the dragon continued. "I won't hurt you, Feril. I would never hurt you. I'll be on my way. I shouldn't have . . ."

The sivak cocked his head, gesturing with a crooked finger. "Is this the woman you wanted to find? A Kagonesti?"

The dragon gave a nod.

"When you mentioned an elf, I pictured some fragile creature with flowers in her hair—or with painted lips and eyelids, like your friend Rikali. Nothing dainty or painted about this one. She certainly didn't need our help with those Knights of Neraka. Slaughtered most of them on her own, she did. Are all of your friends this tough, Dhamon?"

"Dhamon? Impossible!"

Even as Feril said this, she knew it was indeed true. The image of the man she had seen in the dragon's eyes, and saw again now. The image of that rugged, handsome face flickered, then disappeared when she blinked and shook her head. "Impossible," she repeated, though she knew that somehow it was him. Her chest tightened, feeling as though someone had slammed a mailed fist into her stomach. She could hardly breathe. "By all the gods, Dhamon Grimwulf!"

She reached out, shaky fingers tentatively touching the scales on his leg. She pressed her palm against one and closed her eyes, flooded by myriad emotions and questions. Her breath came ragged and fast.

"It is you, isn't it, Dhamon? I never thought I'd see you again and certainly not like this. What strange magic did this to you, Dhamon?"

"Feril, dark magic. Terrible magic. I . . ." The dragon glanced behind him toward the trees where the Knights of Neraka had been hanged. He knew that Feril found him repulsive. He had long rehearsed the speech he might give to her some day, but right now his thoughts were jumbled. "Ragh, it's time to leave. This wasn't . . ."

The sivak shook his head in disagreement. "We're not leaving, not just yet. We came all this way, and you're not even going to introduce me?"

Dhamon looked at the sivak, then down at the Kagonesti, who was still stroking his scales. Saliva dripped from his jowls, and Feril stepped back to keep from getting splashed. After a moment, he tipped his head up, as if he were listening to something far beyond this clearing in the Qualinesti forest. A red-shouldered hawk cried shrilly and cut through the sky above them, then circled a fallen knight on the river bank, where a cloud of insects swarmed.

"Ragh, this is Ferilleeagh Dawnsprinter," Dhamon said at length, "a Kagonesti from Southern Ergoth and once a champion of Goldmoon."

"I prefer Feril," she said, shortening her name, as she stepped back from the dragon to study the draconian.

"Feril," Ragh said, as he met the eyes of the Kagonesti. "Well met, Feril of Southern Ergoth."

At first her eyes were daggers aimed at the sivak then finally they softened as she turned her face away and lifted it to the dragon again. "Dhamon, what has happened to you? How in the world did you become . . ."

"A dragon? It's a long story," Dhamon replied. The faintest hint of a smile played at the corner of his massive mouth.

"Tell me, Dhamon."

"Short or long, let's do it away from here," the sivak urged, gesturing at the dead bodies. "They're going to attract all sorts of beasties once they begin to stink—stink worse than Dhamon even, maybe attract more knights." He waved a clawed hand in front of his face to ward off a gathering mistlike swarm of gnats.

Again, Feril glared at the draconian. "I am in no hurry. I intend to bury all of these men."

"What, are you mad, elf?" The draconian furiously swiped at the gnats.

"Listen, sivak," she started. "I've . . ."

"Ragh," Dhamon said to the Kagonesti. "Feril, he's a good friend of mine."

"Dhamon, his kind . . ."

"I know, my kind eat elves," Ragh finished her sentence, finally giving up on keeping the insects at bay. "Elves are a favorite food of most sivaks, you might say but it's been a few years for me. I've long since acquired other tastes."

She sucked in a breath and pointed south, where tall pines grew far apart and sheltered smaller trees. The shadows were particularly thick there. The sun had nearly set. "Dhamon, if you must go, then I'll meet you over there when I'm finished burying the dead. We obviously have a lot of catching up to do."

Dhamon pawed at the ground, a talon digging a deep line. "I'll bury them, Feril." Softer, he added, "They were once my kind."

———◆◆◆———

"So you knew him years ago when he was human, huh? Probably before he got all high-and-mighty bent on saving the world."

Feril was settled on a carpet of lungwort that grew between the knobby roots of a golden rain tree. She stared up at the clusters of yellow flowers and didn't answer the nearby sivak draconian.

"Certainly before he had a change of heart and fell in with thieves in ogre lands, before he hooked up with Maldred."

Feril rubbed at the back of her neck and rolled her shoulders. She seemed oblivious to the sivak's prattle.

"Well, I met Dhamon back when he was human, too," Ragh continued. The sivak leaned against the trunk of an old gum as he warily regarded her. "He was a good man, for a human. Best I can recall knowing. I have a gap in my memory, but I understand that Dhamon freed me from some of Sable's minions. Sable's the black dragon overlord that rules this swamp," he paused, "but I suppose you know about Sable. I suppose everyone does."

He rubbed his back against the tree. "Anyway, Sable's minions cut off my wings. Dhamon said they were bleeding me to make spawn and abominations."

Still no reaction from Feril. She seemed busy watching a small black bird that was searching for insects in the flowers and along the small branches. Her elf eyes picked through the darkness and noticed the bands of blue on the bird's wings.

"In those days Dhamon had this big scale on his right leg, black as night with a silver streak in it. The thing was paining him terribly. Sometimes he'd curl into a ball and pass out, it hurt that much. We'd watch him with a knot in our stomachs—Maldred and Riki and me. I remember thinking I wouldn't want my worst enemy to suffer so. We thought sooner or later the pain might kill him."

Ragh talked on and on about Maldred and Riki, the ogre-mage and half-elf thief who kept company with Dhamon for a while and who worried over him and his accursed scale. He talked some about Rig and Fiona, without mentioning their deaths, since he realized Feril must have known the pair. Dhamon could deliver those somber tidings when and if he wanted to.

"Somehow the pain got worse, then he started growing more scales. Not as big as the first one—he said that first scale came from the red overlord. Malys, they called her. At first, all the smaller scales were just on his leg, black as night, and he managed to keep them hidden from us. We found out eventually, and Maldred tried to find a cure for him." The sivak paused. "We went to Shrentak, where there was this magical woman Maldred had heard about, some old Black Robe sorceress who was said to be near as powerful as Raistlin Majere. She was powerful, all right, but she was as mad as a nest of rattled hornets."

Again he left out a vital piece of the story . . . that the mad woman indeed could have cured Dhamon, for a price—if Ragh had become her property. The sivak thought the cost too high and killed her when Dhamon was unconscious, hiding her body and later telling Dhamon that the woman could do nothing for him and had wandered off.

"Wasted trip. She couldn't help him," Ragh continued, a little louder. "We left Shrentak, and Dhamon's scales kept spreading. I guess you knew him about the time he got that first big scale, huh? It was some years ago from what I understand. He said it was red at first, just like the overlord Malys. He also said a shadow dragon and a silver dragon broke the hold Malys had on him because of the scale, and in the process the big scale turned black. 'Course, the magic the shadow dragon worked on that scale, we didn't know it at the time, but I figure it eventually caused all those other scales to sprout. It just took time."

The sivak waited for Feril to say something. He scratched at his chin and let out a deep breath. He heard the hoot of an owl, and then a closer owl hooted longer at a higher pitch. The owls were waiting for it to get a little darker, then they would fly in search of mice and ground squirrels. He allowed himself a moment of envy, then brushed a beetle off his leg and resumed his tale.

"It was a little more than a year ago, I'm talking about, when the small black scales had started to sprout like fever blisters. Like I said, we had left Shrentak and were cutting through the swamp trying to help Dhamon. We took a boat across the New Sea and went north through goblin lands and into the mountains. It wasn't an easy trip, definitely dangerous, and Dhamon was hurting more and more all the time. Dhamon wouldn't give up, though, and we stayed with him. He was after the shadow dragon, figured it was his only chance to stop the scales from covering him entirely. Figured, I guess, that since the shadow dragon caused his problem, the shadow dragon could cure him."

"The shadow dragon was in the mountains?"

Ragh bit his tongue in surprise that Feril finally had deigned to speak to him.

The sivak nodded. "Yes, in a lair deep in the mountains, but Dhamon was scarcely human by the time we arrived there." Ragh slid down the trunk and sat cross-legged. "By then Dhamon looked like a draconian, biggest one I ever saw, but he was black as night, like one of Sable's spawn, and he had wings. He started growing even bigger every step closer that we got to the shadow dragon."

Feril was definitely listening now. She leaned forward, intent on Ragh's story, nodding for him to continue.

"Deep, deep under the mountain we learned that the shadow dragon wanted Dhamon to turn into a dragon. The shadow dragon was dying, old and spent, and was looking for a new body—Dhamon's. He had control of Dhamon for a while and almost had him trapped for good, but all of us fought hard to free him."

Feril's lips formed a thin line. "And you won?"

Ragh nodded. "If you can call it that. We killed the shadow dragon and left Maldred in ogre country when it was all over. I'm the only one who stayed with Dhamon. He's not great company, I'll tell you. I don't think he cares for being a dragon."

Neither said anything for a while. Feril rubbed at her palm and looked far into the woods, seeming to watch something the sivak couldn't see. There was a flapping sound, wings directly overhead, a large white owl taking flight.

"You said all of that was a year ago, sivak?"

"About a year, give or take. Hard to mark time when time doesn't matter much."

"Rig and Fiona . . . where are they now?"

Ragh didn't answer at first.

"Did they fight the shadow dragon, too?"

"Fiona did," he said finally. He quickly changed the subject. "Dhamon and I have been living in Sable's swamp. He's built a lair, collected some treasure."

She edged closer, raising an eyebrow. "Wealth never mattered that much to him."

"When he was human, maybe," Ragh said. *Maybe when he was with you and the powerful Palin Majere,* he added to himself. The sivak knew that when Dhamon traveled with the cunning Maldred, it was different; the two were always scheming to rob people or find buried riches. Treasure was at the top of their priorities. "Dhamon thinks dragons have some deep instinct to build a hoard."

"Is his treasure around here? If not, what is he doing here?"

Ragh gave a great shrug of his broad shoulders.

"He came looking for me, isn't that it?"

"Yes," the sivak said. "You mean a lot to him for some reason."

It was her turn to shrug. "Once he meant a great deal to me, too, but it feels like that was a lifetime ago."

"When he was human."

"Yes. I met him even before he had the scale."

"When he was a Dark Knight?"

She shook her head as she stood up. "He was as chivalrous as a knight, though, all puffed up with notions of honor."

It looked as though she might say something else but stopped herself. Her face became hard again and set itself in a scowl, as if she were angry for talking this much to a sivak, a monster without humanity.

"You have a problem with *my kind*?" he said, sensing her discomfort.

She answered swiftly, her words sounding brittle even to her ears. "Sivaks killed my father and sister. I ran away before I could see the beasts eat them, but I was a child, too small and too frightened to do anything except run."

She brushed at her legs and then walked to the edge of the trees and looked out over the clearing. Twilight was starting to claim the sky, and the river was dark and still churning.

She stood there waiting for Dhamon, never once glancing back at Ragh.

———◆———

It took him longer than she expected, but he had fished all the bodies out of the river, too, heaping them all in one mass grave, marked with shields and swords, in front of the trees from which she'd hung them.

Now he was slowly lumbering toward her, his blue and silver scales dim in the fading light, his equine snout pointed straight at her. He had put effort into suppressing his aura of dragonfear, so Feril felt not even a twinge of dread. A few yards away he stopped, letting her finally break the silence.

"The Knights of Neraka have been hunting the Qualinesti elves living in these woods," she said.

"Thus, you've been hunting the knights?"

A new life, a new code of responsibilities.

"And goblins," she said. "Tribes of goblins, hobgoblins, and worse are roaming the forest. Mostly I've been hunting the bandits, but I get my share of knights."

"Bandits?" His eyes blinked questioningly. "Can't the Qualinesti deal with bandits?"

Feril laughed lightly, and Dhamon thought it sounded like crystal wind chimes teased by a slight breeze.

"Where in all the world have you been, Dhamon Grimwulf? Beryl is dead, and most of the Qualinesti have fled from the woods. This land they've held since the Age of Dreams—now it's lost to them. The stragglers don't have enough of a force to fight the bandits or anyone else. The north country is ruled by Captain Samuval, an outlaw who's offering land to any man who'll serve for a time in his so-called army. Samuval's army has been killing or driving away any Qualinesti they find."

Dhamon lowered his head until the barbels that hung from his chin brushed against the ground. He cringed to see Feril wrinkle her nose at his odor. "What about your allies, Feril? Who is helping you fight the knights and the bandits?"

She put on a defiant look. "No one." After a deep breath, she added, "Nature is helping me, Dhamon. You saw how many knights I managed to take down on my own. I've become more proficient with magic since you knew me."

He opened his great mouth and canted his head to the side. "I shouldn't have come here, Feril. I should have stayed in the swamp. It's my home now. I shouldn't have tried to reach back into the past." He paused, glancing beyond her to the draconian. "My friend over there wanted to fly for a bit, so I obliged him."

"How did you find me?"

He drew his head close to his neck and something sparkled in his eyes. "That wasn't so easy," he said. "It was mostly Ragh's doing. Some time ago he was a spy for Sable, and he still has some old contacts in the swamp, including ones who worked for the Knights of Neraka. It took more than a month and the liberal spreading around of steel pieces and pearls that I really had no other use for anyway. Eventually, one of Ragh's contacts told us that a wild elf was waging war in the Qualinesti forest of Wayreth. The description didn't closely match, but Ragh wanted badly to explore, and I wanted badly to . . ."

She raised a hand to the side of her head. "I look different. I have cut my hair," she said.

"And the tattoos?"

"Well, I live a different life now." She looked over her shoulder at the sivak, who was trying to look casual while eavesdropping on their conversation. "It seems you have a remarkably different life, too." Taking a few steps forward, she stretched out her fingers and tickled his lower jaw. "You're an impressive-looking dragon, Dhamon Grimwulf. I'd almost say the scales suit you."

For an instant, pain registered in his eyes. "I've come to appreciate being powerful, Feril. I enjoy flying. I can see and hear better than any man, and I . . ."

Ragh cleared his throat. "Oh, don't listen to him. He's not the least bit happy, elf. The scales don't suit him at all." The sivak came closer to the pair. "Did you bury all of them, Dhamon?"

A nod.

"*All* of them?"

"Yes." There was an irritated rumble beneath the word.

"Damn." Ragh pounded the ball of his foot against the ground. "I wasn't thinking, wasn't thinking at all. Did you . . ."

Dhamon shook his head. "No. I did not keep their coin purses."

"Damn. Damn. Damn." The sivak sidestepped the dragon and squinted back in the direction of the mass grave, seeing little in the growing darkness. "We don't have a single steel piece left. We didn't bring enough from your lair. You should have grabbed those purses. Maybe we can still find some of those swords . . ."

"Let them stay right where they are," Dhamon said.

"Fine," Ragh said. "Fine. Fine. Fine. Now we can't even take the steel and swords we earned." He walked away, muttering, kicking at stones.

Dhamon focused his immense eyes only on Feril. He shook his head, his shadowy horns rustling the leaves of the branches above him. "I couldn't stop the transformation, Feril. Not even an old Black Robe sorceress in Shrentak could find a way to keep me human. Not the shadow dragon, not . . ."

"If it's magic that made you a dragon . . ." she began. "Well, now there's plenty of magic in Krynn again. Perhaps some of that magic can restore you, Dhamon—bring back your humanity."

For an instant she thought she saw a flicker of hope in the dragon's midnight eyes, then nothing.

"There isn't enough magic in the world, Feril."

She shifted back and forth on the balls of her feet. "Maybe not, but you came looking for me for a reason," she said, "and I think it was because you think there is a chance. Ragh is right. You are unhappy. You want to be human again."

"Yes, I wish to be human."

"I know you, Dhamon. You have some plan, don't you?"

Ragh had come back, standing silently nearby, listening. He recalled Dhamon studying the crystal ball in his lair, asking it questions and cocking his ear for hours on end.

"Yes," Dhamon answered, "and I need your help."

"Why? How can I help you?" She searched hard for the human reflection in the dragon's immense, stoic eyes but found only darkness.

"You can come with me to Nalis Aren."

"Just who is that?" Ragh cut in, tugging on Dhamon's dew claw.

"Not a who," Feril supplied the answer, as Dhamon lowered his eyes. "Those are Qualinesti words for Lake of Death."

CHAPTER

4

One hundred and seventeen grape-sized rubies were arrayed on a pedestal beneath a delicate silver candelabrum. The light made the stones shine like drops of fresh blood that had been magically captured in perfect-faceted form.

The light stretched yards away to illuminate a long marble table where diamonds filled rose-colored crystal vases and sapphires were heaped in etched platinum bowls. There were also emeralds, amethysts, jacinths, tourmalines, and more, all of these sorted by size and quality and displayed in polished mahogany chests that rested side-by-side beneath the table.

Against the far wall, gilded urns were crammed with rare black pearls. A small ceramic pot sat on a thin ivory pedestal. There was a silvery liquid inside it—a special presentation from one of the black dragon's most valuable spies, who promised there would be more goodies to come. Rings and bracelets overflowed an old sea trunk that had been captured from a three-masted merchant ship in the New Sea. Necklaces and gem-encrusted scepters crowned mounds of steel pieces stretching deep into the shadows. There were plenty of gold pieces, too, bearing the faces of famous men from centuries past. The common steel pieces in circulation today served as a carpet beneath all the remarkable treasure.

A massive ebony chair that once must have been used as some ruler's throne was one of the centerpieces of the chamber. It was intricately carved with images of centaurs and walrus-men and had a thick green satin cushion embroidered with vines and flowers. On either side of it were life-size priceless sculptures of sea elves that had been recovered from the bottom of the Maelstrom.

There was much more strewn around the treasure chamber—decorative suits of armor, shields, and weapons; paintings so numerous they were stacked rows across and a dozen deep; tapestries from the Blood Sea Isles; ancient books mysteriously preserved and precisely alphabetized on cherrywood shelves; numerous crystal balls, magic wands, and attractive enchanted baubles crafted by the most renowned of Krynn's sorcerers and whose functions had not yet been discovered by their current owner. This was only one of several treasure chambers that was regularly added to and visited by the black dragon.

Sable lounged at the wide end of this underground cavern, staring as the light from the delicate candelabrum flickered and caused the rubies beneath it to sparkle like fat crimson fireflies. The great dragon knew precisely how many steel pieces, gems, and other trinkets were in her favorite lair deep beneath the foul city of Shrentak. She watched with mild interest as more was added to the pile.

A Knight of Neraka commander was directing a quartet of bakali to deposit sacks of steel pieces in the center of the cavern, where they could be inventoried under the overlord's supervision. More precious stones and ornaments were placed near the coins. The weapons and pieces of plate armor that had been gathered would be left outside until an armorer could be summoned to inspect them and determine what was suitable to add to the hoard and what should be discarded.

When the bakali were finished unloading the riches, they stood at attention in front of the overlord, shivering despite Sable having done her best to suppress her dragonfear. The commander gestured to the tallest bakali.

"This one, Mistress Sable." The knight's words were clipped and loud. "This was one of the few creatures who survived the incident at the lake with the shadowy dragon. He was instrumental in helping to find the beast's lair."

Still trembling, the designated bakali stepped forward, its chest puffed out in pride and a strand of saliva spilling over its quivering lip and stretching to the cavern floor. Its eyes glimmered expectantly when Sable opened her mouth as if to speak, but the dragon spewed forth a blob of acid, engulfing the bakali and his brethren. Their scaly hides bubbled, popped, and disintegrated in places so that muscle and bones showed through. They fell to their knees howling and begging to be spared, but their pleas were short-lived, for Sable breathed a second time.

The Knight of Neraka commander barely managed to leap out of the way of the attack, yet he was sorely misted by the acid breath. The acid continued to burn and sizzle on the edges of his black breastplate, marring the lily etchings.

"You will have the bodies disposed of promptly, Commander Bedell," Sable rumbled. "They taint the beauty of this place."

"Of course," the knight was quick to reply. "Right away, Mistress Sable."

"As for the shadow dragon called Dhamon . . ."

"We found no trace of him in his lair, Mistress. It was as though he had abandoned it."

Sable's eyes narrowed to thread-fine slits. She allowed her fear aura to grow stronger, until the knight shivered and sweated. "What makes you so certain it was the Dhamon-dragon's main lair and not some decoy?"

Commander Bedell gave a curt nod, releasing a breath he'd been holding and doing his best not to pass out from the nausea. "We'd been searching for the lair for nearly five months, and we knew it must be near the lake in the lowlands, a favorite haunt of the beast. It was very well hidden. Had the wind not been blowing so strongly to disturb a veil of leaves, we would have missed it."

"Why did you not raid or destroy it then?" A blob of spittle rolled out of Sable's mouth and hissed as it fell to the floor, sizzling between her talons.

He glanced at the still smoking corpses of the bakali. "We found bakali weapons there and took this as proof, Mistress Sable." He held up a statuette of a night bird. "The last force that we sent against your foe carried this . . . uh, item. It is enchanted, and one of our gray robes . . . a venerable Knight of the Thorn . . . used his magic to find it." He placed the statuette next to the mound of steel pieces.

"Like a dog tracks a rabbit," Sable mused.

Commander Bedell stood stiffly at attention. "We thought it best to leave and track the Dhamon-dragon.

Intrude as little as possible. Don't alert the dragon unnecessarily. Perhaps it will yet return to its lair, and we can trap it there."

"I suppose."

The Knight Commander trembled faintly, and this pleased Sable.

"How much of a hoard is there?" Sable asked.

"Nothing compared to what you have here, your majesty."

"So the Dhamon-dragon claims little wealth as far as I am concerned but is intent on claiming more and more of my land," Sable said sulkily.

The black dragon stretched her front legs out and clicked her talons against the stone inches away from the dissolving bakali corpses. It was reminiscent, the knight thought, of the bored gesture a man might practice, thrumming his fingers against a desk.

"It looked as though the creature had not been there for weeks," Commander Bedell told Sable. "It was unfortunate, as this time . . ."

". . . as this time I gave you more than enough bakali and men to deal with the foul fiend," Sable finished. "I underestimated the Dhamon-dragon before, but no longer." The talons clicked louder. "Now that I have given you enough men and bakali, you will leave on another mission right away. This time I don't want you to come back alive until you kill or capture the Dhamon-dragon."

The commander shook his head and blinked at the sweat that was running into his eyes. "I fear the shadow dragon is gone, Mistress Sable. I have scouts near the lake he frequented and others scattered in the lowlands, where we found old tracks of the sivak that is loyal to him. They report no signs of the dragon. There is a Gray Robe attempting to divine the dragon's whereabouts, though so far he has been unsuccessful and claims the shadow dragon has simply left your lands."

Stacks of paintings fell over as Sable roared her discontent. There was a cascading of coins and gems, too, as gold and steel pieces rolled off the mounds and jewels rattled in their various containers.

"Men are so pitiable, especially your gray-clad sorcerers, Commander Bedell! You claim that the Gray Robes are wondrously powerful, yet they cannot find the Dhamon-dragon!"

"We did find its lair," the knight risked saying, trying to assuage some of the dragon's anger, "and we brought you some spoils as proof. We will continue to search for the dragon, though I believe it is as the Gray Robe reports, that he has for some reason left the swamp, wisely surrendering it to your might and . . ."

"Hmm. I will narrow your search."

Sable opened her eyes wide and slowed her breathing. The mounds of coins and display of treasure faded from her sight, and in their place she now saw lofty cypress trees and black willows, spreading ferns and hanging vines, everything shades of green and the air intensely humid. She pushed her senses outward. So close in spirit to the swamp she nurtured, Sable could feel the dark life festering in the blessed fetidness that surrounded her. Her mind touched alligators, young and old and those that had grown to giant proportions because of the arcane nature of her realm. Her mind brushed against birds, snakes, and curly-tailed lizards that scampered along the highest branches of the uppermost canopy. She sensed a few lesser black dragons, all professing their loyalties to her, the spawn and abominations she had created, and the draconians that patrolled the city above and the swamp villages at her behest.

Sable couldn't sense the Dhamon-dragon anywhere—not in the lowlands, nor by the lake, none of the usual places he seemed to favor and where she had sensed him before. She couldn't find the nuisance in the far south near the Plains of Dust, nor to the east where the swamp was encroaching on ogre lands and was wearing away at the mountains. Like Commander Bedell had said, the Dhamon-dragon had disappeared from her sacred swamp. Why?

The Dhamon-dragon could be dead, Sable knew, no thanks to her forces. He could have drowned in the lake or have been swarmed by the giant alligators; he could have run afoul of the lesser black dragons. Sable briefly considered sending the knight and his fellows in search of her fellow blacks to ask if they'd killed the Dhamon-dragon, but as quick as the notion came to her, she dismissed it. The blacks would have been the first to brag of the Dhamon-dragon's demise.

"Yes, the Dhamon-dragon has indeed left my swamp, as you believed," Sable finally purred. The knight relaxed visibly. "Not as good as his death, though acceptable."

"If he returns, we will kill him."

"If he is truly wise, he shall not return," Sable said.

"You pose too great of a threat," the knight said, venturing a lavish compliment.

"He shall attempt to claim other lands, craft another lair elsewhere and fill it with other trivial baubles and steel pieces too few to be of any interest to me. More's the pity you were not able to kill him. I would have fancied his head mounted above Shrentak's gates. Pity that, after all, you failed me."

The knight showed his penitence by bowing his head and rounding his shoulders. "I would be happy to search for him beyond your swamp."

"No."

"Then I willingly give my life, Mistress Sable, and the lives of my men for our failure. Our blood for the blood we were not able to shed in your glorious name."

"You know that you are more use to me alive than dead, Commander Bedell—for the moment." The overlord dismissed the knight with a curl of her upper lip. "Remove the stuff you collected from the Dhamon-dragon's lair," she said. "It is not worth adding to my own. Give it to the destitute in the city above, and make it known that it came from me, that I am being magnanimous to my subjects." She clicked her talons rhythmically. "Return this night for more instructions. Perhaps I shall think of a menial task or two that you will be better able to manage."

The knight was quick to summon more bakali and order them to gather up the remains of their brethren, scour the stone beneath the bodies so that it gleamed, and to take Dhamon's purloined treasure away from the cavern.

"A lamentable hoard the Dhamon-dragon had," Sable said to herself when she was finally alone, "not worthy of even a hatchling's collection."

She focused on the flames that flickered in the delicate silver candelabrum and illuminated the one hundred and seventeen perfect rubies that were as shiny as fresh blood. Soon she was dozing peaceably, dreaming of the inevitable death of her despised foe.

Dhamon often caught Feril staring at him, eyes wide and unable to wholly conceal her disbelief. Though she acknowledged that he was a dragon, he knew she was having a difficult time accepting it, and he knew that as much as she loved all creatures and might have once loved him, a part of her was horrified. Dhamon understood; he knew that he was repellent, even to Ragh, his only friend. All dragons had a particular odor—he remembered Malys the Red smelling of brimstone and ashes; Sable of decaying plant life and fetid water; Brine of the foul sea. His own smell was poisonous; his breath reeked of metal and blood.

Still, the Kagonesti had stayed close. Dhamon intently watched Feril, noting the Kagonesti's slightly upturned nose, her high cheekbones and rounded chin, those gently pointed ears that he once caressed—back when he was human.

When the sunlight hit her eyes, which were blue flecked with green and saffron, they sparkled dark green like emeralds. Perhaps they were whatever color she wanted them to be, he thought, recalling that late at night under the stars they seemed to shift between deep blue and gold. There was a magic about her after all, and perhaps her eyes changed color with her mood or her setting.

Feril's hair reminded him of the rich shade of leaves just beginning to turn in the early fall, and though he at first thought he missed her long mass of curls, he decided that he actually liked this new hairstyle better. Her hair was so short that nothing competed with her face. Her skin was lightly tanned like the bark of a young hickory tree, her complexion smooth and flawless. The only exception was a tiny scar on her forehead where a tattoo once had been. He would ask her later what happened to the tattoos and where she had lived these past few years.

He closed his eyes, in his mind still seeing her vividly, and he offered a prayer to whatever god would listen to a dragon, that he could always see her just like this. He wanted to be able to perfectly recall her image after she left him again forever. He wanted to remember what she smelled like—newly opened wildflowers and sage grass, her hair carrying a suggestion of honey and ginger.

She would leave him eventually—this time permanently, he was convinced, but how soon? Wild elves were solitary figures, and Dhamon thought before that it had been a struggle for Feril to stay as long as she did with Palin and the others when they were all Goldmoon's champions and fought against the overlords.

He just hoped she would stay this time long enough to be of use to him.

Though there had been many women in Dhamon's life—back when he was human—Feril was the only one he truly had loved. He'd come close to settling down once with a half-elf thief named Riki, who bore his child. He had genuine affection for Riki, but he couldn't bring himself to commit to her, not considering his reckless nature, and not considering that Feril was too often in his thoughts.

Feril had changed, other than cutting her hair and removing her tattoos. Dhamon noticed that she seemed more confident, that her arms and legs were muscular, yet somehow she moved even more gracefully than in the old days.

She has changed for the better and I so very much for the worse. How long before she leaves? he thought one last time. Then he pushed his musings aside.

It had been just past dawn when Feril led Dhamon and Ragh down a wide path and into this grove of unusual trees. There were lofty black wattles and spreading rusty laurels, and stretching above them were silky oaks and silver basswoods. Feril pointed to tamarinds thick with bellbird vines, and to clumps of pink ash growing amid red muttonwoods. She slowed her pace when they passed an exotic acacia with huge silver-blue feathery leaves and orange flowers in foot-long spikes. The bark had a scent similar to raspberries, and it cut the sulfur odor of the sivak and the smells of the swamp that still clung heavily to Dhamon.

Feril noticed Dhamon admiring some of the trees, in particular a dome-like giant with heart-shaped leaves and copious clusters of vivid scarlet blooms.

"That one and some of these other trees shouldn't be here," she said.

"Like I shouldn't be here," Dhamon whispered. His soft voice was nonetheless loud enough to be felt by all as it resonated through the ground.

Feril tilted her head back and stretched an arm up so her fingers could tease the soft flowers of the exotic acacia.

"Dhamon, what I mean is that these trees were meant for warmer lands. I know it is hot now this summer, but come winter the snow could lay thick in these woods. They weren't meant to stand such cold, these beautiful trees."

Feril explained that when Beryl ruled this forest, the dragon must have done something to the earth or perhaps to the trees themselves so they could thrive here, but would the dragon's magic eventually fade without her around to nurture it? Did the Kagonesti even want to be in these woods come winter to find out?

Dhamon had offered to fly Feril and Ragh to the Nalis Aren, and at first the sivak had championed the idea.

"What is it about Nalis Aren that might help you become human again?" Feril asked.

It wasn't the lake itself, but what was in the lake, Dhamon explained. Feril wanted to know more, but he dismissed her questions with a shake of his massive head.

"Later, Feril. When we reach the lake."

"Why do you need my help so badly?"

"Later, Feril."

Feril refused to fly with him to Nalis Aren. Dhamon suspected she was just being stubborn; she would insist on taking her time traveling to Nalis Aren, just as he insisted on taking his time revealing everything that had to be done.

"It is not terribly far from here, the Lake of Death." Feril shook her head vehemently when he noted that they could avoid all these trees and fly there directly. "We can walk. It'll take three days at the most if we keep up this pace. We'll follow the river. I want to see if there are any more bandits or knights along the way, and I want to see if there are more burnt places, things we might not be able to see from the sky."

They all knew the land had been scorched by fire and magic, and that here and there were mass graves of Qualinesti elves. Indeed, they ran across a small group of marauders that they dealt with summarily. They had come upon the raggedy men skulking near a long, deep rut that ran parallel to the river. Perhaps the rut had been dug for a reason, but Feril couldn't fathom why. Perhaps it was made by a dragon, Dhamon speculated as he smoothed it over with his claws—after burying the bodies of the bandits they had killed deep in the trench.

They continued on without sleep and so reached Nalis Aren after two days. It was afternoon and the sun, though high and intense, was not enough to burn off the thin mist that hung above the massive crater-lake. It was roughly shaped like a triangle and filled the entire valley. The south end touched the foothills of the Kharolis Mountains, and the center of it was more than two miles across.

"Lovely," Feril said.

It was more than lovely, she thought, it was also unnatural—the color of the water was murky, yet the surface lay as smooth as polished glass despite the White Rage River surging into it. Where the brown foamy river met the lake's edge was where the water changed color and grew still. The sand around the shore was the shade of eggshells and sparkled in places from what Feril guessed were grains of quartz. No trees grew within a hundred yards of the sand and the nearest were old oaks that reached eighty or more feet into the sky.

They stood just inside the treeline staring straight ahead at the strange lake.

There were traces of old roads leading to the water from all directions, though they were now overgrown with milkweed and fennel and a scattering of seedlings. Feril noticed bootprints on the path they'd traveled to get here, and she suspected the tracks were made by either Knights of Neraka or bandits, but in no significant number and not within recent days. There were odd prints, too, goblins most likely, though it looked like they had tried to cover up their tracks. Feril could study the tracks more closely to make sure what creatures left them, or she could ask Dhamon, who was an expert woodsman. These prints, too, were weeks old.

"This lake," Feril said in a hushed voice, "is where Qualinost used to be."

Ragh staggered forward. "Qualinost, the elf capital . . ."

"Yes, the city was right out there . . . somewhere out there. Dhamon, I know you and the sivak have been living in a cave, but don't you know about the elves? Even on the Isle of Cristyne we heard about the demise of Qualinost."

"There's a lot about what's going on in the world that we don't know," Ragh said tersely. "It's not easy for . . . such as Dhamon and I . . . to walk into a city and hear the latest news and gossip. Hard enough finding you, elf. That took a big satchel of steel and lots of threats." He made a tsk-tsking sound and shook his head. "The whole city. Gone? I'd seen it almost seventy, eighty years ago . . . from high above. I thought it impressive for something of elven construction."

Feril's eyes narrowed at the insult as she approached the lake reverently. Her gaze drifted warily between the water and the sand. She glanced down at her feet. The grass was thick and mixed with stunted fennel and felt good between her toes. It reached no taller than her ankles, as if it had been regularly grazed upon. She smelled sulfur and swamp rot and knew Dhamon and Ragh were close behind her.

"You move quietly," she flung over her shoulder.

"No animal prints, Feril." Dhamon had been intently studying the ground. "You'd think there would be creature tracks in the sand, but there are none. Something is cropping the grass around here, though."

"Nothing drinks from the lake," Ragh cut in, "and here I am thirsty. Wonderful."

"That doesn't necessarily mean the water's bad," Feril said. "Let's see." She bent to her knees and took a deep breath. "It does not smell tainted, yet I agree it is unnaturally dark. Perhaps animals are scarce here or do not drink from the lake along this section of shore, but they might drink from it elsewhere."

"Perhaps." The sivak's tone was skeptical. "Dhamon, enough with the suspense. Tell us, how is this lake going to help you become human again?"

Feril raised her shoulders in a half-shrug and tentatively touched the water with her toes. "The lake can't help him, sivak."

Ragh growled. "Of course it can. Otherwise, why by the number of the Dark Queen's heads did we come here? Don't tell me it was a wasted, worthless . . ."

"It's what's *in* the lake that could make all the difference, right, Dhamon?" Feril stepped forward until the water came up to her knees. She'd caused only the faintest ripples when she entered, and the water was still smooth like glass behind her, where she'd already passed. "They say the city of Qualinost still exists here, but it's beneath the water. They say that when Beryl ... they called her the Green Peril ... succumbed to the elven army led by Laurana and Marshall Medan, that she destroyed Qualinost in her final moments. They say the dragon thrashed so hard a crater was created, and the White Rage River filled it up. Nalis Aren was born."

Ragh continued to growl softly, looking up at Dhamon. "Great. A dead city. What *exactly* do you think is in the lake? You saw something in that crystal ball, didn't you? That's why we're here." The sivak ground the ball of his foot into the sand. "Coarse stuff," he muttered to himself, "much coarser than sand should feel. You'd think there'd be dirt here instead of sand this far inland."

Feril thought the water was warm, though not so warm as the summer air. Perhaps the breeze blowing from the south had cooled it a little. It was comfortable, relaxing, and she found herself suddenly looking forward to a swim. It was odd, however, that there was a slight mist above the water carrying a chill.

"Qualinost was in the crystal ball, Ragh," Dhamon rumbled finally, catching Feril's eye with his intense gaze. "The crystal revealed that Qualinost is indeed still here, at the bottom of this lake, relatively intact. The crystal told me there's something down there that can make me human again."

"The city's intact?" Ragh kept grinding his foot, curious to see how deep the sand was. "And there's something hidden in it that will help?" His tone seemed incredulous.

"So the crystal says. Unfortunately, the crystal did not reveal just what that 'something' was."

"I suspect there's plenty of magic left in the city,"

Feril volunteered. "A few Qualinesti refugees I helped on Cristyne told me stories."

Dhamon nodded. "I need you both to help me find the magic."

Feril turned and looked at him as her fingers drew circles in the water. She shivered from the cold mist, and suddenly there was something cold in her eyes. "Dhamon, I would like to help you be human again, but . . . this lake is very big. The city was immense. This would be like looking for one perfect hair on a shaggy dog."

She took a few steps closer to the shore, anger now flitting on her face. The water lapped around her calves, and she stared at Dhamon with an odd expression before speaking again. "As curious as I am about this lake, I get a feeling of dread. This is a dangerous place, and what you're looking for . . . you don't know what you're looking for . . . could well be impossible to find. I don't think . . ."

Dhamon cleared his throat, the sound rough and loud, giving both Feril and Ragh a start. "I realize it's dangerous, but I will make it worth your while, Feril."

The Kagonesti arched a dubious eyebrow.

"You know I have treasure in my lair. It's a fortune on your terms, and you could use it to help your refugees. You can have all of it, Feril. You know you have power to survive underwater longer than my kind. If you explore the lake and discover what is down there that can make me human again, you can have all my treasure."

"Hey!" Ragh protested, before Dhamon swiveled his head and cut him off with a glare.

"A fortune?" Feril wrapped her arms around her chest, trying to ward off the chill of the mist.

"Gold, gems, and magical baubles . . . all of it yours

and all of it certainly worth the risks of Nalis Aren. Think how many refugees you could help."

She stood silent for several moments, weighing the offer. "This is absurd," she said at last, "and too dangerous." She turned and faced the center of the lake and glided farther out from the shore, testing the waters up to her waist. "The refugees do need help, and if the city is indeed at the bottom of this lake, there might be wisdom and magic in it, no doubt many things precious and arcane. When the elves fled, they could take only a handful of possessions with them. They had to leave practically everything behind."

"So the crystal ball might be right," Ragh, excited despite himself, interjected. "There could be a cure down there for Dhamon."

"There were many sorcerers and scholars in Qualinost, the finest elf minds in all of this land." She stirred the water with her fingers, noticing that the swirls were small and the surface was disturbed only briefly before returning to placidity. "Perhaps the finest minds in all of Ansalon." She tried to flick a ripple away from her, but that stopped rippling within a few inches. "Odd."

"Odd that elves had fine minds?" Ragh mused. Much, much softer, "I've respect for elves, Feril. More than they've respect for me and my kind."

"Feril . . ." Dhamon edged forward, his front claws reaching into the shallows of the lake. "Do you really think the Qualinesti's magic could hold the key?"

"I don't know." She shrugged. "They were shrewd in many ways and they defeated an overlord, didn't they? What harm could there be in my looking for things they left behind?" She glanced over her shoulder and up into Dhamon's eyes. "I admit, I wanted to come here anyway, Dhamon. I would have come here alone, eventually, had we not met again. I am a curious soul, and this place, with its unimaginable history of sadness and tragedy, draws me."

"You wanted to see if the tales were true about a sunken city?" Dhamon asked, shaking his head ruefully, the gesture stirring the air and blowing the scent of the swamp in her direction.

She frowned. "No. I doubt I would have thought to enter the water, were it not for your coaxing. I wanted to see the lake. It is said that no elf comes here."

"It may be dangerous, as you say."

"Our world is dangerous." She edged out until the water was above her waist and then nearing her shoulders. "One of the Qualinesti refugees I spoke to mentioned working for a sage who had studied dragons and their magic—said the sage and his students, like so many others, refused to leave Qualinost so likely died there. Perhaps if I could find that sage's workshop, or another's of equal importance, it might help you. I agree with you that it is worth the trying."

Dhamon watched in quiet admiration as the Kagonesti bravely tipped her head back and let the water play around her neck. She closed her eyes.

"Yet I see what you see, Feril. The water behaves oddly. There are no animal prints nearby. I sense, if not danger, then caution signs," he said. "Watch yourself."

"You and the sivak can wait for me in the shade of the oaks. I might be gone a while." With that comment and a last look over her shoulder, Feril abruptly disappeared beneath the surface. Ragh gasped expectantly, meeting Dhamon's gaze.

"The sivak," Ragh said with some irritation, after he was certain she was not going to pop right back into view. "My name is Ragh, elf." He left the sand and walked onto the grass and scowled when he couldn't find the depression he'd made with his foot near the lake's edge. "Damnedest place this lake is."

Dhamon came close to him on the shore, saying nothing

"Your elf-friend can breathe water?" Ragh asked, in a milder tone.

"When she wants to. I've seen her slip inside the minds of sea creatures, and I've seen her grow gills. She can run with any animal too."

Ragh started heading back toward the trees. "I'm not sure I'd want to breathe *that* water even if I could. Hmm, no animal tracks near the lake." Then he remembered he couldn't find his own tracks in the sand. "Damnedest place, and damn you for not telling me about this plan of yours, for not telling me what you learned from that crystal ball. I deserve to know these things. You're risking the life of your elf-friend, but you're risking mine too. My half of the treasure also, if you don't mind my mentioning it."

"Half?!" Dhamon snorted contemptuously. "Feril doesn't know how much treasure we actually have now, does she?" Dhamon said in an amused tone. Ragh's jaw dropped. "Anyway," Dhamon continued, "she's a formidable character, you've already seen that. She can well take care of herself."

"What else did your crystal ball say? Think she'll run into trouble down there?"

Dhamon's eyes glazed over. "Oh, she'll run into trouble all right, but like I say, she can take care of herself. I didn't send her down there to be sacrificed. I still have some . . . feelings, you know, but I want to be cured, to be human again, and then, my friend, the bulk of our treasure will let us live like kings."

———————◆•◆•◆———————

The water was pleasantly warm and relaxing, colored a brilliant blue below the murkier-looking surface, as if some inner light that made it practically shine and glow. As Feril held her breath she felt the water press gently against her ears. She was uncertain how far she was seeing under the water, perhaps only as far as one hundred feet—all intense blue. A minute passed and nothing intruded; after two minutes she saw something out of the corner of her eye.

Turning, Feril spotted a fish with silvery sides and a rosy stripe. A variety of lake trout, she decided, and beyond the first one another fish as long as her forearm. This second was green and brown, its jaw extending just under and beyond its fat eye. Likely a bass, she thought at first, but it swam closer, revealing itself as more colorful and quick, a new species she did not know. Shortly she saw a pair of small, black bullheads with snow-white underbellies.

Then a school of silverfins twisted into view, before darting and disappearing away. Other fish appeared, and with them a soft surrating sound, like a gentle scraping, as if from the larger fish brushing against each other.

The presence of so many fish calmed her. She hadn't told Dhamon, but she feared the water actually might be poisoned to an extent, since she'd not noticed any animal tracks nearby and since it was unnaturally still and so murky on the surface.

She swam forward, still holding her breath, discovering many underwater plants now, which further improved her mood. Dodders, reeds, and delicate looking lake oats reached just inches below the surface. There was the greatest variety of fish where the plants were the most dense. She spied deep-bodied drum fish that were making grunting sounds that carried hauntingly through the water. There were bony-jawed pike hunting smaller fish, and spoonbills and guapotes.

She dived deeper down and struck out toward the center of the lake, finding plenty of bowfin, one nearly as long as she was tall. The mottled green fish had a large, scaleless head and a tooth-filled mouth, and though it could have troubled her, it came close enough only to satisfy its curiosity, then fluttered away.

Feril was starting to get lightheaded as she swam through a bed of plants resembling cattails. She closed her eyes and pictured the silvery trout. For an instant she considered taking that form, but hands might be useful, she decided, so she modified her nature magic. As her chest grew tighter and she felt the first wave of dizziness, she focused her energies on her neck, just below her jaw—still picturing the trout, the way it moved, the flash of its scales—its gills.

The water that flowed into Feril's lungs through the gills she'd grown was tepid in temperature but nonetheless sustaining. *Amazing,* she thought. Each time she called upon her nature magic to fly, breathe water, or perform some other miracle that was beyond an ordinary elf, she was astounded. She would never grow tired of her abilities, never fail to appreciate the gift of her experience.

For several minutes she pushed aside unsettling thoughts about Dhamon and the sivak, the mass graves and the dark forces hunting the struggling Qualinesti. She focused only on herself and this incredible lake. She concentrated on the feel of the water that cocooned her, and how her short hair fluttered as she continued her diving and swimming. She could smell everything below, the fish and the plants, perhaps the very essence of the water, all of it very pleasant and distracting. She savored the sensation of the water flowing through her gills, and she listened attentively to the faint, musical sound of the drum fish. A school of sunfish darted toward her, all shimmering orange and yellow-gold. A lone catfish swam lazily behind. Later, there were more trout, pike, and basslike fish.

Farther out and deeper down, there was only the intense blue and eerie silence. She reached out with her senses, searching for the sounds of the drum fish she had come to rely on, hearing only the beating of her heart and a rush in her ears. She strained her eyes looking for something that might have spooked the fish, but she saw no trace of a predator. The plant life had vanished. She considered returning to the surface just to get her bearings. Instead she plunged even deeper. Feril guessed she was twenty or thirty feet down. There should be some kind of undergrowth here, at least reed thin plants looking like strands of yarn. Perhaps she was deeper than she thought, forty or fifty feet—too deep for plants to grow. The water was becoming a dark blue. Perhaps the light didn't reach far enough for any plant life. How deep could the lake be?

"Just a little farther," she urged herself, "for Dhamon and for the treasure that will help the refugees." It was equally for her own curiosity. If truth be told, she had been headed in the direction of the lake when Dhamon and the sivak crossed her path. She'd intended to visit this place when she'd first learned of it last year, though she'd been taking her time getting here. She'd never been to Qualinost when it was teeming with elves—she had no desire then. There would have been crowds, elves asking the Kagonesti stranger questions, pressing against her on the street. She preferred her blessed solitude—she relished her solitude even here in the lake. "There must be a bottom. Broken homes, shattered towers, and . . ."

The lake changed abruptly, startling the Kagonesti. It had grown darker still, the dark blue giving way to a dusky green, the pleasant warmth becoming instantly, numbingly cold. It was as if she'd jumped into a glacier lake in Southern Ergoth. She blinked furiously as her eyes tried to adjust. There was something below her, just outside her vision—a stark angular shape. A tower?

She pointed herself straight down like an arrow and kicked her feet violently. At the same time she fought to separate the dark colors and shadows and to keep her imagination in reign. Was this the outskirts of the city? Was Qualinost truly at the bottom of this lake, as the tales claimed? Or was she seeing the husk of a dead tree? Perhaps she wasn't seeing anything, her mind was playing tricks.

No, she told herself. There is definitely something there.

She kicked even more furiously, trying to fight off the cold, which was becoming hurtful, streaming through the water and locking her gaze on the angular object. Her heart beat faster in anticipation as she drove herself harder.

No! Only a tree, she realized, one that had been large and wide in life loomed like an obelisk now, but a tree nonetheless. Though disappointed, Feril still had no intention of retreating to the warmth of the surface. If there was a giant of a tree such as this deep down in this lake, there could well be other surprises.

"Qualinost," she whispered, the word carrying through the water not intelligibly, but as bubbles flowing around her ears. Qualinost must be here, she repeated to herself. It has to be here somewhere—the tales can't be wrong.

"It is here," came an unbidden reply. "Just a little farther. I'll show you the way."

Something gripped the Kagonesti's wrists and pulled her. The touch was impossibly cold and impressively strong. Feril struggled against it, but the force tugged her inexorably down, down, down—where the cold was all around.

CHAPTER

6

An hour later, Dhamon was half in, half out of the lake, his tail twitching on the sand and creating patterns that the sivak could watch disappear.

"You said the elf could take care of herself."

"She can, Ragh."

"Then why worry?"

"I'm not worried."

Dhamon stared into the water, seemingly looking at his own scaly reflection through the top layer of mist, but truthfully staring at something far beyond the lake and beyond this day. He saw himself six years ago, when he boasted wheat-blond hair and as much honor and stout-heartedness as any knight. He'd not been long-removed from the Dark Knights, as they called themselves then. His soul was shiny then, after being polished by an aging Solamnic Knight whom he'd come to know as a mentor and friend. His heart had been pledged to helping Goldmoon and her companions against the dragon overlords. Feril was among those companions: he, Rig, Palin, and the others . . . all of them believing they could make a difference in the world and were looking for a way.

Dhamon thought he loved her from first sight, even though, smiling inwardly, he knew he initially had rebelled against that notion. She as an elf after all, and he was a human; their lives were so differently fated, and his years on the earth would be so short compared to hers. She was a Kagonesti, a wild elf, a loner. He was a former Dark Knight with so much blood on his hands. Still, they did become swept up in each other, at least for a little while. The memory of that time was the sweetest thing that kept him going. Did he still love her?

Could he ever be human again? Dhamon looked at his reflection and shuddered. Unspoken always was the faint hope that if he was human, he could—perhaps—be with Feril again. Unless she chose to leave once more or truly expected him to part with his hoard to help refugees, because he might still love her, but not enough to part with the riches and what they could bring him.

As much as he was repulsed by his dragon-self, did he truly want to be human? A part of him relished the amazing power of this body, savored the sensations of flight. A part of him didn't want to give up being a dragon.

"You said the elf could breathe water, could turn into a fish if she wanted to." Ragh was standing at the very edge of the water. "You said that."

"Yes," Dhamon snarled, irked that his thoughts had been interrupted.

"Then let's wait for her back by those trees like she asked us to. Maybe she can find whatever it is down there that can make you human again. Too bad that crystal ball wasn't more precise, didn't tell just *what* you needed to find. Hope the elf can figure it out. Sure is taking her a while." The draconian looked over his shoulder. The shade was inviting. "It's hot out here in the open, Dhamon, and I think the shade would do us both some good. We could cool off some."

Dhamon suspected this summer heat didn't at all bother Ragh. He knew the draconian preferred the camouflage of the shade, however. It was too easy to be spotted in the open, especially against the starkness of the sand and the lake here. The sivak once had been a spy for Sable and was used to keeping to the corners and shadows, so his anxiety had nothing to do with the heat of this late summer day, Dhamon decided. Ragh simply wanted to be safe from any prying eyes.

"I'll wait for Feril right here, Ragh. You go ahead."

"Fine. Fine. Fine." The sivak ground the ball of his foot into the sand and watched until the depression smoothed itself over. "You wait right here for your precious elf, where it's all hot and . . ."

"You're the one who persuaded me to leave the swamp. Ultimately, this flying around and exploring was your idea."

"My idea? Yeah, but I'm not the one who was looking in the crystal ball looking for a cure. Whoever's idea it was, it isn't such a bad one, eh? Not so humid here as in the swamp, and the trees are different. The smells are different." He wrinkled his nose at Dhamon. "No giant alligators nipping at our heels. You're back in touch with the love of your life, and she's trying to make you human again . . . even though she doesn't know you're not going to keep your part of the bargain, even though this elf-lady hasn't a clue that you won't donate all your treasure to refugees. All in all, I'd say this is a good venture, huh?"

Dhamon wondered if he detected a touch of melancholy in the sivak's tone.

"We got out of the swamp and far away from Sable," Ragh continued aimlessly, as he edged back toward the shade, "at least for a while, and I got to see something I never had before . . . a lake where the mighty elven city of Qualinost once sprawled. It was definitely a good idea, this . . . holiday away from the swamp. Another good idea is waiting for the elf in the shade, which is just what I'm going to do. You can go ahead and stay here if you want . . ."

Dhamon slid partway into the water. "She's been gone for too long a time, Ragh, too long for my liking. I think I'd better try and look for her."

Ragh stopped in his tracks, letting out an exasperated sigh. "You said she can take care of herself, that she can breathe water, be a fish if she wants."

"I'll just take a look. You know I'd rather not."

"Yeah, water's not your favorite element, Dhamon."

"Perhaps she needs help."

"If she's some sort of trout swimming around down there, you're not going to find her. You may as well stand here and burn in the sun."

"She can find me. I think I'll be rather easy to spot," Dhamon said as he moved out into the warm lake water. He shuddered, though not from the chill of the mist. No, he didn't really care for water. "I can hold my breath a long time."

"Fine," Ragh cursed, kicking at stones on the beach. "Fine. Fine. I'll wait for the both of you in the shade." He struck out toward the oaks and only once glanced over his shoulder. He noted that the surface of the lake was as flat as glass behind the dragon, not even a ripple remaining in Dhamon's wake. The sand had also smoothed itself again. "Like you say, dragons are easily noticed."

The shadows cast by the thick oaks felt cool washing over the sivak's scaly hide. But he couldn't enjoy himself. He looked out at the lake, muttered a string of curses, and grudgingly headed back toward the bank. "I'll wait for you, Dhamon Grimwulf. Just don't be down there too long. I like this place less and less."

<hr>

The deep lake water was painfully cold, and whatever had a hold of Feril's wrist was strong and equally painful and only added to her misery. It continued to pull her down swiftly. The pressure against her ears tightened, and the water that coursed through her gills felt like ice. She focused on her wrists and saw what at first she mistook for wispy vines, as if emanating from some plant that grew in the watery depths, but as she peered closer, she realized that the tendrils were instead ghostly, gloved fingers. She fought against the grip, staring harder into the dark blue below her and finally making out the specter of a man. The specter was wearing transparent armor, with the faintest mark of a lily on his breastplate.

The ghost of a Knight of Neraka, she thought, as she struggled even more futilely. How could something that looked so insubstantial be so strong? How could those no longer a part of this corporal world hold and hurt the living?

"Join me." The words came from the specter, sounding thin and hollow.

No, Feril raged.

"You are not strong enough to resist," the dead knight insisted. "Join me. Together we will protect the Fallen Queen."

What Fallen Queen? Feril thrashed wildly, trying to pull herself free from the icy grip of the strange specter, but the ghostly fingers only tightened, and Feril felt her willpower, her life, slipping away.

"You are not strong enough to fight me, elf. Join me in the Lake of Death."

The water became an intense green color as she was pulled farther down.

"Join the Fallen Queen."

By Habbakuk's fist! Feril looked, blinking furiously. The green stretched as far as she could see and was coming more into focus the closer to it the dead knight pulled her. The green appeared to be the bloated corpse of the overlord Beryl.

She couldn't see all of the huge carcass—only the head, neck, and just beyond its shoulder blades. Its front claws were outstretched and its head rested between them. It looked almost as if it was sleeping. Its horns curved up, looking pale like the specter and breaking the wall of green. Its massive eyes were closed, and for a moment she thought it looked peaceful and beautiful. How big the corpse was, she could only guess. A green mist and dark waters concealed most of its bulk.

Scales glimmered faintly along the dragon's neck, and in places some of them were broken apart—with elven long swords lodged between some of them, spears, and the rotting shafts of arrows sticking out of the dragon's head. From a closer look she could tell that two talons were broken, and there was a long slash in one of the front legs.

The dragon had died a long time ago, Feril thought to herself, wondering why the beast hadn't started to rot; that was puzzling, but something Feril decided she would mull over later—after she was far away from the dead knight.

"Join me," the ghost droned, still pulling her down deeper. "Join my brothers in service to the Fallen Queen."

Other images were coalescing around the spines that ran down the dragon's neck. More ghostly Knights of Neraka, floating shoulder to shoulder as though in formation. There were a few elves among them, and Feril wondered if these were the spirits of Qualinesti who died in the battle against Beryl or other visitors to the lake who had foolishly entered the water and been conscripted into the dead army.

I'll never join you, Feril thought, redoubling her efforts to squirm free. Despite her considerable strength, she couldn't break the specter's grip. In that instant she finally realized brute strength alone would not work, so she opted for a different tactic. She closed her eyes and pictured one of the catfish she'd seen earlier. She began to change her form—waver and shrink, arms thinning and receding, gradually slipping out of the dead knight's grasp. While the process was not painful, it was uncomfortable and unsettling, and the intense cold made it even more precarious. Her teeth chattered and she shivered uncontrollably as her legs grew together to form a tail, her feet flattening into fins. Her tanned skin turned black and her leather clothes and elf features appeared to melt away.

Smaller, she urged, *much smaller.* The specter made one last grab at her as the still-mutating fish-creature finally darted away and up, beyond its clutches. *Smaller still*, she commanded herself. Only a foot long now, the fish-Feril swam faster, angling sharply away from the carcass of the overlord.

When curiosity got the better of her and she finally looked back, Beryl's head was all she could make out, that and the small wispy forms of the dead knights clinging like moss to her scales. The dead knight intent on capturing her seemed to have vanished. After a few moments, she turned around and swam closer to the dragon's nose, cautiously, so she could get a better look and so she could see if the undead paid her any attention. The water was still painfully frigid, but her catfish form tolerated the cold much better. She was quick to learn that the spirits of the knights and elves were uninterested in any small fishes.

There were decaying trees just beyond the dragon's snout and what looked like the remains of a marble fountain. There were plenty of bones, too, human or elf, Feril guessed, deciding not to get that close to find out for certain. Pieces of plate mail, shredded tabards, shields, helmets, quivers, and more were scattered around.

The dragon probably collapsed on her Knights of Neraka and the elves, on the fountain and who knew what else as it died. Feril tried to picture the dragon's final minutes and its fall, the impact its massive body made and that caused this huge crater near the White Rage River and the creation of this—what did the dead knight call it?—this Lake of Death. An apt name, Feril mused to herself.

How was there so much magic in the dead dragon that it kept the corpse perfectly preserved and kept the lake so still? Feril wondered. It was so oddly cold at this depth, yet warm and still and inviting near the surface.

Perhaps it was the unnatural cold that kept the fish away from these ghostly depths, or perhaps there was some other magical boundary that separated the realm of the living from Beryl's realm of the dead. Nothing seemed to prevent Feril from exploring deeper, though the cold was threatening to drive her away.

Despite her trepidation, she swam closer still, until the dragon's visage filled her vision. Her eyes searched the broken objects on the lake bed amidst the traces of the undead. Feril's catfish eyes were acute, so she could tell that everything around the dragon was rotting, and therefore had been there for some time. Everything but the dragon itself was rotting. She couldn't get over the size of the overlord's head. She'd seen Beryl once before, when the dragon was alive. It was at the Window to the Stars but that was years ago, another lifetime it seemed.

Even in death the overlord looked impressive. Feril wanted to swim all the way around the dragon, inspecting the items and objects scattered around it and studying the diaphanous knights and elves. The murkiness and green mist that cloaked much of the dragon and the faint glow coming from its depths was unsettling.

Not worth pursuing at the moment, she thought. Feril wasn't sure what she was looking for and wished Dhamon would have given her some specific clue. She didn't see anything that looked like a magical item lying around. Perhaps she ought to go back and find a sorcerer who could more aptly consult Dhamon's crystal ball. Perhaps, after all, Dhamon was better off as a dragon.

Yes, maybe Dhamon is better off as a dragon, Feril mused as she finally turned and sped away from the dragon's snout. She wondered if she could find happiness in such a form, but she sensed that Dhamon wasn't very happy and that being a dragon didn't suit him. Didn't she prefer Dhamon as a human?

Feril suddenly realized she was disoriented. She didn't know where she was, where to swim, or even how far out and deep down she was in this well-named Lake of Death. She swam closer to the bottom and started circling outward, passing over more decaying tree trunks and dead bodies, shattered weapons, then bigger, fallen columns and strewn rubble from homes. Beyond this—beyond all this—she could see several virtually intact buildings.

Qualinost.

She stared wide-eyed. The city beyond these first destroyed buildings appeared as though from a lost dream, artful spires rising from the lake bed, courtyards sprawling, exquisite statues attesting to the talent of the greatest of Qualinesti artisans. With her catfish eyes she could make out the colors through the water, the buildings ranging from white to pale brown, all of them with pastel trim and intricately carved doors and shutters, all of them slimed with algae and rot. She half-expected to see dozens of elves walking from place to place carrying out the routines of their lives, but nary a fish swam by, and she knew the water was as cold and tainted as it had been next to the dragon's corpse.

She couldn't see all of the city, suspected she was seeing only a small outer portion of it, and she felt her emotions well up, a great pang of sadness, wishing that she had visited this glorious place years ago when it was full of life.

There would have been libraries to explore and sages to greet in their homes, places where the greatest of elf sorcerers once lived and apprentices studied. Qualinost would have been a good place to spend hours researching practically any subject, she thought. It was such a magnificent city—once. Now it lay deep under the Lake of Death, smothered by the dark blue water.

Where to start? Where in all of this do I start?

She swam toward a low building with curved sides. A row of twisting tree trunks paralleled what looked to be the front of the structure. Feril imagined they were once birches, judging by the few papery white pieces of bark that clung to their bases. Nearly all the trees she saw were black and gray sticks, looking like silhouettes against the pale buildings and deep blue of the water, like charcoal slashes on a canvas. Like a winter scene, with the leaves missing.

The leaves and the life gone forever, she thought. Qualinost, one big cemetery, the buildings and trees markers attesting to the greatness of elven dead.

Sadness overwhelmed her as she wove around the twisting birch trees and followed the wall of the curved building. Perhaps this was a library, certainly a building meant to be used by citizens, its design inviting. A place to start her investigations? She wished Dhamon was here to see this and advise her. Though it was depressing to think that centuries of civilization were buried in this lake, the sunken city retained some of its former allure, and she wished to share that with him.

As she neared the building, she reached inside herself and found the familiar magical spark. She coaxed it to brighten and forced the energy into her tail and fins, regaining her legs and arms and elf size. The catfish skin became her leather tunic again, and her fingers pulled her through the water. She retained her gills, a necessity, but released her acute catfish vision and took back her own eyesight. Despite the depth, she could see well enough. The cold was still intense.

The building she approached had carvings arching above a skewed, ironbound wooden door. The carvings were tiny and precise, showing elf children playing with small catlike creatures. A stately elf matron supervised them. Other carvings running the length of the door showed children carrying runes of an Elvish dialect Feril was only passingly familiar with. "Senaril t' Deban," she made out. "Deban's gifts," she thought it meant. It would be better if it translated as "warm inside," she thought to herself wryly.

She wrapped her fingers tightly around the door handle and pulled. The iron was rusty, the wood warped, and coupled with the water pressing against it, she couldn't budge it open. Odd, there were no windows. She swam up to the roof, looking for a window or skylight and finding none. The Kagonesti told herself she should move on. A hundred buildings were in her line of sight, but this one had aroused her curiousity, and so she returned to the door and pressed her fingers against the wood.

Move for me, she implored. *Damn my curiosity. Move!*

Her energy spread from her chest and down her arms to her fingertips and into the wood. Her magic warped the panels just enough in the frame so that it burst open on its own accord. Soft yellow light spilled out, and Feril slipped in.

Amazing, she thought, again wishing Dhamon were here to see all this. The building consisted of one large room, and it was filled with a multitude of sculptures. At first glance she could tell that most of them were elves, and most of them were artworks of children caught in various poses of play. The nearest child stretched for a butterfly; another was of a young boy with a large frog in his hands. Beyond these pieces were sculptures of older children, and at the far side of the room Feril saw the adult figures. Perhaps this showcased the stages of childhood. Paintings on the walls, faded terribly by water, were of elf infants.

The other sculptures were of woodland creatures, centaurs, and small winged fey that Feril suspected lived only in the artist's imagination. The works, so similar in style, she could tell were all created by the same individual. A lifetime of sculptures and work this room represented. There were hundreds, she realized after staring into the far corners of the room, most of them small, but many life-sized, and some double and triple the size of a natural subject. It would have taken hundreds of years to produce all of this art in such detail, Feril knew. A lifetime of work ruined with the dragon's death and swallowed up by the lake.

She forced herself to ignore the persistent cold and wound her way through the gallery, touching the elf boy with the frog and finding the stone pleasingly smooth. Feril ran her fingers over each sculpture she passed, discovering that some were of the same individual, though captured at different stages of childhood. Occasionally she glanced up, marveling at the light that shafted in from the ceiling. It came from an enchanted crystal that hung by a gold wire and cast an even glow over the artworks. She'd seen such magical baubles before, but when she swam up to inspect this one, she discovered that it was especially meticulous—pear-shaped with silver leaves and a stem. From her ceiling vantage point, looking down over the room, she spied small crystal figurines arranged at the bases of some of the larger statues—pieces of fruit, diminutive animals, vases, and mushrooms. She stole another glance at the enchanted, pear-shaped crystal.

I will borrow this bauble, she said to herself, as I doubt that all the buildings are so magically lit, but I will return it when I am done.

Feril tucked the pear under her belt, which dimmed the glow only a little, and then dived down to the floor again. She took a long look at the statue in the middle of the room as she swam around it. It was of a Qualinesti boy standing with a crossbow, a quiver of bolts propped between his legs. He had the face of the boy holding the frog—perhaps the same boy, only older, perhaps a brother.

Maybe the statues tell a story, she thought, or recorded important moments in the lives of individuals who were precious to the sculptor. Maybe when she was finished with searching the city and after she had discovered a way to help Dhamon, she might return and study this room at length. There was certainly nothing in here that would help Dhamon or would help her puzzle out the magic in the city. She swam toward the door with a sudden pang of regret.

When she turned for a last look at the sculptures, she noticed a wispy figure rising from behind the boy with the crossbow. It was thin, like an elf, and as it drew closer its features became clearer. It had the image of a man, but with long graceful arms and delicate fingers. Mist swirled around the wispy figure, serving as a robe. Translucent feet poked out, sandaled and narrow. Its face was narrow, too, and Feril imagined that in life this dead elf must have been gaunt.

Somehow she was not frightened.

"Join me," the ghost said. "Enjoy my art forever."

CHAPTER

7

Dhamon didn't like water, and he especially didn't like deep lakes. He had almost drowned in a lake once. He shuddered at the memory.

This one in particular was unnerving. The blue was too intense to be natural, and he saw there was a depth beyond which the fish would not swim. The water turned cold deeper down, an aberrant, disturbing cold that swirled around him. He had to find Feril, of whom, thus far, he had seen no sign.

Nalis Aren indeed, he thought, half-expecting to see chaos wights in the frigid water. He cursed himself for his fear of water and for not immediately joining Feril when she dived in, for hesitating and letting her take on his possible salvation alone. If something happened to her he would never be at peace with himself, and he might never have another chance to regain his humanity.

He searched for the Kagonesti for several minutes, at first seeing only the blue, then plunging deep, but without seeing anything out of the ordinary. He could have searched much longer before surfacing for air. His lungs were immense, and he likely could hold his breath for an hour or more, but he wouldn't stay down for more than a dozen minutes at a time. He couldn't.

Dhamon dived again, hunting Feril erratically not methodically, going over the same area again and again. For a while he swam along the surface and tried mingling with the fishes, thinking one of them might turn out to be Feril, but they were all frightened of him, despite his suppressed dragonfear, and soon darted away.

At last, admitting defeat, he climbed out onto the bank and saw Ragh sitting in the grass just beyond the sand.

"You weren't down there very long, were you? I know you're not overly fond of the water."

Dhamon stood in the shallows and gave a shake, the water spattering all over the decidedly disgruntled sivak.

"Didn't happen to see any elves down there, did you?"

Dhamon shook again, arched his back, and let the sun warm him. "It's a big lake, Ragh. She could be anywhere. I should have asked her in what direction she was going to swim."

The draconian shrugged. "Still, you didn't look very long for her."

"I keep telling you, Feril can take care of herself."

"So you're not worried."

"No, Ragh, I'm not worried."

"Could've fooled me."

Dhamon's eyes narrowed. "This is not a game, Ragh." His tone was suddenly angry.

"Fine, fine. I agree that she's perfectly capable, Dhamon. I saw her hang those knights from the trees, and if she can swim with the fishes like you say, then we might have a long time to wait—no reason to get impatient."

Dhamon pawed at a plant caught around a talon. "I might try again later, if she doesn't come back in a short while."

"Fine by me. I'll wait in the woods, as far away from this peculiar lake as possible. I like the water maybe even less than you do. I can't even swim like you do. I sink like a rock."

"Stop talking about it and go to the woods then."

"I intend to." Ragh headed toward the trees again, glancing over his shoulder. "I'm going to take a long nap, Dhamon . . . in the cool shade. Wake me up if or when you find the elf . . . or when you give up waiting for her."

"She'll be back," Dhamon said.

The Kagonesti had obviously managed well enough without him these past several years, he thought, and she certainly had faced worse dangers in her life than this unnaturally cold lake.

"Yeah, fine, but of course there's a chance she already has drowned, Dhamon . . ." When Dhamon shot him an angry look, the sivak added, ". . . so might want to keep an eye out for her body floating to the surface. Wake me up if you do, then maybe we can get out of here, pronto. Sable's swamp is starting to look mighty attractive compared to this damnable lake."

"Join me," the elf specter repeated. "Live in my gallery forever." The wispy figure floated toward Feril, arms spread out in a greeting. "I am Deban Nildareh, and I would love to add your beautiful form to my works of art."

Not today, Feril said to herself. She would have liked to say aloud, "I'll not ever join you," but she didn't want to rile the strangely mild-mannered ghost. Instead she swiftly kicked her feet and swam past the sculptures and outside the building. She followed the wall as it curved toward a slate-tiled street.

Residences stretched in a line far into the dark blue water. One was missing a roof, and another had decorative stones knocked off along one side, as if a great windstorm had swept down the row of homes. The largest had a broken fence and shattered window boxes everywhere. A few had sheer curtains hanging out of opened windows. There was minimal damage on many of the buildings that she saw, though she suspected that she would see considerable damage if she really inspected things closely, but she wasn't going to slow down in case the elf ghost was pursuing her. She kicked her feet and drove through the water faster.

Feril tried to keep her mind off the cold by imagining what it was like in the final moments for the Qualinesti who had refused to leave their beloved city. It must have been a time of pure terror, the sky darkened by the great dragon Beryl cutting across it. The overlord must have breathed on the elves, her deadly green cloud choking the ones caught in the open. Beryl's forces were probably scouring the streets. She pictured the elves fleeing, some of them fighting desperately.

Did they die by Knights of Neraka or by the great overlord Beryl? Did they give the last measure of their strength in defiance of the dragon, or did they fall as they were fleeing? Did they drown when the dragon struck the earth and the White Rage River spilled into the crater to create Nalis Aren? Had they known there wasn't a chance of victory and stayed till the end because Qualinost was all they had and all they ever wanted, and they couldn't bear to leave their dreams behind? Or did they imprudently believe there truly was a chance to save their city?

Feril would have stayed and fought alongside the bravest warriors to defend the nation, not the city, of Qualinost. The city was merely graceful towers and elegant homes to her—a physical home. She was thankful she'd never become attached to any home, any one single place; indeed, she had very few possessions. Clothes, memories, and woods to walk through, that was all she needed. *Perhaps Dhamon Grimwulf,* a piece of her heart murmured.

Was there something down here that could help him? Was this all a waste of her time?

Feril headed straight toward an artful tower that had caught her eye. It looked to be five or six levels and seemed to have escaped any serious damage. Her arms churned through the water faster, as the cold relentlessly seeped into her very bones. It seemed to be getting worse, and the feeling was leaving her feet.

As strong as her will was, it couldn't keep the cold away. In the span of a few city blocks, Feril's teeth were chattering senselessly. She imagined this must be as cold as the icy lakes created by the white dragon Frost on her Kagonesti homeland.

She angled herself toward the top of the tower and its roof that reminded her of a turnip. The roof was lighter than the stone of the outer walls, and it glimmered faintly as if embedded with crystals or precious metals. Directly beneath her was a circular manse and next to it, an impressive home that looked like it had been built around a much older courtyard. There was a fountain in the center, with two long-finned fish twisted together in an embrace. Water must have sprayed up all around from the mouths of smaller fish that ringed the bowl. There were tall, leafless trees in a runic pattern throughout the courtyard, and benches with posts carved to look like the legs of wild cats and horses. Someone with wealth and influence and an appreciation for art had lived here.

She passed over what she suspected was a small merchant district. The buildings were more colorful and a few had decorative awnings that hung limply without a current to stir them. There were numerous signs, all wooden and all rotting, the paint faded by the water and making their words illegible from this distance. Gowns and cloaks lay half-out, half-inside one shop window. Slippers were strewn outside another; a headless doll lay on its back in front of a likely toy store. Runes above a second-floor window suggested a sage or herbalist had lived there.

She would return to visit this district later, she decided, as perhaps that herbalist and others—scholars and healers with storefronts—had left some of their goods behind. Perhaps if the materials were stored in stoppered pots, not all the contents would have been ruined by the lake. Feril might bring Dhamon along. He'd been a battlefield medic and so could describe potent healing salves and such that could be salvaged and handed out to the Qualinesti refugees.

And some clothes for herself, she thought impulsively, considering that her only leather tunic was growing thin and was in need of replacing. Some garments the water wouldn't have ruined; these she could lay out on the bank and let the sun dry. A light cloak would be nice, as the evenings would be getting cooler soon. It was so terribly cold here, she was reminded. She would look for a good knife, too, she decided, remembering the Knights of Neraka attacking her back by the White Rage River. She'd wished then that she carried a knife.

She spotted skeletons everywhere—at the corners of streets, near marble benches, at the doors to a few shops, and around the base of the tall trunks that lined the district. She noticed only occasional bits of armor, and these were silver, not black, likely marking the wearers as Qualinesti warriors. There were spears and javelins and a few shields, the markings on which were partially ravaged.

Feril could barely move her numb fingers by the time she had cleared the small merchant district and reached the high tower. She knew there must be other merchant quarters . . . somewhere. The city was immense, perhaps it had been scattered by Beryl's fall, and she knew it could take her weeks to explore this area, months perhaps.

Her slender arms had become so heavy that she could scarcely lift them anymore, scarcely keep swimming. She glanced up, seeing only the never-ending blue, and realized that she should head toward the surface—at least for a little while.

How deep is this lake? How many feet down am I?

Feril angled upwards, swimming more slowly. Warm up thoroughly before returning. She was so terribly, terribly cold. The city and the lake would be here forever, so Feril knew she would have time to regain her strength and tell Dhamon what she'd discovered, perhaps wait until tomorrow to return.

Then she found herself close to the tower, and there was an open window a few feet away. She had the enchanted crystal still tucked into her belt to light her way. What is in the tower? Feril's curiosity won again, and she decided to take a quick peek inside. Just a few moments, she told herself, as she managed to force herself to keep swimming. A few moments will not make a difference, then I can be on my way and be warm for a while. She pulled herself through the window, her enchanted light revealing a room that at first appeared to be filled with fog, but the mist was actually layer upon layer of parchment, she was quick to discern, all the sheets hanging suspended from floor to ceiling. She stretched her arm forward, touching several sheets. They dissolved into shreds, looking like fragments from a crushed eggshell.

She waved her arms to scatter the pieces drifting like snow before her eyes, so she could see farther into the room. She saw shelves on the far wall, all loaded with books. Likely the water had destroyed all these, but there was always a chance some pages could be dried out and preserved. If by chance, the books offered any magic spells or lore, the water shouldn't have caused any harm—this she had learned during her time with the great sorcerer Palin Majere.

So many books, and this is just one tower.

They could be accounting ledgers for all she knew, or histories of Qualinost's oldest families. They could be blank books, waiting to be sold to some scholar or statesman, to be filled with their imperious ruminations. They could all be ruined. Hoping against hope, she reached for one of the books, a short, narrow volume bound in red leather. The cover floated open, spilling its pages onto the floor where they dispersed in every possible direction.

Worthless. Like this notion of finding a cure for Dhamon here is worthless. By Habbakuk's fist, why did he ever think to suggest I search this lake? Search for what? What?

Feril tried to reach for another book but couldn't; all of a sudden the numbness had taken a greater hold of her arms. It's the cold that's making me despair, she thought, the cold is making this all seem so futile. There's an answer here, I know it. The Qualinesti had some of the brightest savants and sorcerers on all of Krynn. They had to have left something behind that might help Dhamon.

So terribly, terribly cold.

The sun above would feel so good against her skin. She dreamed of the warmth as the shredded parchment floated up and danced before her eyes, yet there was still no current to stir them, and she wasn't moving her arms to disturb them. Why did they move and sparkle so? She realized it was her mind playing tricks on her; the numbness had her seeing things. Though she continued to breathe the frigid water, felt it flowing in and out of her gills, she couldn't even turn her head now. It felt frozen. It was as though she was turning into ice.

The colors of dancing parchment shifted to gray now, and her enchanted light dimmed. The room grew steadily darker. She felt as though she was sinking.

Too long, she told herself; she'd stayed down here too long. Damn my curiosity. Once more she tried to push her arms and legs into movement, backing out of the window. She might have made some progress, but she couldn't be certain. The room was darker. It was hard to make out any of the details anymore.

No hope for Dhamon now. Feril didn't mourn her own demise; she knew every living creature lived and died, but she felt sad that she hadn't been able to help Dhamon. She did wonder what death would be like, however. The Kagonesti revered Habbakuk more than any other of Krynn's gods, and she wondered if she would meet him when she passed from the world.

One last desperate attempt to budge.

The tower room at the bottom of Nalis Aren grew ever colder and blacker.

CHAPTER

8

Dhamon Grimwulf was human again, tall and tan, his wheat-blond hair fluttering about him. He was sinking in a lake, one far to the north of the Qualinesti Forest. The water felt cool against his skin but not unpleasantly so. It would have been comforting, were it not weighing down his clothes and boots and tugging him relentlessly and inescapably down.

He'd been fighting a dragon—his once-partner Gale—and in the height of the battle he had plummeted into the lake, the impact against the surface driving the wind from his lungs and knocking him senseless.

The water pulled him deeper, his eyes fluttering open. He couldn't see much, just dark blue-gray patches and occasional glints of silver-gray—fish swimming past. His hand touched something soft and slimy, and he grabbed for it. It came away in his hands—a plant.

Dhamon heard a loud thrumming in his ears and realized it was his heart beating wildly. He could hear nothing else, and after a moment he could no longer register the cool water. He was drowning. He tried to move his arms and legs . . . commanded them to propel him to the surface, but he couldn't even move a finger. He could only sink deeper and watch everything grow dark around him.

He'd always told himself he wasn't afraid of death. When he was with the Dark Knights he often embraced the notion of meeting death bravely on the battlefield, dying honorably and heroically for whatever cause his unit was embracing at the moment. Death would not be so bad if met head-on, but drowning was ignoble. He felt his chest tighten, then everything went black.

Dhamon woke up from his daze, shaking his head to clear the image from his mind, his barbels lashing the surface of the lake and spattering water.

"That was years ago," he growled to himself, but the image of his human self drowning in that northern mountain lake was as clear in his mind as if it had happened yesterday. He knew that even now he had panicked, reliving it.

Only Dhamon hadn't drowned A dragon living in a cave at the bottom of the lake had spotted him. That dragon had saved his life and presented him with an enchanted glaive to help in his fight against the Overlords.

"I should have died then and there," Dhamon muttered. He thrust a claw into the water and shook his head again. "I really should go look for Feril."

He stayed in the shallows, however, and stared at his scaly reflection through the cool mist for more than an hour before he finally took a deep breath and with a shudder dived back into the Lake of Death.

"By Elalage's silver braids, I've seen nothing like you before!"

The old elf's voice carried clearly through the water as he knelt over Feril, smoothing at her face, pasty fingers gingerly brushing her eyelids. He scowled when she didn't wake up. She was stretched out on the stone floor of the tower room in front of the largest bookcase, bits of parchment floating all around her. Her head was resting on a pillow that he'd retrieved from another room, and her hands were folded on her stomach. She looked like she was sleeping peacefully.

He stood and paced, his thick hair flowing into a mass of bright white curls that hung below his shoulders, his thin lips working, mouthing over and over, "What to do, what to do." His thumb came up to rub against the crooked bridge of a nose that looked a little too long for his narrow, deeply wrinkled face.

"An elf with gills, an amazing sight. An elf who's obviously been to visit Deban's place and stole one of his lighted crystals." The pear-shaped crystal Feril had tucked under her belt was now perched on the bookcase, clearly illuminating the entire room. "Perhaps you only borrowed the crystal, elf lady, or maybe Deban gave it to you as a gift. Toward the end, just before the dragon came, he became quite charitable. Maybe he knew what was fated for us, and maybe he thought being neighborly might put him in better stead with the gods in the world beyond. You are certainly pretty enough to catch Deban's eye, though you've no hair to speak of. What, by the memory of my dear Elalage, are you doing down here? How do you breathe water?" He made an annoyed sputtering sound and shook his head, the gesture causing his hair to fan away from his pale face.

"Not a sea elf. No, not Dargonesti or Dimernesti. Seen plenty of them before, and you're obviously neither. Certainly not Qualinesti, and you're too far from home to be one of those argumentative and pretentious Silvanesti. A Kagonesti, you look to be from your dress and the color of your hair. Seen Kagonesti, too, and you're the type. Except no tattoos and here you are exploring underwater in a place you'd best not be roaming around in without a map. So a puzzlement is what you are. Gills *and* flesh *and* elf ears. Remarkable."

He stopped pacing and looked down at Feril, studying her as if she were a rare specimen in a laboratory. After several moments he bent, his face inches from hers. He shook his head again, this time the curls spilling down over his shoulders and brushing Feril's cheeks. "What to do, what to do," he mouthed again. "You're alive, my elf-fish. I see you breathe, but for how much longer? I think you are fast fading."

He touched his lips to hers. "Like I faded." A second kiss, then he pulled back. "They're cold as death, my puzzlement. Cold as this graveyard. Your skin is so white, when I don't think that is its natural state. The cold has got you in its grip, little elf-fish." He stroked the bridge of his nose again. "The cold cannot have you. No, no. Not yet. You are a refreshing mystification, and if the cold takes you now, my questions will go unanswered, so you must live, my pretty puzzlement. Somehow I must stop you from fading . . ."

He stared at her for several minutes more, then the old elf seemed to come to a decision. He closed his eyes, spread his arms, and floated above her, parallel to her form. His lips moved, forming clipped and precise Elvish words, though no actual sounds emerged. His fingers danced rhythmically, as if he were playing an instrument. Motes of saffron and green light appeared in shimmering globes that enveloped his hands. The globes grew larger then receded, seeming to grow and dim, breathe as if in rhythm with Feril's breathing. The silent words came faster, and the water began to circulate in the tower room.

The bits of parchment started whirling then dissolving, pages from the books on the shelf joining them and dissipating. All of this turned the room a milky opaque color, then the water churned itself clear. The globes glowed with a fierce intensity now and broke free from the old elf's hands. They hung poised between him and Feril for several moments, the motes of color winking on and off erratically. Then the globes dropped onto Feril and melted into her prone form.

A moment later, her eyes fluttered opened, and the first thing she saw was the old elf standing at her side, extending an insubstantial hand as if to help her up. Feril's mouth dropped open in surprise, and she skittered away from the apparition, bolting to her feet and looking toward the window she'd come in.

"Nothing to be afraid of, little elf-fish," the strange old man cooed. "I won't hurt you. Indeed, it is I who saved you." He beamed and tipped his chin up, proud of his efforts. "I had to save the pretty puzzlement."

Saved me, Feril thought.

"Yes, indeed I did," he said, folding his arms across his chest. "You were dying of the cold, and we just couldn't have that. I cast a spell to keep you warm."

Feril looked back and forth between the apparition and the window. She wasn't cold any longer, and she certainly wasn't dead. Her last thought had been that she was joining the ghosts of Qualinost and would never see Dhamon Grimwulf again.

How . . .

". . . did I save you? A spell, just like I told you, and not a terribly difficult one, once it came to mind. I've still some magic in me. I can even look . . ." he paused and scratched at the bridge of his nose, searching diligently for the correct term. "I can even look like I am alive if that makes you more comfortable." His lips worked and his body took on color and substance, but there were a few spots where he was still semi-transparent. The venerable age he had reached in life was evident from the many deep creases on his face and the numerous spots on his hands and neck. "If I concentrate, I can almost look like my old impressive self."

Thank you for saving me . . . .

"Obelia was my name," he interjected. "Obelia Durosinni D'l'athil of House Evner of Qualinost."

So . . . you're dead, Obelia.

"Yes, like everyone else who stayed when the cursed dragon and her forces came to call. My dear sister Elalage urged me to leave, but I would have nothing to do with the notion. I said I was too old, said she was too old, and that we should stay here. Said it would be safe in the city, great Qualinost would never fall. She called me an old fool and left that night, but Elalage was right; I was an old fool. Now I am a dead old fool in a city that is crushed to the bottom of a very deep lake."

And . . . are you reading my mind? Is that how you know my questions?

"Not exactly, my elf-fish, but when I try hard, I can hear what you're thinking. It would be hard to communicate with you otherwise."

So you're a sorcerer. Feril, beaming, couldn't hide her pleasure.

"Well . . . I was a sorcerer, back when I was alive. Of some renown I might add." He stepped between her and the window. "But to the matter of you. I find you a pretty puzzlement, and I must know what exactly you are and what brings you here to this dangerous lake. Why do you have gills *and* skin? Why do you brave this cold, cold graveyard to come poking about in what used to be my books?"

Feril glanced around the room, noting that the empty leather bindings of many books lay askew on the shelves and the floor. She was glad to be alive but didn't like that Obelia was standing so close, blocking the quickest way out.

I am Ferilleeagh Dawnsprinter, she thought.

"A Kagonesti name! I was right! But you've got gills, Ferilleeagh Dawnsprinter. Gills! Such magic you must have. You must tell me everything, my pretty puzzlement."

Feril wasn't sure she trusted this dead sorcerer, but after all he had saved her life. Maybe he would be able to help Dhamon, so she told him everything, going back to when she first met Dhamon, to the torment he suffered because of the dragon scale inflicted upon him, to the time she spent alone after the incident at the Window to the Stars, to her affinity with nature magic.

"Such wonderful magic you possess! Ah, little elf-fish, were I alive I would beg you to teach me all that you know."

Dhamon, she concentrated. *He's the reason why I'm here and . . .*

She finished her long story. "Those two dragons, that shadow dragon and that silver dragon . . . they broke Malys's control, and the scale on Dhamon's leg turned black. The shadow dragon was a trickster, and his magic later caused scales to grow all over Dhamon." Obelia was engrossed in her tale, pacing in front of the window and worrying at the bridge of his nose. He'd become wholly transparent again. "So this Dhamon fellow . . . a human . . . eventually turned into a dragon. Strange predicament. Now you're hoping to find some magic here in this graveyard of a city to help him become a human again."

Yes, Feril thought. There must be a way to save Dhamon. *He looked into a crystal ball, and something there told him the answer rested in this lake.*

"What an astonishing yarn you've spun for me, elf-fish."

Is it possible?

"To help your friend? With something in this lake? Well, I really don't know. This is a very big city and an even bigger lake, but looking for a remedy could be an interesting diversion for me. It could take a very long time."

So you'll help me?

"I insist on it!" Obelia made a tsk-tsking sound, wagging an insubstantial finger at her. "You shouldn't seem so surprised, my pretty puzzlement. You're the only living creature I've talked to since Qualinost sank. Of course I'll help you. In fact, I'll *have* to help you if you're to have any chance of success. Who else will keep you warm down here in the deep cold waters? Who else will show you this city . . . without trying to make you a permanent part of it?"

<hr />

Feril wanted to visit the home of every sorcerer and sage Obelia knew. The old elf said he could do just that, if she really wanted to—but there were a great many of them, and he would show her some of the city first to prove his point.

As they left the tower and glided above this section of the city, Feril saw that indeed the search would take a very long time. The city spread out beneath her like a graveyard of spires, manors, businesses, and small homes jutting up like tombstones from the lake floor. Qualinost looked at once peaceful and eerie, with spirits of the dead floating idly everywhere. The dark blue water distorted some things, making some buildings and objects appear larger or farther away than they really were.

"Serilait lived there many decades ago," Obelia said, pointing at a three-sided building and interrupting Feril's musings. "I fancied her once, and she had some interest in me, but magic took too much of my time, so Sirilait found another and moved to the artist's quarter." He released a sigh that sounded like a long-held musical note. "She escaped the disaster with the dwarves through the tunnels under the city. I'm glad she and her family got away. She and Elalage and so many of my friends . . . I should have gone with them. I had some good years left to me."

They passed over a park where the tree limbs had been trained to grow in attractive patterns, some in the shapes of animals, now distorted by ruin and water. Feril tried to picture what they would have looked like in the past and guessed one was a horse rearing, another a winged beast. There were sculptures in the center of the park, similar to the ones she'd seen in Deban's gallery.

"Yes, they are his work," Obelia said, answering her unspoken question.

Feril touched the enchanted crystal that Obelia had returned to her and which she'd tucked back under her belt. Obelia didn't need any enchanted light to see, but the crystal helped her make out some of the details. She saw clearly now that many of the buildings had been damaged by magical attacks; doors and shutters had been torn apart. Broken vases, stools, and candleholders lay amid the bones outside a fanciful residential district. Perhaps the elves who stayed until the end had fought their enemies with any belonging they could wield like a club.

"Ilit-Ivo's place," Obelia said, pointing to another house. "One of the finest archers in Qualinost competitions. He won most of them, year after year after year. He finally tired of the trophies and the lack of any real opposition. He quit in the middle of a match one day and provided the best arrows for all the challengers thereafter. I thought he would have remained in the city, but he was persuaded to leave with the others, despite his hatred of the dwarves. Many of those who stayed broke into his weapons shop, looking for things to defend their homes. If you need a sword, my little elf-fish, we can . . ."

I wouldn't mind one, Feril thought, *but first I need to help Dhamon.*

Another musical sigh, and Obelia led her toward the very center of the city, where the buildings looked older and smaller. As the city grew it spread outward in a circular pattern. The streets beneath her appeared as spokes on a wheel.

"I knew many sorcerers in this district—and philosophers, too. Some of them were close to my age, and some of them stayed to die with the city. Maybe we can stir up a spirit or two, little elf-fish. Let's do a little looking here."

He dived toward a dark shape, a narrow three- or four-story place that looked simple compared to its neighbors. As they got closer Feril could tell it wasn't so much a building, as a tree. The place had been fashioned out of the trunk of a giant ebonwood, with doors and windows carved into it and a tile roof laid across the top. Colorful carved bricks rose up one side of the tree, likely more for design than for stability. However, age and the lake were taking their toll—she could see where the wood was rotting at the base and midway up.

"I'd say we should go in the front door. The polite thing to do and all. Join me?" Obelia didn't wait for her response. He floated through a door that Feril had to struggle to open.

By the time she had tugged it open, she could see no trace of Obelia. There was only an empty room which looked like the inside of a hollow tree. The floor was gravel, and there was no furniture, but at the back of the room there was a rotting wooden ladder that led to a room above and another below. Feril hovered by the ladder, her enchanted light revealing a cavernous lower floor that was filled with scroll tubes and colorful glass flasks, most of them intact. She started to head down but heard a musical sound from above, Obelia's sigh. She reluctantly pulled herself up into a room filled with numerous elf spirits.

"Join us," said a reed-thin apparition.

Feril felt a chill as she spun to go back.

"Don't leave, elf-fish." Obelia said, cocking his head bemusedly, his diaphanous eyebrows raised. "I thought you wanted help with your dragon problem."

Feril clung to the ladder, looking up at the ghostlike face of an aged elf standing close to Obelia and peering curiously down at her.

"This is Kalilnama," Obelia continued, nodding toward the thin ghost. "His wife was a fine sorceress. She left him when the dwarves led our people from the city, but he stayed."

So he stayed and died, Feril thought. She was growing cold again, and she wrapped her fingers tightly around one of the ladder rungs. *I'm getting cold, Obelia. I have to leave, go back to the surface and get warm, recover my strength.*

"Yes, he stayed, little elf-fish. He could not leave all his books and scrolls . . . his life's work."

The cold surrounded her, and the room above grew darker, the ghosts ever more transparent.

"He studied dragons. For more than a hundred years, elf-fish." Obelia's fingers were twirling in the water, and motes of saffron and green were appearing. Globes of warmth formed around his hands then sped toward Feril. "Oh, here. I almost forgot. We don't want you getting all frozen again . . ."

Let me tell you all about Dhamon Grimwulf, Feril thought, after the cold was banished again.

Kalilnama glided closer as Feril repeated Dhamon's saga, with Obelia chipping in comments and things she forgot to mention. The other ghosts crowded in a little closer, peering at her and murmuring amongst themselves.

The thin ghost named Kalilnama was enraptured by Feril's story, and more than once he excitedly wrung his hands, the fingers passing through each other. When she was finished, Kalilnama asked questions so fast that Feril's answers blurred together.

"Were I alive!" he cried, his voice thin and high-pitched. "To touch this creature you speak of, a dragon who was once a human. Such a thing has never before lived."

"Kalilnama knew Beryl was coming." Obelia was at Feril's shoulder, his words musical whispers in her ear. "He predicted the great bloated beast would destroy everything."

"But I stayed," Kalilnama said. "I thought we might find safety in the catacombs."

"He drowned there," Obelia said matter-of-factly. He waved an arm at the other hovering spirits. "The others drowned with him; some of them were his students, some were elves from the outskirts of the city who had fled here for protection." The ghost gave a laugh that sent goosebumps down Feril's back.

There was a reverent look on Kalilnama's insubstantial face. "The dragon was evil, but a truly magnificent creature to behold. I'm glad I stayed, if only to glimpse her. I'd never seen an overlord before, and I thought to record everything about her." He wrung his hands together again, sadly shaking his head.

Can you help Dhamon? Feril floated face to face with Kalilnama.

The ghost grew thinner, folding in upon itself until it looked like a sheet of parchment, then thinner still, until he was a mere wisp of white rising from the floor. "A dragon scale turned him into what he is now. Perhaps the magic in dragon scales can undo this terrible thing. Your friend's own scales would not work, of course—you would need unspoiled magic to break the old magic that remade him, and very powerful magic, naturally—so the scale of a greater dragon is my guess. That makes it all the more difficult. I have notes in the catacombs, sealed in scroll tubes that keep the water at bay. They are yours."

His airy form flowed down the ladder and into the room far below. Feril and Obelia followed him, while the roomful of ghosts watched them go.

Kalilnama, what kind of dragon would have such scales? Feril prompted.

"We'll work on this mystery together," Kalilnama was quick to return. "I hate to say it, but I think a scale from an overlord would provide the best chance for success."

"Hmmm. Beryl's corpse is not far away," Obelia suggested. "Perhaps that is the cure in the lake that your friend is looking for."

Feril pictured the green carcass and the ghostly Knights of Neraka that hovered around it. She shuddered and felt something tighten around her heart.

CHAPTER

9

This time Dhamon swam farther out, diving and surfacing, until finally he caught sight of the edge of the sunken city. His eyes widened at the sight.

He circled above a tall building. He was surprised it seemed so well preserved, looking almost as though it were purposely built on the deep bottom of this lake. The bones, bits of armor, and possessions he could see strewn below on sidewalks clearly marked this place as an abandoned graveyard.

Wispy ghosts of elves spotted him and hid in door-ways and pressed against walls. Though no longer alive, they still feared dragons, and they recalled all too vividly how Beryl brought about the death of their beloved Qualinost.

Circling widely, Dhamon also spotted the horns of Beryl's carcass but did not swim close, especially because the overlord was mired in the depths. He swam and searched for hours before feeling the old anxiety and tightening in his chest. Then he returned to the surface, gulping in air and relishing the warmth.

Three days went by without any sign of Feril. Three days of Ragh's griping and repeated entreaties to leave. Three days before Dhamon decided to risk another swim farther out and deeper down into the Lake of Death.

It was the afternoon of the third day since Feril had dived into the lake, and on that day Feril returned, just as Dhamon approached the sunken city from above. With tremendous relief he spotted her swimming in a straight line toward the surface. He shot up, surfacing not far away, and followed her to the shore.

"Dhamon! You're shivering! You've been in the lake looking for me? Isn't that . . . sweet. Ack, but you smell even worse when you're wet. Move away!"

He gave a nod of his massive head, water dripping off his scales. Wet, they shone almost brilliantly in the setting sun. "Three days you've been gone. I feared you had drowned," he rumbled ruefully. Ragh was plodding toward them.

She ran her fingers through her hair and stretched in the fading sunlight. "I was fine, Dhamon Grimwulf. You know I can well take care of myself." A pause, then: "In truth I didn't realize so much time had passed." She wondered how long she'd been unconscious in the tower room before Obelia warmed her. "Elves do not have to sleep very much, you know, though I am terribly hungry." She offered him a wistful smile, showing she appreciated his concern.

Dhamon wanted her to tell him everything, especially if she'd found any magic to help him in the sunken city, but he stopped himself from asking directly. He knew Feril and knew that she talked about things in her own time.

"I saw Beryl's horns," he began.

Feril nodded. "I found her, too."

She said nothing else, causing Ragh to roll his eyes. Dhamon glared at the sivak, who backed away, holding his hands up, leaving the two alone. She tipped her face up and breathed deep, taking in the smells of the late summer wildflowers and the grass. The breeze was drying her, though it would take some time to thoroughly dry her leather tunic. She was reminded of her private vow to visit the sunken shops below and find some new clothes. First, however, she intended to return to Kalilnama's tower.

"Don't worry. I'm just taking a breather. I'm going back down shortly."

"Not alone this time. Let me go with you."

"I can take care of myself," she said, shaking her head, "and I know that you are afraid of water."

Dhamon winced. "Let me go with you anyway," he said. "What's down there that's so urgent?"

She glanced away, avoiding his question, not wanting to raise his hopes. "I missed you, Dhamon."

He was going to say something else to her, but he was surprised by her candid emotion, and his words caught in his throat. He glanced awkwardly over at Ragh, who had simply gone back to sleep against a tree.

"I shouldn't have left you after the Window," Feril continued softly. "I thought I needed time alone, away. Apart. I thought putting distance between us would help clear my head, but it only troubled my heart. I have missed you."

She didn't say anything else for quite some time. She stood at the edge of the lake and watched the thin, low-hanging clouds turned gold by the setting sun as they slowly dissolved. The sun set, and in the growing twilight a pair of owls sailed low over the far side of the lake then turned east as they flew off for night hunting.

The air was cooling, the wind dying down. Feril and Dhamon continued to stand on the bank as the breeze carried new, faint scents to them—the mustiness of raccoons and possums that must be hunting at the edge of the treeline, along with a subtle hint of blood, suggesting something had been killed in the nearby woods.

Stars gradually winked into view, and Lunitari was the first moon to peek over the canopy and reflect palely on the surface of the ever-still lake.

Feril walked forward until the water teased her toes.

"Don't go back in tonight," Dhamon said. There was an unusual pleading in his voice. "I know elves don't have to sleep very much, but you look tired."

Feril turned away from the lake and looked straight up into the night sky. Then she took a deep breath, and another, starting toward the trees to the southeast. "All right. Do you think your sivak friend will mind sharing the forest?"

She bent and tugged at something in the grass, some type of root she was brushing the dirt from. She was quick to eat it.

Dhamon caught up to her and walked slowly at her side.

"I found . . . something . . . in the lake that might help you," she finally said, just as they approached the sivak, one eye open, resting propped up against an old white oak. "Let's consider the matter in the morning."

The sivak was on his feet, eyes drifting up to meet Dhamon's gaze, then catching the Kagonesti's. She looked tiny next to the dragon. "Welcome back. After so long I figured you'd probably drowned, elf. Dhamon thought so, too."

Feril walked right past the sivak without so much as a word of greeting and stretched out on a bed of ferns.

Dhamon stayed back near the clearing with Ragh. As Dhamon watched her, he offered a silent prayer to the gods. He had never prayed so hard for the return of his humanity, never prayed so hard for anything.

If he were human, he could have rested at her side, draped an arm around her and held her close. If he became human again, they could use the treasure in his hoard to buy a mansion anywhere they wanted. Hire servants. Nothing would be too expensive. He relished his dragon power . . . but he was not happy this way.

He noticed Ragh scrutinizing him.

"Well, I'm glad the elf didn't drown," the sivak said.

Ragh paced behind Feril and Dhamon. The draconian kept telling Dhamon that it was time to move on to another part of the Qualinesti forest. He was achingly bored with sitting under oak trees and watching birds and insects while waiting for Feril to finish up with whatever she was doing deep in the Lake of Death. Now she was planning on going back . . . and for how long?

"So you found something that might help Dhamon. What is it?" The sivak pressed.

The Kagonesti didn't reply.

"Well, how long are you going to be down there this time?" Ragh raised his voice but still didn't get an answer. "How do we know how long we should wait or whether you've been killed by an octopus or something?"

"Stop it, Ragh," Dhamon said after a few moments. "You don't have to wait for us."

Ragh gave a soft growl. "Fine, fine. Just where am I supposed to go?" He waggled his scaly fingers toward the trees. "All right. I guess I'll go back to sleep over there until you're finished with your little quest." The sivak took a dozen steps away and looked over his shoulder. "Dhamon, I truly hope she finds something down at the bottom of that lake that can . . . that might . . ."

"Make me human again."

The sivak nodded.

The sun was rising and the trees were already throwing shadows. Dhamon touched a talon to Feril's shadow and arched his back. His glossy black scales turned darker and dull, the blue and silver scales disappearing. He had come up with this idea last night. He could transform into a shadow dragon; he had that ability from the shadow dragon who had birthed him. That way he could accompany Feril into the lake, protect her even, though he didn't dare say that to her.

This way, he had argued, they could team up and double their efforts to find what she was seeking.

His fear of the lake was lessened when he was a shadow dragon.

Dhamon's form shimmered slightly, then flattened until he looked like a dragon-shaped pool of oil. A few moments passed, the pool shrinking and melding with Feril's shadow.

The Kagonesti breathed deep, the air heavy with wildflowers and the hint of rain. No trace of the odors of stagnant water and rotted plants remained. As a shadow, Dhamon lost his scent.

"You said you'd be able to hear me, Dhamon." Feril waded into the water, "and that you could stay underwater with me the entire time, that as a shadow you don't breathe." Feril was up to her waist now, relishing the feel of the warm water and knowing the cold would come soon enough. "We're going to an old section of the city, Dhamon. I've met some . . . some people . . . there."

Then she was swimming ahead of him toward the center of the lake and diving. She chased schools of small sunfish and perch, and as she did she grew gills almost immediately. She was invigorated after a night's rest and reflection, and she kicked fast and strong, angling like an arrow toward where she knew Qualinost reposed. She watched pike, bass, and silverfins swim by, then the fish and plants disappeared abruptly and she braced herself for the cold. It wrapped around her, and she felt her heart being squeezed. She glanced over her shoulder to see if Dhamon had the same reaction, but she couldn't tell, though he was close behind.

She was impressed, though not astonished, that Dhamon could attach himself to her as a shadow. Feril could assume the forms of most living creatures—something she thought preferable to becoming a shadow. Did he feel this horrible cold? She thrust her worries aside and threw her efforts into fighting off the numbness and looking for a glimmer of light amid the dark blue water.

She'd placed the enchanted crystal on the roof of the philosopher's home, as a beacon. Kalilnama and Obelia promised to wait for her there, and she hoped that they hadn't drifted off somewhere during the hours she'd lingered above.

Ragh stomped grumpily toward the white oak. He'd hollowed out a spot between the knobby roots of the tree, and the depression made it comfortable enough to sleep there. That was virtually all he'd been doing for days—sleeping.

"Hope they find something down there to help him," Ragh said. "Make him human again. No more flying, no more swamp. No more smelling the swamp on his breath all the time. He was all right when he was human. He saved me when he was human. He might still want me around, but I wish they'd hurry up. It's boring around here. Boring, and I still think it's strange and dangerous."

The sivak looked over his shoulder again. The surface of the lake was placid as usual. No sign of either the elf or Dhamon.

"Now I'm talking to myself. Nothing else to do around here." He chuckled and ground the ball of his foot against the earth. "No one to talk to, no one to fight with. Nothing good to eat. Nothing to look at, but trees and trees and trees and that damnable lake." His head jerked up and he scanned the treeline.

Hey, something was moving up there. He heard leaves rustling, but there was no wind to speak of. Shadows shifted, and he swore he could smell something foul.

———◆———

The enchanted light showed the way, and Feril swam fast toward the beacon. Obelia and Kalilnama could easily be spotted waiting in the tree-home, along with more than a dozen other Qualinesti spirits, some of whom she recognized from her previous visit.

Obelia cast a glance at the shadow which trailed her but said nothing. "Here are things we've found that might help, elf-fish." Obelia summoned his globes of light and used them to chase the chill from Feril. "Unguents from Rosemoon's, powders and crystal shards that Kalil-nama's wife left behind. Her laboratory is at the top of this place. There are scrolls with spells in Jerlin L'oile's shop, and these should be safe from the water. Jerlin used to heavily wax the edges of the tubes. There'll be more things in the library at the east edge of the city. Though I suppose nearly all the books are ruined." He stroked the bridge of his nose and stared long into her eyes. "We'll tell you precisely where all these things are, my elf-fish. I'll take you to them, but you'll have to do the gathering. You see, our hands . . ." He sadly passed his fingers through her. "We cannot pick any of these things up. I alone of my dead friends can hold any semblance of a physical form, and I cannot hold that for more than a breath."

You'll show me where all of these things are?

Obelia nodded. "I'll be your guide, and show you those things and more, elf-fish. All precious and enchanted, things the lake couldn't destroy. I don't know if they'll be much help in obtaining an overlord's scale, but it's worth the trying."

Dhamon saw the elf spirits through Feril's eyes and heard everything Obelia and Kalilnama said. Dhamon wanted to ask them questions about how an overlord's scale might help return him to human form. Too, he wanted to know what kept these ghosts in the city and why they hadn't passed to the spirit realm where dead folks were said to drift near the gods. The only one he could speak to was Feril, and she had cautioned him to keep his tongue around the spirits.

The sorcerer-elf had been ancient in life, Dhamon reckoned. He'd seen plenty of elves, but none with wrinkles so numerous and deep, fingers and limbs that had they been flesh would be bony, pale, and sprinkled with age spots. Hundreds upon hundreds of years old the spirit elf was, maybe a thousand or more—in Dhamon's early days with the Dark Knights he'd heard campfire tales that elves could live that long. Not so long as dragons, though, he thought smugly.

He continued to observe everything through Feril's eyes, marveling at her acuteness of vision as they passed over a once lavish neighborhood. The huge head of Beryl came into focus, and he recalled the one time when he had laid eyes on the overlord at the Window to the Stars. That was years ago, and Beryl had been dead for years, too, so Dhamon guessed it was the unnatural cold of the lake that kept the carcass so preserved that it looked alive and merely sleeping. Conversely, it was likely the magic in the overlord's carcass that made the lake so cold. Here the depths were truly murky and at the same time tinged green.

The ghosts of the Knights of Neraka appeared among the overlord's neck spines, difficult to see because they were more translucent than before. They didn't make any hostile moves toward Feril, and as she and her dead Qualinesti companions came closer, the knights' images wavered and dissipated.

"I would think any scale from Beryl would do, elf-fish." Obelia, speaking conspiratorially, was close at Feril's shoulder. "Perhaps you should take two . . . as a fail-safe, in case your first attempt to help your friend fails."

Three, Feril decided. Or perhaps four. However many I can pry loose and carry to the surface.

She kicked harder and drove toward her target, speeding past Obelia and Kalilnama, so close to the overlord now that all she could see was a wall of emerald scales that made up its jaw. She hovered for a moment, regarding the corpse's scales and wary of the knightly ghosts.

The smallest scales were on its claws and along a ridge above the dragon's closed eyes. She darted in and gripped one of the smallest on the dragon's head, just above one of its huge nostrils. Her arm muscles bunched and a vein stood out on her neck as she yanked. She gritted her teeth and pulled harder, but the scale would not give way. Feril doubled her efforts and was rewarded with the palms of her hands being sliced by the sharp edges of the scale. Blood trailed away and a string of curses tumbled through her head.

Silently, Dhamon encouraged her, half thrilled, half disconcerted to be this close to the great dead Beryl.

"You're hurt, my elf-fish," Obelia said consolingly. He appeared at her side, his heavily-lined face thick with concern. "You must bandage your hands. There is exceptional, thick cloth in the city and . . ."

I'm fine, she thought to him. *I'll go back to Qualinost and bandage my hands after I get some of these blasted scales.*

"But you're bleeding—that's not good."

I've had cuts all over in my time, she returned. *The scales first.*

Good for you, Dhamon thought.

Obelia nodded and floated away. Feril turned back, studying the ground around the dragon's talons until she found what she was looking for—a long sword lying amid the bones. There was still no sign of the dead knights who had evidently vanished. She swam down to the sword and gripped the pommel in her slender fingers. The leather wrapped around the crosspiece was rotting, but she could use the blade to pry loose the scales, though she'd have to be careful not to damage them. Her goal was to extract scales in the most flawless possible condition.

This one first, she thought, eyes locking onto one of the deepest green scales. It was tiny compared to some others, about the size of a serving platter, but she thought it might be easier to get loose for that reason. She slipped the tip of the sword beneath the scale and, using it like a lever, carefully tried to pry it.

It shifted slightly, to her exultation. She nearly had it free when an icy wave surged over her; the cold shot down her back, and the sword slipped from her fingers—a cold more intense than anything she'd experienced before, instantly numbing her. Whirling she faced a row of militant ghosts, all spirits of the Knights of Neraka. The closest had needlelike claws instead of hands, and though he looked transparent, he'd somehow managed to pierce her. Though the cold was vicious, she also felt some warmth and guessed this was her own blood.

"You dare mutilate our mistress," the knight with the claw hands cried. "Defiler! Despoiler!"

"You will die for your transgression," another knight added. He reached toward her, his hands turning to wispy claws.

Obelia! Feril's mind screamed. *Obelia! Help me!*

The specter of the ancient sorcerer appeared above and behind the line of knights, his sage companions forming a foggy cloud near him. Obelia's hollow eyes met Feril, and he sadly shook his head.

"We cannot help you, elf-fish."

Dhamon! she wanted to scream.

Looking around wildly, she could see no sign of her shadow.

Feril reached for the dropped sword, held the pommel tightly, and swung it wide. The blade harmlessly passed through the approaching ghost knights.

"You will die," they said as one.

One smiling ghost knight floated so close that his form brushed against her. "Your spirit, too, will help guard this sacred dragon."

CHAPTER
10

Ragh hadn't smelled a skunk in some time, spending so many months in the swamp where the creatures weren't normally found, but the foul smell made him think that a family of skunks was headed toward him and his favorite white oak. Ragh growled. He wasn't afraid of skunks, wasn't afraid of much of anything. Dragons, he had to admit, scared him some. He was definitely afraid of dragons, particularly Sable . . . and any significant number of Knights of Neraka.

He fished around in the grass and managed to find a handful of pebbles. These Ragh heaved toward the noise that was rustling around some ferns near the base of a tree, not quite finding his mark but getting close enough.

Still, the rustling grew louder, the offensive smell stronger, and when a small feather-decorated spear poked out above the ferns, he realized the smell was coming not from skunks but from something else entirely. A shrill cry cut through the morning sky and the woods came alive with the pounding of tiny feet.

"Goblins!" Ragh snarled and braced himself, holding his clawed hands out to his sides.

Less than three feet tall, the goblins in question were manlike in form but had scaly skins like lizards. Their faces were drawn forward, giving them a ratlike visage, and their ears—though some had been bitten off—were pointed. Some of the goblins were the red-brown color of dried clay; others were dark brown or dirty yellow. There was one white-skinned goblin in the mix. Scraggly clumps of hair grew on top of their otherwise bald heads, and their wild, wide eyes were black as night and fixed belligerently on the draconian as they attacked.

"An army of stinking goblins." There were several dozen of them that Ragh could see. He couldn't outrun them, as goblins were fast and agile, and he certainly couldn't fly away, but he could fight them, and he relished the opportunity.

"Stinking rats." Ragh snatched at the first goblin to reach him, his scaly fist closing about the creature's throat and squeezing until he heard its neck snap. Ragh hurled the dead one into another trio of goblins that was rushing at him, spears thrust out as if to skewer him. The corpse bowled over the others, and Ragh crouched and turned his attention to a barrel-chested goblin who had come up close and was wielding a small axe.

"I'm not afraid of you," he spat. "I'll wet the ground with your putrid blood."

Ragh's voice was craggy, a rasping whisper that would have hinted at weakness or age had it come from another creature, but it got that way from many throat wounds earned in battle. His neck was thick with the scars. "Goblins come to bother me, fool thing for you to do. Stink up my tree. Last thing you'll ever do."

The draconian fought hard—not only against the goblins, but to keep from gagging, the stench from the goblins settling hard on his tongue and filling his nostrils. He'd traveled in the company of goblins before when he, Dhamon, and Maldred were heading to the mountains on the other side of the New Sea. They'd struck up a temporary alliance with some goblins, and those had looked up to Ragh as if he were some sort of general. Those goblins were from dry lands, and though they smelled bad, they didn't stink so much as this bunch.

"By the memory of the Dark Queen! What did the lot of you roll in? Rats, you are! Stinking, filthy rats!" One of them jabbed at him with a spear. He cursed at the goblins in an old language he knew and kicked out at the one who dared jab him, the force of his blow caving in the small creature's chest.

He slammed his fist down on the skull of another, smiling when he heard the bones crack and saw the goblin crumple. Ragh grabbed two more, one of them the white goblin he'd spotted, wringing both their scrawny necks. Tossing the two bodies over his shoulders, he picked up a fallen spear with his right hand and started skewering the red-skinned goblins. He alternately batted goblins away and bashed in their skulls. He had to step over a growing pile of bodies to keep fighting.

It was exhilarating to Ragh, after all these days of boredom. He threw back his head and howled, the sound quieting the goblins for a moment and giving the front rank pause. The spear slipped through his fingers, his hands were so coated with their black blood.

Ragh kicked one goblin so hard it sailed over the heads of his surprised fellows. He could read the hesitation on the faces of the closest goblins and the scent of their fear mingled with their stench.

"Stinking rats, come to disturb my morning!" the sivak cursed. His eyes sparkled darkly and a big grin spread wide across his scaly face. "I'll kill all of you and let Dhamon toss the lot of your dead bodies in that damnable lake!"

Another goblin managed to get close, chattering maniacally, and jabbed a spear deep into his already-wounded leg.

"Foul little beasts!" Ragh hollered, stepping back and shaking his claws dripping with goblin blood. "What are you doing in these parts, anyway?"

The goblin tugged the spear free and stabbed again at the same wound. He chittered at Ragh and eluded the sivak's grasp, lunging at Ragh's stomach.

One of the tallest goblins shouted long and loud in its spitting guttural tongue. Ragh had spent enough centuries on Krynn to learn most languages. The tall goblin had said, "Hurt him, yes, but don't kill the wingless one. We need him alive!"

Alive? Ragh redoubled his efforts, though his arms and legs were moving slower from wounds and fatigue. What in the memory of the Dark Queen would a pack of goblins want with an old, scarred draconian without wings?

Another wave of goblins rushed out of the trees. Ragh guessed there were a hundred or more of the disgusting creatures. In general, goblins certainly weren't anything to fear . . . but how many more of them were lurking nearby?

An uncharacteristic chill raced down Ragh's spine, and he risked a glance over his shoulder at the lake. The surface was still and there was no sign of the elf or

Dhamon. Calling for help would do no good; he doubted anyone would hear him underwater.

Ragh slammed his teeth together and growled from deep in his chest. He fought against the fatigue and clawed at every goblin within reach. He didn't cry out for mercy, even when they gradually circled and cornered him, jabbing at the back of his legs with their tiny spears and knives.

Mere pinpricks, he told himself. They can't hurt me. Ragh ripped open the chest of the tall goblin whom he'd heard ordering the others not to kill him. Then he trampled the body and tore into a couple more. The draconian's eyes were watering fiercely—from the exertion, from the strong smells of blood and the reeking goblins. He batted at his eyes and shook his head to clear his vision.

He caught sight of a huge figure looming behind the goblin throng. It was a man with broad shoulders and an imposing build. Ragh couldn't make out any details, as the man clung to the shadows of the oaks, but he was certain the man was guiding the goblins, else they probably would have attacked him, too. Ragh swung at the goblins blindly now, keeping his eyes on the man, mentally daring him to step out from the shadows of the trees where he could be contested.

More goblins died; more were crushed or went flying. Then, abruptly, Ragh was brought to his knees and all he could see was the press of little leathery bodies, a veritable wall of scaly red and dirty yellow, shot through here and there by broken-toothed grins. The stench of the creatures' sweat, blood, and whatever else clung to them overwhelmed him and he choked. The air in his tightening chest was hot and fetid, and he twisted his head up, gasping for fresh air.

He continued to swing and flail while the goblins cried shrilly and stabbed at his arms and legs. They were careful not to pierce his chest or stomach, having been commanded by the man, now stepping forward, that this sivak had to be captured alive.

"Take him down." The man spoke in the common human tongue, and the goblins moved as one. "Break him, but do not kill him, not yet."

Ragh was pushed onto his back with the pack of goblins climbing on and pummeling him with their weight. He managed to kill a couple more before the strongest of them drove spears into his arms and legs to pin him to the ground like an insect collector might pin a butterfly. A few of the goblins spat on him then, while others produced thick twine and crisscrossed it over his limbs and chest. The ends of the twine were tied to daggers that were thrust into the ground.

The sivak struggled but refused to cry out from the pain. He pitched his head from side to side, seeing the spears thrust into his arms and the blood that was spilling from his wounds. A particularly repulsive-looking goblin with one milky eye and patches of sores on his chest held a short sword to Ragh's throat.

The draconian finally lay still and the goblins chittered their victory.

"We did as you asked," Ragh heard one goblin say in the common tongue. "We did not kill him."

"He'll die anyway," another said. "Look how he bleeds."

"Work fast, Bedell," a grizzled red goblin said. "Make him talk before he dies."

Ragh saw a face above him. It was clean-shaven and handsome for a human, a man with short black hair and dark blue eyes. There was a faint scar leading from the center of his chin and disappearing under his ear. He smiled, revealing a row of even teeth as white as the lily emblem on his coal-black tabard. The man's plate mail made a grating sound when he bent over the draconian, and Ragh could see that the armor was marred from acid. The Knight of Neraka drew his sword and touched it to the ropy scars across Ragh's chest.

"I see you've been in many fights, sivak. Scars are the best badges of honor, are they not? Battle marks to wear for all to see." He touched his own scar with his free hand. "Better than medals, don't you think?"

Ragh struggled and the knight drove his heel down on Ragh's chest.

"Commander Bedell," a goblin risked. "You said he wasn't to be killed. Our mistress will be angry if he dies . . . uh, accidentally."

"I risk her anger just by being here," the commander answered, "but no, the sivak is not to be slain . . . yet." He traced the scars on Ragh's chest and neck with the sword. Then he pressed just hard enough to cut a bloody trail across the sivak's chest. "I think I should add to his badges of honor first." Another long cut, as he watched Ragh's eyes, wanting to see them narrow in pain, wanting to see them plead. "Answer some questions for me, sivak, and I'll make your death relatively painless. Resist and I can draw it out for days upon days."

A goblin leaning over Ragh wrung his hands and grinned gleefully. Others pressed closer to watch the entertainment. Ragh felt bile rising in his throat, the stench of the creatures turning his stomach. The stench, coupled with the pain from the cuts and the spears that held him in place, was nearly unbearable. The smell . . . he placed it now, a mixture of sweat and the creatures' own rank odor, but above all that was the stink of a swamp bog. These creatures must have come all the way from the swamp. Didn't the goblins mentioned a mistress? Sable?

"The shadow dragon that calls itself Dhamon," the Knight Commander coaxed, holding his sword poised for another cut. "Tell me where he is."

Ragh shook his head and clenched his teeth as the commander sliced at him.

"You're his boon companion, my Mistress Sable says. The shadow dragon that carves out more and more of the overlord's swamp for his own . . . where is he?"

"I don't know," Ragh spat fiercely. "I'm here alone."

"I can see that," the knight shot back. "You're alone now, but you weren't a little while ago. There's dragon spoor. You're always with the shadow dragon called Dhamon. Where is he?" The knight jabbed the sword into Ragh's shoulder, twisting it. "I could take the chance that he'll come back here eventually—he wouldn't abandon his pet for long—but I'd rather know where he is right now."

The draconian snarled his reply. Ragh knew they wouldn't find a trace of the dragon or the elf on the bank of the lake . . . for the sand perpetually erased all tracks. He prayed to the memory of the Dark Queen that Dhamon and Feril would stay down in the lake for days, like before. Ragh knew he would be long dead, and the knight and his goblin army would be gone by that time, searching for the dragon elsewhere. Dhamon would be safe and would have his chance of someday becoming human again. Dhamon would avenge him, Ragh thought.

If, by chance, Dhamon surfaced while the knight and the goblins were still here, that was all right too;

Dhamon would finish this bunch faster than he had the force of bakali. Only Ragh didn't want Sable to know where they were.

"What do you want with Dhamon?" Ragh asked, meeting the knight's icy glare.

"I intend to deliver his head to my Mistress Sable," Commander Bedell returned. "My goblin army will make of it a surprise for the overlord. She thinks I am running simple errands south of Shrentak. She will be pleased to discover I instead gathered this army and went after her hated enemy."

So Dhamon was to be killed. That meant that Ragh, too, didn't stand a chance of surviving his torture. He had nothing to lose now.

"Going against Sable's instructions? That's not healthy," the sivak pressed, thinking he might learn something else interesting from this stupid, talkative knight.

"She'll reward me, not punish me."

"Isn't it enough that Dhamon's left her damnable swamp?"

"That might be enough to satisfy my Mistress Sable, but it doesn't satisfy me. I need to curry favor with the overlord, and this is my best chance." The knight smiled maliciously. "I want to ensure that the Dhamon-dragon never comes back to her lands. I've enough goblins here to take care of him for good this time."

He patted his belt. Several small flasks hung from it. There was also a small totem decorated with tiny black feathers and chips of obsidian. He pointed to the latter. "I borrowed this special item from a vault in Shrentak to bolster my army's courage, and I brought something extra with me from the swamp that will ensure his defeat."

Bedell drummed his fingers on one of the flasks and paced in a tight circle around the draconian. "Now tell me, sivak, where is your shadowy friend?"

CHAPTER

11

The specters of goblins floated amid the Knights of Neraka, and Feril thought she could see the ghostly outlines of war horses in the distance.

By Habbakuk's fist! Her mind reeled. *Dhamon, can you see them? So many dead! An army of the lake's dead! Dhamon, where are you?*

"An army of the lake's dead, and soon you will join them, little elf-fish." Obelia, his wrinkled, translucent form hovering well above and behind the knights, spoke in a voice laced with regret. The Qualinesti ghost was still shaking his head, and his insubstantial fingers reached up to rub at the bridge of his nose. "You will join them, my pretty puzzlement, then I must watch you die."

Feril's face contorted in pain as a Knight of Neraka drifted into her body. Icy needles stabbed at her all over, and though she screamed, no sound came out.

Dhamon, uncertain how to deal with the otherworldly threat of the knights, had merged his shadow with her form, so that no one, not even Feril, could see him. He could see and hear everything through her senses, and maybe he could help her; he could speak to her now without Obelia suspecting his presence.

Feril! Hear me! You can't fight them with a sword! Use your mind! Use your mind!

The Kagonesti couldn't hear Dhamon. She was overwhelmed by the whispery voices of the ghosts and the pounding of her heart. She fought to stay conscious. Feril raged against the pain that pulsed through her body as a second knight melted into her. Trembling, her fingers tightly gripping the pommel of her sword, she swung the weapon with every last measure of her strength, trying to keep the rest of the ghosts at bay, but as one, the ghosts inched closer.

Her vision swirled. She could no longer make out the blue of the lake; she saw only ghosts, their ephemeral features blurred as their ranks thickened. She couldn't even tell the difference between the knights and the Qualinesti any longer. They formed a solid, chilling wall of white, with voices keening.

"Defiler! You who dared to deface Beryl will perish at our hands."

"You must join us."

"You will help us guard Beryl for eternity."

"You should die slowly and with great pain, as Beryl did. Then you will feel what our blessed Overlord felt!"

"Poor, poor elf-fish."

Betrayer! You're the betrayer! Feril thought. *Obelia, I gave you my trust! You said you'd help me!*

"I intended to, my elf-fish. I . . . I didn't know . . ."

Know what? Feril felt stiff, her limbs impossibly heavy. She tried to bring her sword up again but couldn't lift it and it slipped from her fingers. *You'll not defeat me!* she thought, wanting the Knights of Neraka to hear her thoughts. She meant to claw their eyes out, but she could see nothing but white. She was surrounded by an eerie whiteness and a cacophony of cries. A moment later she fell to the lake bed, her head striking against one of the overlord's talons.

"I didn't know I couldn't help you, elf-fish. Something keeps me from following my heart. I am sorry. Something inside me demands that I serve this overlord."

A chorus of apologies came from Obelia's group of companions, but Kalilnama raised a dissenting voice. The Qualinesti philosopher strove to be heard above the others, his words virtually shouted inside her head: "Do not let them win, Kagonesti! You cannot overcome them, but you can escape! Flee, Kagonesti! Win by escaping!"

I've no intention of lying down and surrendering, Feril thought, silently thanking Kalilnama for giving her hope, but the ghost knights who had entered her body were pinning her to the ground, holding her down as firmly as any anchor. *Do you hear me, knights? You'll not claim me! You'll never claim me!*

Feril slammed her eyes shut to blot out the ghostly horror. She ignored the cold. Instead, she reached deep inside and found one last spark of magic. She coaxed it brighter, felt it blossom in her chest and course down her arms and legs.

She pictured a silverfin, lithe and fast and likely of no interest to the dead Knights of Neraka. Such a fish would not threaten the dragon's remains, she thought, remembering that when she'd turned herself into a catfish days ago the ghost knights had left her alone. Feril sensed her legs growing together and shortening, her arms melding into her sides, her skin giving way to scales. She was so cold she couldn't be sure of everything that was happening, and so she prayed to Habbakuk as she vividly imagined her magical transformation

When she opened her eyes, her vision had righted itself. She was still hemmed in by white, but with eyes situated on both sides of her head, she also saw beyond. *Move!* she told herself. *By the breath of Habbakuk, move and live!*

She flipped her tail and pushed away from Beryl's corpse, leaving behind the two startled knights who had merged with her elf body and now found themselves staring at each other. She swam through their brethren. She pushed past one rank and into another, this one comprised of dead goblins and other creatures. The chill from their ghostly forms struck her like a physical blow, however, momentarily stunning her. She floated amid the spirits, gills barely moving.

I've failed Dhamon and myself, and both of us will be cursed to join this undead army. She struggled to regain her strength but instead found herself sinking down, a dead weight. *I thought being a fish would work. I thought . . .*

"Look! The wild elf is over there!" Feril heard someone cry. The ghost-voice was familiar . . . Kalilnama's or Obelia's, she wasn't certain.

"The elf-defiler has tricked us and is now on the other side of the dragon. We must stop her! We cannot let her harm Beryl's precious body!"

Obelia's voice—Feril recognized it now—but he was pointing the ghosts in the opposite direction.

"Hurry, before she mars the magnificent Beryl! We must slay her!"

The cold receded, if only a little, as some of the ghosts moved away from her. However, not all of the undead warriors automatically heeded Obelia.

"We can't let the elf harm the Overlord!"

A few more ghosts were prompted to follow the rest. Enough of those closest to Feril believed the Qualinesti ghost's cries, so that, gliding away, she revived a little. Feril summoned her strength and kept swimming. Somehow she found a path through the undulating mass of white, angling away and rising up from the lakebed in search of the blue water that indicated an absence of specters.

Feril heard the voices of the undead behind her. Their words flowed together and sounded like the wind blowing strongly through the trees. Faintly she heard Obelia, who was continuing to mislead the spirits, with Kalil-nama helping him.

Then she heard nothing else from the ghosts, as she had swum far enough away from the dragon corpse and its undead protectors and was surging through the unnaturally cold water toward the surface. It felt like hours had passed before the dark blue gave way to a lighter, brighter shade and the water turned obligingly warm. She was in the company of other silverfins now, swimming with them toward shallow waters, feeling the caress of soft tendrils of broadleaf water plants.

Every inch of her ached; over and over she recalled the knights melding into her and chilling her beyond feeling. For all she knew, Dhamon was still down there, but she was so incredibly tired and sore, she had to get to the shore.

Thus she pictured her elf body and swiftly felt her scales smoothing to become tanned skin, the fins separating to become legs, her eyes returning to normal. Gasping, the Kagonesti crawled out onto the bank and collapsed on the sand. It was early evening, but Nuitari and Solinari were low in the sky, and they cast just enough light for faint shadows to fall against the white sand. That was when she noticed her own shadow pulling away, flowing like oil into the grass and thickening. It expanded into an inky cloud, then began to assume the shape of a dragon. It grew larger still and some of its blackness gave way to specks of shiny blue and silver. Scales and spiky ridges rose from Dhamon's back. The dragon's head, all angles and planes, lowered, the barbels brushing Feril's back.

"Dhamon . . ." She raised her head. "I feared you had abandoned me. I feared you were lost or captured by the ghosts. I'm ashamed. I might have left you down there." She laid her head back down, letting exhaustion claim her.

"I was with you, Feril, but I didn't dare reveal myself, and I couldn't break free. I wanted to help you fight the ghosts, but I trusted you would find a way."

He was frightened of the depths of the lake too, he would have admitted if he was being entirely honest. His voice rumbled through the sand. "I'd never felt so helpless. There were no shadows down there, and . . ." He suddenly jerked his head around, hearing something and suddenly remembering Ragh. He didn't see the sivak in his usual resting place, but just beyond, a line of goblins with a Knight of Neraka towering behind them was emerging from the trees.

"The beast!" the knight leader shouted.

The goblins issued their guttural war cry as they attacked, waving their weapons.

"Kill it!" the knight shouted above the din. "Slay the creature and be rewarded!"

In a thick wave they poured across the clearing. Dhamon shook Feril, then he didn't give her another glance as he turned and thundered toward his foe. He released the full brunt of his dragonfear, expecting to see the goblins freeze, whirl, and flee into the trees. Though they looked briefly shaken, not one of them quit the fight. They yelled all the louder, coming at him brandishing their heavy weapons.

Dhamon batted wildly at the first to close with him. These goblins flew off into the skies as he waded into the front ranks. He tried to reach the Knight of Neraka shouting orders, but there were too many goblins between him and the human. Across the gap the knight cursed at Dhamon, an odd smile playing on his lips.

Dhamon brought a clawed foot down on a dozen goblins, but a dozen more shoved forward, pricking at his feet and legs with their weapons, though the wounds were nothing more than fly bites to Dhamon. He raised another claw and trampled his torturers, then leaped forward close to the Knight Commander.

The knight didn't budge, using two hands to swing a greatsword in a high arc, not quite close enough to strike Dhamon, only taunting him perhaps. In the same instant the knight barked more orders in goblin-speak, and droves of the hideous little creatures streamed out from the woods to attack Dhamon.

They were no more than ants to him, however, and he swatted some away with his claws, squished others beneath his massive frame, slapped more down with his thrashing tail. Some he swallowed, chewing on the disagreeable creatures just a little before spitting them out. There seemed to be hundreds of them, Dhamon guessed. The crude symbols on their shields and on the bits of armor they'd cobbled together marked them as being from the same region. He wondered briefly if Feril was all right, if she was even conscious.

Glancing over his shoulder, he couldn't see her, but she must have collapsed on the beach, or else she would be here. The Kagonesti never shrank from a fight.

The Knight Commander backed away, still issuing orders in the goblin tongue, keeping his eyes locked on the dragon's, while grasping a feathered talisman that hung from his belt. There was no trace of fright on the knight's face. Too late, Dhamon wondered if his fear aura had been diminished somehow, as not a single goblin had panicked and the knight wasn't even trembling.

He had crushed and killed goblins galore, but the reinforcements continued to defiantly prick him with their small spears and swords. They'd drawn a little blood here and there.

"Pests! An annoyance," Dhamon muttered. "I'll not save any of you for Ragh." That reminded him—where was his loyal draconian friend?

"Ragh!" His roar vibrated through the earth and pitched several goblins right to the ground. The vibrations raced outward in all directions, even jarring Feril awake. The Kagonesti opened her eyes wide and a minute later struggled to rise.

She looked toward the trees and saw the goblin army. "Dhamon!"

"Ragh!" Dhamon bellowed over and over. "Ragh, where are you?"

Feril shakily got to her feet, nurturing her inner resources and sending her senses into the tall grass around the forest. "Aid me," she murmured to the plants and trees lining the beach. "Snare the creatures that assail the dragon."

Meanwhile, Dhamon was distracted by a new mob of goblins rushing to confront him; he lashed them with his tail, clawed and snapped at them as they swarmed him from all sides. As the minutes passed, however, the grass around him began to grow to unusual lengths; nurtured by Feril's magic, the tall grass whipped around the legs of the goblins, holding them in place and making them easier to trap and kill. Ferns and wildflowers spiraled up and twisted around the creatures' flailing arms, keeping them from using their weapons.

Feril! She has recovered? he thought gratefully. The grass grabbed at him, too, but he was too large and powerful to be pinioned. With a massive swipe of his claws, he finished off the last group of goblins still managing to mount any offense, then cast his gaze about for the Knight Commander.

The Knight of Neraka had disappeared. Dhamon knew he must be proving his cowardice by hiding somewhere in the woods. He sniffed the air, picking up the scent of wildflowers, goblin blood, and his own rankness. He didn't scent the knight or the draconian. Again Dhamon wondered about his friend.

"Ragh!" Dhamon's serpentine throat had gone hoarse. "Ragh?"

He scanned the still-rustling foliage, peered through the mounds of goblin corpses for a glimpse of the cowering Knight Commander or Ragh. The tall grass and ferns, spreading evergreens and bushes were swaying hypnotically. It made his head spin.

"Ragh!" Though he had won the day, he felt spent, defeated. "Ragh . . ."

Had the goblins killed him? If they had, where was the body?

The tall grass was wrapping around his talons and twisting around his tail. His head felt so heavy that he lowered it, feeling the tendrils of flower vines ensnaring his barbels. He rested his head on the ground, his collapsing jaw crushing goblin bodies. Long blades of grass edged over his lip and entwined his teeth.

Dhamon closed his eyes and let out a great sigh, feeling almost comforted and cocooned by the enchanted nature.

"Dhamon?" Feril stepped over dropped weapons and dead goblins, feet slipping in the copious blood. She stilled the grass with a silent command and peered ahead, looking for goblins or worse.

She didn't see anything moving, though with her elven eyesight she saw better than the dragon, and under an old white oak she spied the prone form of the sivak. He was pinned to the ground with spears, and she thought him dead.

"Dhamon?" She hurried to the dragon, tripping over dead goblins. Slender fingers traced the scale pattern on his snout. She gagged at his odor, made a hundred times worse combined with the stink of all the slain goblins. "Dhamon!"

She shook off the fatigue from her journey in the lake and stared wide-eyed at Dhamon. It didn't make any sense. The dragon wasn't breathing.

From deep in the woods, the Knight Commander surveyed his decimated army. Despite the massive bloodshed, it was total victory. Though all but a handful of the goblins had died, goblins were cheap fodder to the Knight Commander, and he had managed to slay the dragon called Dhamon.

"Mistress Sable will be greatly pleased." He imagined she would bestow a magnificent reward on him. True, he wouldn't be able to bring the dragon's head to her as he'd originally planned—he didn't have enough goblins to cut if off and carry the heavy head—but he would do something to show proof of his success.

The draconian was also close to death, but sivaks were hardy creatures and this one might survive. If he did, the Knight Commander would drag him back to Sable's lair, a witness to this evening's triumph who could testify about the knight's genius and the dragon's momentous death. Then he would end the sivak's suffering in front of Sable or maybe let her dissolve the draconian with her acid breath. Sable would have to reward him then. Hadn't he killed the great Dhamon and his pet? He would be so terribly, terribly rich.

The Knight Commander would sneak back to this place in the morning, just to see if the sivak pulled through. If the sivak didn't live the night, too bad, then Bedell would have to settle for a small trophy from the Dhamon-dragon. Perhaps he'd cut off a small piece of the body—evidence of the kill. A few scales would do, a barbel, or a tooth. The pathetic elf woman would have slunk off by first light, then he could be on his way back to Shrentak. Without his army of goblins, he didn't care to deal with the elf. She was a tricky one; she had brought the woods to life and held the goblins fast, thus she was a sorceress of considerable power. Confronting her would be above and beyond the call of duty. Sable didn't know or care about the elf sorceress. Besides, she might figure out how to enchant him or tangle him up in the plants or trees like the stupid goblins, then he couldn't return to Sable and gain his tremendous reward.

No, he would retreat to a deserted village a few miles away. A couple of the homes were reasonably intact, and he would pass the rest of the night there.

Then he would return in the morning for his precious evidence.

CHAPTER
12

Dhamon tucked his long hair behind his ears, then stretched and worked a kink out of his neck. He was in his lair, deep in Sable's swamp, and he was ogling all the riches he had collected when he was a dragon, thinking how he would carry them all out of the cave to a safer place—build a mansion and live there happily. He would need a wagon and sure-footed mules that could navigate the marsh. Several wagons, he corrected himself, as he looked into an alcove, the floor of which was covered with gold coins. Coins such as those had not been used on Krynn in a long time, and collectors would pay highly for them, especially in this marvelously preserved condition. He tried to remember where he'd gotten them—ah, yes . . . a few months ago he'd lumbered across an old ruin and Ragh had delved into a tunnel. The draconian came back with the gold coins and a handful of egg-shaped pieces of marble strung together on a thin cord.

He had gems more precious than all those gold coins. Four matching sapphires that he claimed off the body of a Knight Commander were faultless and were the prize of his collection. Those walnut-sized gems couldn't have honestly belonged to the knight; Dhamon suspected they had come from Sable and were to be used as a gift or a bribe. Those four gems alone would be enough to buy him a fine house and furnishings in whatever city he eventually decided to settle in. Perhaps he would build several mansions in different cities, opting to travel between homes whenever he felt like a change of scenery. Some of the baubles he would save for Feril, of course. Even a Kagonesti appreciated jewelry. He fancied her wearing a thin strand of pearls he'd taken off the corpse of a female knight.

"It wasn't proper in my day," Dhamon mused, thinking of that knight who had died easily by his caustic breath. When Dhamon was a Dark Knight no jewelry could be worn, and certainly no jewelry was taken off dead bodies—save the odd memento. The knighthood had changed, for the worse as far as he was concerned. There wasn't as much honor, and loyalties were divided. "Shouldn't be proper now." He bent and ran his fingertips over a bowl filled with polished onyx chips, then turned and went to inspect other riches at the far end of his cave.

There was one of his favorites—a long sword displayed on a stack of shields. The sword had been taken from the same Knight Commander who had carried the four sapphires. The sword was as strong and fine in its craftsmanship as any Dhamon had ever seen, and he ached to be human again, to properly hold it and feel its balance. Dhamon knelt and almost reverently touched the pommel. It was made of a hard metal that gleamed like silver but was far more precious. It felt comfortingly warm to the touch. The grip was etched with runes and studded with blue topaz cabochons. When he studied it closely, he could tell that the runes and gems had been set to represent constellations. The crosspiece was inlaid with gold and crushed pearls, and it curved at the ends, looking like the horns of a bull. His fingers wrapped around the pommel and he picked it up, briefly feeling the regret that a good sword never felt the same gripped in dragon's claws.

"Beautiful," he said in a hushed voice. The blade was made of the same metal as the pommel, hammered to a fault, extraordinarily sharp. The balance was perfect, all of it feeling impossibly light and so easy to wield. "To battle with this! Wonderful!"

Dhamon decided he would hang this favorite sword above the mantel in his favorite house, wear it into town on certain days, wield it against any who caught his eye with a challenging glance. He vowed this particular sword was one prize he would never sell. There were plenty of other pieces of treasure that he also didn't intend to part with: some fine pieces of armor and an impressive shield edged in platinum and bearing the visage of Reorx the Forge. There was that nightbird statue that Ragh thought was magical and a pair of exquisite throwing daggers.

It was going to be hard to decide what to sell and what to keep.

"Ragh," Dhamon mused. He would keep the daggers for the sivak, and probably give him a few sacks of steel pieces too. Nothing too valuable or too extravagant, he thought, but the sivak deserved something for all his help building this hoard.

Dhamon made a slashing gesture with the sword and watched the blade gleam and flash in the light . . . the light of what? Where was that light coming from?

He spun, looking for the source and seeing moisture glint off the walls of his lair. What was that unaccustomed smell? He should be smelling the swamp, rotting plants and stagnant water, overripe blooms and dank earth, but he didn't smell anything, not even his own glorious sweat. Neither could he hear anything, all of a sudden. He listened hard for the usual sound of leaves shushing outside, the omnipresent trickling of water—everywhere there was water in the swamp. He couldn't even hear the clicking of his boot heels against the stones of the cave. He froze, holding his breath, concentrating. Then, faintly, he could hear a gentle thrumming, regular at the beginning, then growing softer and erratic.

"Oh, it's my heart," Dhamon realized. He felt his heartbeat slow down, the thrumming difficult even to detect now. "I must be dreaming. I'm dying."

Feril's nervous fingers fluttered over the scales on Dhamon's legs. Dead? He couldn't be dead, she told herself. Impossible. A dragon as ferocious, as beautiful as this one, could not have been felled by mere goblins—not even by a limitless army of them, yet no question about it, Dhamon wasn't breathing.

Nothing was breathing within her line of sight. There must have been nearly two hundred dead goblins spread across the clearing and into the woods, all smashed, broken, skewered, or otherwise killed by Dhamon, yet Dhamon was dead.

"How could he be dead?" Feril fought back tears. The scent of the dead dragon was intense, and coupled with the stench from the dead goblins and all the blood, it was overwhelming. "To lose Dhamon again. This can't happen."

Perhaps it was the Lake of Death, she thought. Maybe even though Dhamon had been part of her shadow when she was in the lake, the cold and the touch of the undead had so weakened him that the goblins were able to conquer him in the end.

"You can't be dead." Her lips brushed the top of his claw. "How could . . ."

Several small goblin spears were wedged between scales on Dhamon's claw, and in the light of the moon she saw that something other than blood glistened from those wounds. Feril felt the substance with her fingers. It was dark and oily, smelling like decaying plants.

"Poison!" She felt a stab of realization, of deep pain. "The vile creatures poisoned you!" She spat on the oil on her fingers and wiped them off thoroughly on the grass. Then she spat on her fingers again and again, wiping them furiously on her tunic. The pain persisted but spread no farther, and she clenched and unclenched her fist as she climbed onto Dhamon's snout and put her ear to a cavernous nostril. Her heart leaped. There was the faintest hint of emission, he breathed only very slightly, and she cursed herself for being a fool and thinking him dead. She splayed her hands wide on the ridge of his snout.

"Dhamon, I pray I have not dallied too long to save you." Once again the magical spark blossomed inside of her, grew warm and moved down her arms until her fingers felt hot too, then the ache in her hand vanished. "I'm not a healer like Goldmoon and Jasper were. I don't have their strength of healing magic." She did have certain curative powers, and she'd called upon them several times when she was in the company of Dhamon and the others years ago. She'd cultivated that power in the years away from him, helping wounded refugees.

Refugees on the island of Cristyne who were ill, starving, some with broken limbs, she had always done what she could for them, and though she mourned the ones who were beyond her help, she had tried to learn from her mistakes. Once, long ago, Feril had aided wolves on Southern Ergoth that had eaten contaminated meat left by herders. She remembered the healing she had used on that occasion, summoning the memory of one favorite wolf she had saved. She'd coaxed his heart stronger, and she tried to do that with Dhamon now. She imagined his heart, huge and muscular. The energy flowed from her fingers and into his snout. Her mind pushed the energy down his neck and into his chest. As the Kagonesti worked, she bent her ear and listened for signs that her tactic might be successful.

"Be stronger, Dhamon Grimwulf. Stay with me."

At first she heard only her own heart beating, the faint rustling of a soft breeze teasing the trees, the buzz of insects being drawn to the goblin bodies. For a moment, she thought she heard a man talking, an unfamiliar voice coming from the trees behind her. Then it was gone, and she heard Dhamon's faint heart beat.

"Take my strength, draw from it," she breathed, pushing the energy, augmenting it, and breathing in time with Dhamon. Now there was more force in each breath he took, and she could sense his heart slowly growing stronger.

At length Dhamon gave a loud snort, and after long minutes his eyes eased open. Feril turned so she could look into them, straddling his snout, fingers still splayed and working their spell. She gazed at her reflection in his dark eyes. She searched for the poison, finally sensing it, dark, oily, and potent, deep down.

"The poison's strong, Dhamon. You need to be stronger than death."

Feril pictured the poison, as real and as threatening an enemy as the Knights of Neraka she had stalked in this forest, and like the knights she'd hung by the trees as punishment, she would vanquish this menace. Her arcane energy continued to pulse into Dhamon, and after nearly an hour it gradually diluted the poison until it was no longer a serious threat. Her skin was slick with sweat from the exertion, the slight breeze doing little to soothe her. She was exhausted.

"You'll be all right now, Dhamon." She pushed herself off him and slid down, collapsing when her feet touched the grass. "I'm so weak." She was careful not to have taken any of the poison into herself, as surely anything strong enough to fell a dragon would certainly kill her. Perhaps they'd used it on the sivak.

Where was Ragh? Looking around, she remembered—oh, over there.

She dragged herself up and staggered across the goblin bodies, falling more than once and coming up slick with blood. Feril finally reached the sivak—out of responsibility to Dhamon, who had been his friend, she should at least bury the strange creature. Peering at him now, she realized the draconian wasn't dead, not yet anyway. He stared up at her, his mouth working. Surprised to find him alive, she bent over him so she could understand what he was saying.

"They had poison, the goblins did." His voice was unusually soft and forced. "Took me unawares, the poison. Is Dhamon . . ."

"Unwell, but he will survive. It was indeed a virulent poison. And you? You don't look very healthy . . ."

The branches of the white oak towering above them were thick, and not much moonlight was filtering down. Feril could see the many wounds lacing the sivak's chest, the goblin spears holding his limbs to the ground.

"They tortured you," she said, wondering how best to free him.

"I didn't tell them anything," the sivak said.

He grimaced as she tried to twist the spears off that were trapping his left arm. "Ouch! That hurts." After a moment, with a dry chuckle, "Of course it, hurt before, too."

"Why didn't they kill you?"

"I don't know. They wanted to know about Dhamon; they were waiting for him to come back. They didn't know about you."

She'd worked the spear free and moved on to another. Two more to go on this arm. The sivak had lost a lot of blood to the spears and the cuts. His blood had a sulfurous odor and was oddly congealed. "The goblins wanted to know what about Dhamon?"

"The knight leading them, he wanted to know where he was, what he was doing. He'd been looking for Dhamon, I guess. I didn't tell him anything, though. To the lowest level of the Abyss with all of them." He spat, choked, and coughed.

Two more spears came free, and painfully, Ragh began to move his left arm. "There were dozens, probably a hundred of the stinking goblin rats. I saw them running past me on their scaly little legs, all of them whooping and . . ."

"Shhh. I don't need to hear your prattle. Only Habbakuk knows why I'm doing this anyway. You are no friend

149

to me or to my kind," her voice softened, "but Dhamon seems to like you well enough." She continued to pull out the spears, breaking some of them off and working his legs free. At the same time she called upon her healing energies again, directing the warmth down her arms and into her fingers, which were gently stroking the sivak's main wounds.

He ground his teeth together to keep from crying out. Feril knew he wasn't about to show weakness in front of her. Some of his wounds had already started to heal over. In spite of herself, Feril felt a twinge of compassion for him.

"I wonder why they were so intent on finding—and killing—Dhamon."

Ragh was still flat on his back. He clenched his fists, testing his muscles, and slowly moved his arms and legs, muttering and grimacing. "I thought they had killed me, too," he said. "I thought I would bleed out my essence all over the ground." He tried to sit up, but she pushed him firmly back down on the ground.

"They weren't only looking for a dragon, they were looking for Dhamon by name? How is that possible? I thought you were the only one who knew that Dhamon was a dragon."

Ragh closed his eyes and let out a deep breath. "That Knight Commander, the one who was leading the goblins, did Dhamon manage to kill him?"

He didn't see Feril shake her head.

"I don't like this place." Feril was talking to herself, carefully prodding the sivak's wounds to make sure none were infected. "I don't want to stay here."

"Finally we agree on something, elf."

"Yet in this lake I may discover a chance to give Dhamon his humanity back." Still, it was as though she were talking to herself. "I need to be about that business as soon as possible, if we are to get away from here." She nervously smoothed her tunic with the palms of her hands, spreading the blood around. Then she turned and surveyed the battlefield; not a goblin stirred.

"Can you stand, sivak?" She held out her hand to assist Ragh.

The draconian lumbered to his feet on his own power, wincing when he took a few steps on wobbly legs. "So we're leaving soon? I'm all for that, but it doesn't look like Dhamon's going to be able to move for some time." He nodded toward Dhamon, then started limping in that direction, stepping over goblin bodies.

"Stay close by his side, sivak. He'll probably sleep for a few hours yet, and I intend to be back by the time he wakes up. You need some rest, too."

"What about you? You should rest too, elf."

"Not me. I have unfinished work at the bottom of the lake." The elf's face was an emotionless mask as she stepped by Ragh and headed toward Nalis Aren.

Feril dived quickly through the blessedly warm water and swam through schools of sunfish and perch. It didn't take her long to reach Qualinost and locate the enchanted crystal atop Kalilnama's home. The cold seemed far worse than before, especially brutal and draining, but as weary and weak as the Kagonesti was, she wouldn't retreat. She swam through an open window and down through the stairwell opening until she reached the second floor.

Obelia was there, as she'd hoped, along with Kalilnama and four other Qualinesti spirits.

The spirit of the aged elf rushed forward to warm her with a spell. "Elf-fish, elf-fish, we feared you were lost to Beryl's protectors. We . . ."

Beryl's protectors? For a brief instant she worried about provoking the spirits, suspecting they could harm her if they wanted. Still, she couldn't contain her ire. *You were among them, Obelia! You protected the accursed corpse as much as the ghost knights! You told me to take a scale from an overlord! You followed me to Beryl's corpse! And then—despite your promises—you did nothing to help me. Nothing! It was as if you had gleefully handed me right over to . . . to . . . .*

Obelia hung his insubstantial head apologetically. "We didn't know what would happen, elf-fish. Something . . . some force tied to the dragon and to the lake . . . maybe even tied to us, prevented us from helping you."

"It's the evil magic that's left in the dead dragon," Kalilnama explained. "It obviously sustains this lake and the spirits of those who died here. It also must have compelled us to protect the dragon's remains. I find it most interesting that in death a dragon still has such great power. It bears studying, don't you concur? Now that I know, I think it will give me something to occupy my time."

Obelia came nose-to-nose with Feril. "There is certainly some evil force making those knights and goblins guard the body. Perhaps a spell cast when the dragon lived and whose power endures, and something caused us . . . forced us . . . to safeguard Beryl's body. I can't explain just what it was . . . something . . . maybe Kalilnama's right and it's the magic left in Beryl. Maybe it's something inside of us."

Scales . . . that was all I wanted, and what you told me I needed. You agreed, no—volunteered—to help me.

"I will help you this time, elf-fish. I promise."

Feril's expression softened a little.

"The powders and scrolls, we'll take you to them," Obelia continued. "Anything we can think of that will strengthen magic. Maps and items that will help you locate other scales without alerting the dragon who possesses them. Some dragons shed scales like snakes and lizards shed their skins, you know."

Kalilnama rubbed his hands together, the fingers passing through each other. "We'll help you find another dragon's scales—not Beryl's—to aid your cause."

Beryl is so close! To leave now when that huge carcass is . . .

"There are other overlords, elf-fish. They're not all dead like Beryl, are they? I believe that Beryl is too protected. Your chases will be better elsewhere."

Thinking of the dead, bloated white beast that had destroyed the Qualinesti homeland, Feril saw that the elf spirits were right. She'd willingly go back and try again, no matter the odds, if it would help Dhamon, but she might be able to find dragon scales elsewhere without endangering herself. After all, there were other overlords—dead and alive—besides the one that ruled the Lake of Death. She nodded.

"The closest, if my memory does not fail me," Kalilnama noted, "is the black called Sable. She lives somewhere on the other side of the mountains. The climate of the swamp will be easier to manage than the evil magic of the lake."

You'll tell me where these powders and scrolls are? And how I might use them?

"We'll take you to them," Obelia reiterated. His translucent fingers passed through her hands. "As before, you'll have to do the gathering, elf-fish."

Let's be about it, then. Decisively, she opened her mind and flooded the elf spirits with images of the dead goblins and Dhamon, so they would understand how urgent her need was. *I've spent too much time here already.*

"I used to know an expert herbalist on Wildarth Lane," Obelia said, nodding slowly as he saw what had happened to her, Dhamon, and Ragh. His fingers came up to work at the bridge of his overly long nose. "He had amazing powders on his shelves. Balms and unguents that elves would travel hundreds of miles to buy. Let's go there and see what we can find to help you—and your friends."

Kalilnama visibly brightened, and he wrung his hands together faster than ever. "Yes, Halarigh Starsong, the herbalist was. My wife spent much of my gold on his curious wares. Fine spell components he carried—at high prices. Halarigh and his family were a little greedy, but they sold only the best." The ghost paused and his face took on a wistful aspect. "He couldn't have carried everything off with him, and the lake couldn't have ruined everything left behind."

"And I remember a few sorcerers," Obelia continued, "whose houses we should visit."

"Don't forget my wife's scrolls," Kalilnama said, "and then there's . . ."

They moved quickly for ghosts, but not as quickly as Feril would have wanted. For one thing, the insubstantial ghosts could not physically propel themselves through the water. They floated like flotsam and seemed ignorant of time.

From one abandoned shop they took her to, Feril selected two large satchels made from the hide of a beast she wasn't familiar with. In the bottom of one she put a pair of leggings and a tunic for herself, then she found something that she thought might fit Dhamon . . . when he became human again. The other satchel she filled with jars, scroll tubes, and well-stoppered vials that Kalilnama, Obelia, and their ghostly associates insisted contained promising materials.

She also gathered a handful of small, jeweled trinkets that she guessed might be valuable and filled a small pouch with steel pieces. Little was free in the world above, and now she would have a means to pay for things if the need arose.

"One more place to visit," Obelia told her.

They were on the roof of Kalilnama's home again with more than a dozen curious Qualinesti spirits fluttering around them. Feril plucked the enchanted pear-shaped crystal off the roof and stuffed it under the clothes in the satchel. The water surrounding them instantly became eerily darker without the magical light.

"Follow me, elf-fish. We will be going alone now, just you and me."

Feril said good-bye to Kalilnama and the others, shuddering from the cold when their hands passed through her. They begged her to return and tell them if she was successful in her mission to turn the dragon into a man again. Though she detested the notion of coming back here, she agreed she might, because after all, they had been so helpful. They would show some of the famous sights of the city then, they insisted. She offered a word of heartfelt thanks to Kalilnama, then she followed the spirit elf Obelia as he beckoned her toward his watery home.

"Believe me when I say I am grateful you did not die by the spirits of the knights. I had prayed to all the gods, elf-fish, that you would come back to this lake and would not give up just because you failed to obtain one of Beryl's scales."

Feril didn't reply. She was looking around the spirit's rooms, trying to figure out why she had been brought here—what might be important to her goal.

"There is so much life and hope in you, my elf-fish, a determination and fire that I find envious."

Feril froze in fear. Was Obelia going to betray her again? She whirled to look for his diaphanous form, finding it hovering above a pile of brittle-looking bones.

"I think I would have faded away to nothingness, elf-fish, had you not come along and given me a fresh sense of purpose."

What do you want? She tensed, ready to push past him and out the door.

"To come with you."

You know that's not going to be possible, Obelia, she said sadly, watching his expression change and harden.

Suddenly, Feril felt the warmth leave her body.

CHAPTER

13

He felt a pleasant rush, a fuzzy taste, reminding him of the spiced ale he used to order on visits to town—when he was human and running in the company of his old friend Maldred. The ale would slide down his throat and warm his belly, the feeling slowly spreading to his arms and legs. His tongue would seem thick, his judgment and vision would blur, and he would be blissfully oblivious to his problems for a while. He'd not had an ounce of ale since his transformation into a dragon, but when the last vestiges of the pain and poison fled and his strength began to return, he had a familiar feeling which brought memories of drinking and his old friend. He wondered what Maldred was up to. Was the ogre-mage in ogre lands, getting primed to become king one day after the passing of his father? Or was he walking around some human city, looking handsome and human, and scheming, as always, to garner riches?

Dhamon's talons tingled. He still felt a bit dizzy. Then everything began to clear and he could feel his senses becoming acute again. He dropped all thoughts of Maldred, and focused on Feril and Ragh—and himself.

What had happened to him? He remembered an army of goblins that he was cutting through like a scythe through wheat. Then he remembered feeling overwhelmed by sleep. Goblins were piled all around him, smelling worse than usual because they were dead. The scent of blood filled his nostrils, along with the hint of sulfur, meaning Ragh was nearby. He remembered looking around for Ragh and being worried that the goblins might have killed the sivak while he and Feril were away, busying themselves deep down in the Lake of Death.

"Feeling better, my friend?" Ragh stepped out from the shadows of an old oak, careful to pick his way over goblin bodies as he walked toward Dhamon.

"Better?" Dhamon opened a bleary eye. "Aye, a little."

The draconian read the puzzlement on Dhamon's face and so brought him up to date—telling him all about the goblin spears tipped with poison.

"You'll soon be back to your old self," Ragh said upon finishing the story. "You've amazing recuperative powers. Of course, it was a good thing the elf was around to help."

Dhamon relished the surge of strength in his limbs. He effortlessly dug his talons into the hard ground, raking furrows. He rolled his shoulders and opened his huge wings, feeling refreshed and powerful. Did he truly want to give up this dragon form? he wondered. He couldn't call himself happy now, but would he feel any better as a man? Did he want to return to a body that was an insect in comparison to this greatness? Then he pushed such thoughts aside, telling himself the questions were irrelevant until he knew for certain if there was a cure to be had. His muscles bunched as he stretched his front legs out toward the old oak.

"The elf thought you'd be sleeping for a few hours at least." Ragh looked up to catch the dragon's gaze. "I tried to tell her to stay and wait, but she was impatient. I tried to tell her nothing keeps your kind down long."

Your kind. Dhamon's eyes narrowed as he stared at his friend, for the first time registering Ragh's numerous wounds.

"Oh, I'm all right—now," Ragh said, anticipating Dhamon's questions. "Same army that went after you . . . yeah, they got to me first, but they didn't use that on me, thankfully. Must have been nasty stuff if it could knock down a dragon. Bet that stuff would be worth a good turn of coin in some dark places."

"How long have I been . . . how long has Feril been gone?" Dhamon's head swiveled around and his neck reached forward into the trees, eyes peering into the shadows and nostrils quivering at the stench coming from the goblin bodies. The sound of flies and other feasting insects supplied grim background noise.

Ragh ground the ball of his foot against the earth, a gesture that usually told Dhamon the sivak was either frustrated or disappointed. "A few hours. Said she had things to tend to. I told her to stay and wait, but she wouldn't listen to me."

Something rustled the trees and Ragh watched a small flock of night birds scattering. He eyed Dhamon, who was looking off into the distance, toward the lake.

"You've no idea what's down there, Ragh," Dhamon said angrily, turning back to stare at the sivak, his tone making the ground shake. The insects' drone quieted for a moment, and the few straggling night birds swiftly vanished.

"I wasn't exactly in any position to stop her." Ragh pointed to his deepest wounds. Much softer, "No one listens to me anyway."

Then Ragh walked past Dhamon and headed toward the lake, doing his best to step over goblin bodies and nearly slipping in the gore. He idly glanced at the corpses, scanning for gold or silver neckchains or jewels. He knew it wasn't likely pathetic creatures such as these would carry valuables, but the sivak couldn't shake the habit of looking.

In a few steps Dhamon was past him, stopping at the shore of Nalis Aren and craning his neck out over the mist-draped water. He could dive in after her, would dive in after her, he decided—if she wasn't back by the time the moon was directly overhead. Ragh soon came up behind him, plopping down in the sand.

Ragh stared at the water. Even more than Dhamon, the sivak had a pronounced fear of water—especially of deep water; he couldn't swim worth a damn and knew he would sink like a rock in the Lake of Death. Still, trying to show Dhamon how much he too was worried about the elf, he stood and waded bravely into the shallows, until the water was up to his knees. Standing there, looking around, he caught Dhamon's eye and nodded. The two of them stood there for a long time, looking out across the water for any inkling of Feril.

Dhamon just stood there, watching and waiting. After a while, Ragh washed the goblin gore off his feet and the dried blood away from the edges of his wounds. He was thirsty, but he didn't drink the strange lake water. When he was finished, he came onto the sand and took up a position on the bank a few yards away from Dhamon's right claw. He leaned back on his elbows, closed his eyes, and listened to the flutter of wings, a bird flying over the Lake of Death.

The blue was darker than Feril had remembered. The cold was oppressive. She was swimming up to the warm part of the lake as fast as possible, but Feril couldn't stroke very well with her arms, as she was carrying the heavy satchels.

So tired, legs heavy. But it won't be long, can't be far. I can rest next to Dhamon.

She was making progress, she knew, only it was slow progress. The satchels were soaked with water, adding to their immense weight. Her magic gave her extraordinary strength, otherwise she wouldn't have been able to lift both of the satchels, especially after Obelia had taken away the nurturing warmth, but the Kagonesti was sorely tempted to drop one of the satchels.

She *was* making progress, she told herself, putting more distance between herself and the sunken city. She was ascending, yet the cold somehow intensified, and the water was beginning to turn an eerie midnight blue.

Stay, she thought she heard someone say from somewhere far below her. *Staystaystaystaystay*.

My mind teases me! Got to get out of here. Her legs pumped even more furiously.

Stay.

There was no imagining it—she had heard something. Only this time it came from close by, over her shoulder. Feril's eyes went wide with horror. It wasn't the voice of a single ghost—not Obelia or Kalilnama or any of their companions. No ghost was in sight, only the still-darkening blue waters.

Stay. The word was much louder this time.

But it wasn't one voice, it was several, she realized after the word had been repeated several more times.

Stay.

Repeated, magnified, and distorted. A dozen voices, hundreds of voices. Perhaps it was the voices of all the spirits trapped here, loud, powerful, and persuasive, in one chorus. Perhaps it was the true voice of the lake itself.

Staystaystaystaystay.

Stay? She pondered the temptation. She couldn't, could she? There were things to do, like saving Dhamon and helping the refugees. Important things.

Staystaystaystaystay.

Earthbound duties weren't *that* important. Maybe she should stay. It wouldn't be so bad to join the elves in Qualinost, she mused, as she'd made many nice ghostly friends there. She hadn't seen enough of the city, and she could explore it all at her leisure if she remained underwater. She would have all the time in the world to see everything. She could go back to the building with all the sculptures and talk to the artisan who had fashioned such remarkable images.

Stay, Ferilleeagh. Staystaystaystaystay.

Tempting.

The water started to thicken around her, embracing and cocooning her. It no longer felt hurtfully frigid; it was beginning to soothe her. The chorus of voices came from all around now and became superbly melodious.

Stay, Ferilleeagh. Stay.

Not so bad to stay here. Not so bad . . .

Stay.

Yes, I . . . not ever! she suddenly raged. *I'll not be tricked!* The Kagonesti finally recognized that some magical force was trying to muddle her senses and seduce her into staying. *Dhamon's fate is entwined with mine, and if I die, he'll never be human again. You'll not keep me here. Important things to do.*

She kicked her legs harder, holding tight to the straps of the satchels. They were anchors slowing her down, but she couldn't lose their contents, so she continued to struggle, hoping the lake would not overpower her.

You'll not defeat me, Nalis Aren, and you'll never see me again.

Sadly she thought about the Qualinesti spirits in the city. She'd promised to return and tell them if Dhamon had become human again—and she had sincerely intended to keep her promise. But now, she realized, she could never come back . . . provided the lake and its spirits would let her leave in the first place.

Feril cursed the dead overlord that had settled at the bottom of the lake, that had caused all this ruin and somehow cursed and warped the water. Her anger gave her strength and helped ward off the cold again suffusing her limbs.

So dark. So cold. Why haven't I reached the warm part of the lake?

Stay Ferilleeagh. Staystaystaystaystaystay.

Why haven't I . . .

She barely made out the form of a sauger-fish swimming past her face. In the midnight water, its body was dark; all she spotted was the white of its belly and lower jaw. Higher, and she saw the pale olive stripe of a pike. Spurred on by hope, she put all her concentration and energy into reaching the warm surface.

Eventually she was rewarded.

Dhamon was listening to the birds, insects, and wind. He'd told himself he'd go looking for her when the moon was overhead, but he'd lingered on the shore past that time. Feril was wise and powerful and could take care of herself, he told Ragh more than once. He believed that, though he had to admit he was afraid of the lake. He'd wait just a little longer, he kept telling Ragh.

Finally he heard a soft splash and spotted Feril swimming toward him. Ragh jumped up. Dhamon breathed a sigh of relief as she made it to shore.

"We're leaving," she announced peremptorily, after nodding to the sivak and dropping the two satchels on the sand. She was gasping and took several deep breaths. "I'm never coming back to this accursed place."

"Can't be fast enough for me," the draconian said. "Hope you collected Dhamon's cure in one of those packs." He reached for the satchels. Water poured out of the gaps as he put one over each shoulder. "I've a few suggestions on where we can go. I've been thinking about far, far north, or maybe the Dragon Isles."

Feril shook her head, the droplets of water caught in the moonlight looking like liquid silver. "Not there. We're not going in that direction at all."

"Where?" This came from Dhamon.

"To Sable's swamp," she told them. "I'll explain along the way, but the best chance for a cure is in the swamp . . . and in those bags . . . and in one of Sable's scales." She touched a scale on Dhamon's leg and looked up at him. She couldn't see his eyes from where she was standing. "If the two of you are feeling all right, I'd like to get started now. I truly don't want to stay around this place."

Ragh kicked at stones, muttering. "Fine, fine. Go back to the swamp and get ourselves killed or worse. I don't even get a vote anymore."

Dhamon craned his neck to look in her eyes. "I'll fly us there, Feril. It won't take long. Perhaps it would be . . . safer."

She shook her head. "I want to go by land at least for a while . . . if you don't mind. I'm through with swimming for a while—and flying too. I need to feel the ground beneath my feet."

CHAPTER 14

The bear was a rich shade of cinnamon brown, with a lighter brown concave muzzle and a large white patch on its chest. It was more than six feet long and half again that high at the shoulders, likely weighing about seven hundred pounds. It was wading downstream from where Feril and Ragh were studying the contents of the satchels. It was diligently looking for fish, curved claws and long teeth flashing when it finally caught a thick-bodied salmon.

Around a bend and a few miles farther down the stream were two more bears, larger and stockier, and of a different breed. Their dense fur was yellow-brown, the hair tipped silvery-white in places. Each had a pronounced hump above its shoulders and claws a half-dozen inches long. Their heads appeared disproportionately massive because of long ruffs, and each weighed well more than a thousand pounds. They had been feeding well this morning and were finishing the last of the salmon they'd caught.

Dhamon suppressed his fear aura and slid closer to the two bears.

166

Though the trees were thick in this part of the Qualinesti forest, he managed to slip through clumps of river birch without making a lot of noise. All dragons possessed magical abilities, and Dhamon knew magic let him move almost noiselessly when he truly wanted to. He just rarely put the effort into it.

The trees ended only a yard or so from the stream, giving way to the rocky bank. Dhamon stopped to watch the bears more closely, the shadows from the trees effectively hiding him; the wind was blowing toward him strong enough to keep his stench from giving him away. They were beautiful animals, fast for their size and powerful, but they would not be long for the world, as Dhamon was hungry.

When it looked like the bears were about to move farther down the stream, he sprang forward, jaws snapping, the talons of his right claw flexing. He slammed the smaller of the two animals against the ground. Though grievously wounded, the bear roared and tried to writhe free. Its mate made a huffing sound and bared its teeth, hair rising on its back in defiance. It looked once at its trapped mate and then raced across the stream. It gave a roar that trailed off into a wail as Dhamon reared back and struck, his neck stretching out, jaws opening wide.

He snatched the second bear in his maw and lifted it, muscles straining in his neck from its weight. He threw his head back, biting down hard, and broke the bear's back, killing it quickly. Because of its size, he couldn't swallow it whole, so he had to chew on it for a while. When he was finished, he attacked the first bear, still pinned under his weight, and devoured it more leisurely.

Then Dhamon drank his fill, savoring the taste of the bears. They were far more palatable than anything else he'd eaten lately. After a few minutes of washing his claws, he headed upstream and made quick work of tracking the cinnamon brown bear. He wouldn't need to eat again for some time.

———◆◆◆———

Feril and Ragh sat across from each other on a large rock at the headwaters of the stream. They were at the edge of the Qualinesti forest, the Kharolis Mountains looming to the east. Strewn on the rock were the contents of the larger satchel—colored ceramic vials, clay jars, scroll tubes sealed with thick gray wax, small leather pouches filled with crystalline substances, and an assortment of metal and bone beads and tiny figurines carved from soft green stone.

"All of this is going to help Dhamon?" The sivak was studying Feril as intently as he was regarding the assortment of objects.

She didn't meet his gaze at first as she moved the figurines around with her index finger, lingering on one that resembled a raccoon. "There is some faint magic in these pieces, and in these." She was touching the beads now. "Stronger magic in the bone. Honestly, I don't know how these things are going to help." She raised her eyes. "I will find out, I promise you." Feril stood and reached for the other satchel, rummaging around in it until she pulled out a stoppered flask. "Leave these things be, sivak," she ordered, pointing to the objects. Then she slid off the rock and started toward a weeping cedar, the main branch of which looked like a robed man, one arm outstretched as if pointing to something.

Ragh had seen her holding that particular flask before on and off during the journey here. Sometimes she cradled it like a baby, other times she studied her reflection in its polished sides and cocked her head toward it, as if she were listening to something. At no time did she let the sivak take it in his own hands.

"Hey!" Ragh quickly caught up to her, pointing at the flask. "What's so important about that flask? What are you going to do with it?"

She slowly let out a deep breath. "I keep telling you, what I'm going to do is none of your . . ."

"Concern? Business? I'm tired of your attitude. You bet it's my concern, elf, because it concerns Dhamon. He's the only friend I have, and I want him to be human again as much as you want it. He *needs* to be human before whatever's left of his humanity slips away, and it is slipping. You can see it, if you've a care to look, so you don't need to be keeping secrets." He pointed again at the flask.

"You have no secrets, sivak?" Her eyes seemed to float inward, and she ran the fingers of her free hand across the stopper. "Do you *really* want Dhamon to be human? Would he still remain your friend? You can't go everywhere with him, you can't fly around with him, sivak, if he becomes a man."

A meaningful silence passed between them, and when, after a long pause, the draconian spoke again, his whispery voice came from somewhere deep inside him. "Dhamon was the only man ever to treat me fairly. He never treated me . . . never talked to me . . . like I was a monster. He treated me, still treats me, as an equal." His voice contained a mix of pride and pain. "We've been friends for a long time. I trust we will remain friends, no matter what. Whatever you're going to do with that flask—if it concerns Dhamon—I want to know about it."

Feril stood motionless for several moments, then nodded. In the light of the late morning sun her wide eyes had taken on a hard blue shine. Those eyes were severe, forbidding. Ragh stared, as though seeing her for the first time—noticing faint lines around the corners of her eyes and also at the corners of her mouth, a thin crease on her forehead. Those facial lines were something new, something she'd acquired since her dives to the bottom of the Lake of Death.

The Kagonesti had aged considerably since they first met, the sivak realized. Something in the Lake of Death had added more than a few years to her look. Those added years were *noticeable*. Her eyes, with hard bright edges, had seen something terrible, or she'd been through something that stole part of her life.

"What happened down there ... in the lake?" he found himself asking.

She glanced back at the rock and the assortment of magical treasures she'd collected from Qualinost at the bottom of Nalis Aren. She didn't answer; Ragh heard only the stream flowing along at a fast pace, churning white around the knobby roots of a long-dead willow. The sunlight sparkled gold against the water and cut into the stream, illuminating patches of dark greens. In other places the stream looked clear as glass, with colorful pebbles strewn under the shallow water.

Feril was gazing at the stream, but Ragh wondered if she was staring at something remembered from the depths of Nalis Aren. She still didn't answer. All right, then; he changed the subject. "Are you going to tell me what's in that flask? A magical potion? Some arcane elixir Dhamon's supposed to drink?"

Another length of silence.

"All right," she said finally. "You deserve to know. It's nothing like that." Feril returned to the rock and sat cross-legged. She waited for the sivak to join her before, watching his reaction, she pulled the stopper off the flask.

The air shimmered and a face formed between Feril and Ragh, looking like a cloud settling to the earth. Ragh edged back and the muscles in his arms tensed. The misty face grayed to take on the substance of smoke, then details appeared—pronounced wrinkles, long pointed ears, deep-set eyes that looked more like vacant sockets. Thin lips parted and a pale blue wisp snaked out.

The misty face broke into a wide grin.

"Glory be, elf-fish, I am free of the lake!" The spirit face brightened. "Mountains! Magnificent land! Trees! It worked, my pretty puzzlement! Free!"

Wide-eyed, Ragh tentatively reached to touch a clawed finger to the apparition, then quickly pulled it back, shivering. *Cold,* he mouthed to Feril. *Like ice.* "What in the deepest levels of the Abyss is that thing?"

"Ah, a draconian! In life I was never close to one, only saw one of gold from a considerable distance once. You are a sivak, right?" The spirit didn't wait for an answer. "Yes, obviously a sivak, but I thought your kind had wings."

Ragh glowered at him. "What are you, wrinkle-face?"

"Obelia," the apparition said proudly. "I once was a Qualinesti sorcerer of considerable renown. I died in the heart of Qualinost's Old City when the great dragon Beryl descended on us and ruined our good and noble home. Now, freed from Nalis Aren, I have a new purpose. I am going to help the friend of my elf-fish become human again, then she is going to help me find my dear sister

171

Elalage." He hovered excitedly inches in front of Feril. "We have much work to do, my pretty puzzlement." To Ragh's astonishment, he then read over her shoulder as she carefully pulled the first scroll out and smoothed it against the rock.

For the next hour or so, Feril and the spirit went through each object and scroll, discussing various magical theories and spells. Ragh, keeping at arm's length, listened carefully. Though Feril was only passingly familiar with the kind of magic that Obelia and his peers had practiced in life, Ragh boasted more understanding, having associated with several sorcerers over the centuries, so he paid attention and learned to heed the words of the ghost sorcerer.

The ghost of the old elf went on at length about diverse patterns of magic in the world and where they lay the thickest, discoursing on all sorts of ancient places such as the Window to the Stars, where the magic was more substantial than the very stones that comprised the ruins. Ragh intently listened. In all his centuries on Krynn he'd seen some very unusual things, so he told himself the spirit of a dead Qualinesti sorcerer shouldn't rattle him. The spirit did not seem malicious like other undead creatures Ragh had come across. Still, the sivak decided not to entirely trust the entity, and he could see that Feril didn't either.

Though Dhamon turned up in the late afternoon, he kept far enough back and stayed down wind so the three barely noticed him. The elf sorcerer gave the dragon a quick look, and Feril nodded to him, *yes, that's the one,* but they were preoccupied with their discussion. As for Dhamon, he didn't look surprised to see a ghost conversing with Feril and Ragh. Ragh wondered if he didn't already know about the spirit sorcerer;

perhaps, the sivak thought resentfully, it was another one of the many secrets between the Kagonesti and his old friend.

Truth to tell, for the first time in a long while, Dhamon was truly tired. With a pleasantly full stomach, he felt bleary-eyed. He tried to listen to the magical discussion, the sweet taste of bear tarrying on his tongue. It wasn't long before he was dozing.

Obelia became even more transparent as he put his energy into his voice rather than his form. "Elf-fish, do you remember when the gods were absent and magic was a memory? Some thought there was nothing arcane left on Krynn. The famed human sorcerer Palin Majere discovered a way to weave certain enchantments. He relied on magical swords and daggers, magical talismans that would power his spells. The magical items were often destroyed in his casting, but they made his spells possible. We can learn many a lesson from Palin Majere . . ."

Feril nodded. She was familiar with Palin's expertise, having spent quite some time in his company. It was hard to follow some of Obelia's circular logic. Her eyes searched the pale mist for the expression on his wizened features.

"Magic is vibrant again, elf-fish, but we will need something especially strong to break the spell that turned your friend into a dragon. The scroll you first looked at, we can use that as counter magic, and all the talismans you've gathered . . ."

"What about Sable's scales?" the impatient Feril cut in.

Ragh's eyes grew wide and he cast a quick glance at the sleeping Dhamon. He opened his mouth in protest. A stern look from Feril kept him quiet.

"Yes, the Black's scales. We should get two, just to be certain. Three, four if we can, whatever we can manage, just to be certain. Since it was an overlord's scale that began your friend's woes—as you tell the tale—such a scale will be a vital component in the breaking of it." He drew an insubstantial finger up to rub the bridge of his nose. "For the best chance of success, we should perform this spell . . ."

"At one of the temple ruins, where the greatest magic persists."

The spirit beamed. "You are an excellent student, bright beyond words, elf-fish. Much of this work will fall on your shoulders, as my hands can, of course, hold or carry nothing. Death robbed me of many ordinary abilities."

The draconian snorted. "I have good hands . . ."

"Such sorcery is foreign to me," Feril interrupted. "My magic comes from nature and by Habbakuk's grace."

"You do have magic about you," Obelia argued. "We will work from your strengths, coupled with all of these magical items, a scale, and my wisdom."

"I know some magic, too," Ragh said sulkily, "not much, but some. I can help too, but I think we should find a different overlord to snatch a scale from and not pick any ruins in the swamp to execute this ritual of yours. There's the Window, the Silver Stair on Schallsea Island . . . I know of a few more."

Obelia gave Ragh a thin smile. "The three of us will perfect the spell together, then. We'll work on it during our journey to the dragon's swamp. When your friend is human again, elf-fish, you will keep the other part of our bargain and take me on a search for my sister Elalage. I will scry on her to discover where she went. Oh, she will be most surprised to see me."

Ragh growled softly. "*Another* overlord, Feril. Not the Black. Not Sable. This would be suicide. There's the White in Southern Ergoth. They say that beast's not as large. I don't think Dhamon or I would mind the cold, and I think your undead friend would probably like the cold. Dhamon could fly us there and . . ."

The Kagonesti shook her head, the sunlight touching the ends of her hair and making her locks look afire. "No, my instincts tell me that Sable is the one. Besides, this place is closer, the swamp. Dhamon knows this territory."

Ragh stood up, clenching and unclenching his fists. "Elf, I don't think you understand how formidable Sable is. Sable hates Dhamon. He's taken pieces of her swamp, killed her creatures, taunted her by his very existence, and she will kill all of us if we even get near enough to try to pluck a single scale from . . ."

"You don't have to take the scale *from* the dragon," Obelia interjected. He was looking down his overlong ghostly nose and talking in a condescending manner. "All you need is a scale . . . one, two preferably . . . they might have dropped off the dragon somewhere. Dragons shed, you know, like a common reptile. I suppose . . . uh, your kind even sheds skin from time to time."

Ragh glared first at Feril, then at the specter before hopping off the rock. "Fine, fine, fine. You want one of Sable's scales, I'll get you one. Try to get you one, even if it kills me. I'll crawl right into her damnable lair and . . ."

Suddenly the ghost opened its misty mouth and emitted a low whistling sound that caught Feril and Ragh off guard. It was a high-pitched, haunting noise that raised the hairs on the Kagonesti's neck and caused the sivak to shudder. They exchanged wary glances. The sound went on for some time, quieting the birds and leaving only the splashing of the water around the half-submerged willow root.

"No," Obelia said at last, closing his mouth and ending the strange whistling. "Sad to say I can't manage it."

"Can't manage what?" This came from Ragh, somewhat angrily. He was standing so close to the specter that the cold it gave off caused the sivak's breath to puff away from his face. "Just what can't you manage, dead one? Helping us?"

A shake of the gossamer head. "I tried to cast a useful spell just now, a relatively simple one that would allow me to look for Sable's lost scales. Scrying, the magic is sometimes called. Too bad, because if I can't locate a scale, I don't know how I'll be able to find my sister later on." Obelia let out a wheezing sigh. "Perhaps I can figure out how later. I certainly won't give up on helping you."

Feril touched the raccoon figurine. "Maybe I can help you, Obelia, calling on my own magic."

The lines deepened along the edges of the specter's eyes. "Elf-fish, what a splendid notion! Carry me close to that stream over there, and we'll use the water for a window. Find a quiet spot if you can. Your wingless friend may join us."

"I don't understand all this." Ragh sounded dubious.

"We'll use the water like a crystal ball, right?" Obelia said, beaming. Feril nodded.

The sivak looked no less skeptical.

Carefully holding the flask, Feril stood and walked over to the stream. The current was swift, but there was a spot near the headwaters where the stream slowed around a fallen elm long since stripped of its leaves and small branches.

"A pond would have been preferable," said Obelia, who had followed Feril, trailed by Ragh. "Quiet water is the best, but this will have to do."

Feril knelt on the bank and Ragh followed suit behind her, dropping his voice conspiratorially.

"Elf-scrolls and jars, powders, a ghost, and an overlord's scale. You continue to amaze me. How'd you bring a ghost up from the bottom of the lake anyway? I always heard that such lost spirits were held to where they died."

"Fingerbones," she explained. Feril was leaning over, studying her own reflection in a patch of relatively still water. "I have Obelia's fingerbones in the flask."

"And some water from my home," the ghost volunteered. "I thought that would be enough. Blessed am I to be free of that lake. Even being tethered to an old flask is preferable to being imprisoned in Nalis Aren." Obelia then directed Feril to stir the stream and concentrate. As she did so, the dead Qualinesti concentrated on bonding with her energy, doubling her magic with his own.

"Now tell me, sivak Ragh," Obelia said in a hushed voice, "where would these dropped scales likely be? That is where we should start our search."

Ragh stared at the patch of water, thinking he saw motes sparkle beneath the surface. "Shrentak," he said after a few moments. "It's a city in the swamp, a vile dark city. Underneath it sprawls Sable's home. That is where you might start."

The clear water darkened and swirled, and all of a sudden an immense cavern was reflected on its surface. Gems and jewels, gold and silver bars, weapons and armor glimmered faintly in the light of a few oil lanterns hanging on the walls.

"That's it! That's one of Sable's lairs—her favorite, I believe," Ragh announced in an awed voice. He was at once in awe of the wealth and afraid of the prospect of returning there. "I happen to know a way in," he said hesitantly. "More than one way, there is. Can't afford to go through the city, though. Dhamon caused quite the ruckus there a while back, and I was with him. Not safe to go through the city, but there are hidden ways. I'd stand the best chance of slipping in and out. If I fail, elf, you can always try it yourself. Dhamon can't show himself in the city no matter what. That would alert Sable."

Feril was pointing to different sections of the chamber. "Too dark to see it all clearly," she muttered to herself. "Sure can't see any loose scales."

Obelia made a tsk-tsking sound. "Remember, we don't know for sure if there are any scales, dear elf-fish. Maybe Sable isn't like other dragons. Maybe Sable doesn't shed. We have to consider that possibility."

"Then why risk it?" Ragh growled, turning at a noise.

It was Dhamon edging forward. His nap had been brief but enough to refresh him. He'd been listening to the last of his companions' exchange. The wind shifted slightly at just that moment, and the smell of the swamp that still clung heavily to him assailed Feril and Ragh. Obelia beamed to see the dragon. Ragh grimaced to note the blood still staining Dhamon's jaws from the bear meal.

"I'll make Sable shed," Dhamon announced. He tossed his head and snarled, revealing more blood on his teeth. "I'll rip her scales from her bloody carcass."

Ragh suddenly went weak in the knees.

"Y̶ou can't kill Sable, Dhamon, but she can kill you. You can't scare her or pose even the smallest threat to her. You can make her mad . . . just like you were doing before we went searching for your elf." Ragh was pacing on the bank, stopping just short of Feril before whirling on his heels and stomping back in the other direction. "I used to be Sable's puppet, remember? I know just how powerful she is. You saw her, too. High, mighty, and huge! You told me all about it. You were human in those days, and one time you crept into the bowels of Shrentak and lost yourself. Ended up in her lair by accident and spotted her foul magnificence draped over mounds of coins. You were lucky she didn't wake up. You wouldn't be here now if she'd waken up, and now you want to go back?!"

Dhamon spoke calmly. "As you said, Ragh, I was human then, and I've seen her twice—there in her lair and at the Window to the Stars. I survived both times, and I was *human* then." He dug his claws into the earth and his muscles rippled. He snarled again and his noxious breath spilled out, withering the plants on the bank and making Feril and Ragh gasp for fresh air. Obelia, chuckling, seemed to find the smell amusing. Dhamon exhaled again, seemingly enjoying his friends' discomfort, then bent to drink deep from the stream.

The sivak stared at the elf. She glared back, refusing to back him up.

"I don't believe you ever were *only* human, my friend." Ragh let out a breath, the air hissing between his teeth. He continued, louder. "You don't need to see Sable a third time unless you have a death wish." Ragh slammed his fist against his hip for emphasis. "I, for one, don't, and she'll kill all of us."

Dhamon disdained any reply, allowing a low rumble to escape his lips.

"You can't win," Ragh said, again gasping for air. "It would be suicide."

"Yes, suicide," Obelia agreed, to Ragh's surprise. "A unique dragon, you are. Alone. Singular. Beautiful. If only Kalilnama could see you. If only all the elf spirits in Qualinesti in the lake could behold you." He appraised Dhamon for several long minutes. "Maybe not suicide," he said finally, undead eyes fixed on Dhamon's sword-sharp claws, "but not worth risking in any event."

"Not worth it," Ragh agreed.

"Not necessary in any case. My elf-fish has already gone to far too much trouble to help you, Dhamon, for you to squander her efforts on a needless battle against the overlord. There is a safer course for getting one of Sable's scales."

"Yeah? What if there aren't any scales, like you were

saying?" Ragh, shifting back and forth on the balls of his feet, nearly spat out the words.

"Let him talk, sivak," Feril said.

"Perhaps there are no errant scales in the beast's lair," the spirit continued, his insubstantial nose wrinkling at the sivak, "but I was rash to say the black dragon does not shed at all. Even if Sable does not shed, she still might lose the occasional scale for odd reasons. Let us take a look elsewhere, before we despair."

The ghost returned his attention to the stream, again supplying Feril with energy for the scrying spell. Dhamon and the sivak both edged closer. The water swirled and the motes of light Ragh thought he saw before became prominent again, floating to the surface, then rising above it and winking out like lightning bugs.

"Together we must concentrate on the scales, elf-fish, only on the scales—the lone, solitary ones. Dropped. Shed. Scales as black as the dragon's heart. Perfect ones. Scales that have not been cracked by weapons or age or magic, that have not been fashioned onto armor and shields. Untouched, perfect scales."

Feril tingled all over as her fingertips touched the stream. The sensation reminded her of the nights she used to run along the sea cliffs of Southern Ergoth. A storm would be raging, rain hammering down. Lightning would dance through the sky and charge the air with energy. Such dangerous energy always made her feel exited.

"Sable's scales," the Kagonesti murmured. "In Habbakuk's name, please show us one of Sable's scales. A perfect scale. A lost or shed scale."

The water swirled faster, the lights sparkled dizzily. Then they suddenly dimmed and tumbled, sinking into the water; after a few minutes the water stilled. Instead of pebbles at the stream bottom, they saw the image of a mountain range.

"The Kharolis Mountains," Ragh noted. He was standing close behind Feril. "Hey, I think I know that particular formation. We're not terribly far from it."

Two spires twisted together toward the sky. The twin spires were said to symbolize two dwarves from feuding clans who fell in love and turned their backs on their families, climbing to the highest point in the range to escape the conflict. The clans came for them, and in trying to get each to return home, the feud intensified. Swords were drawn, and several dwarves from both families were slain. The lovers stood at the high point of the mountains, fearing for their lives and praying to Reorx the Forge to be spared from the pointless bloodshed. Legend said Reorx reached down and touched the dwarf lovers, spinning them into the rock formation that has stood there all these centuries, forever safe from wars and forever part of the mountains they considered home—forever together.

"Aye," Dhamon agreed. "I also know that part of the mountains well. There's a pass near the spire, cleared a long time ago to make travel easy for merchants."

Feril continued concentrating on the vision, a part of which was looming larger now. For an instant an odd image intruded. The faces of people appeared—a dwarf with steel-gray hair and a nose spread wide across his stern-looking face. Behind him were grouped a handful of dwarves and men, all looking careworn and haggard and determined. Then the faces winked out and once again there were only the twin spires. She focused on a crevice that drew her attention.

"Closer to that opening," Dhamon urged. "I think I see something interesting."

The scene shifted slightly, and the crevice came into better view. Wedged into the narrow gap was what at first looked like a shield. Dhamon thought it might have been dropped by one of the men they'd caught a glimpse of, but on closer inspection, the object proved to be a glossy black scale the size of a shield.

"A scale from Sable," Obelia proudly pointed out. "Looks like one that has been shed, not broken or ripped off. So the black Overlord sheds after all! That means there must be other scales lying about that people have not absconded with or spoiled. Let's look some more, shall we?"

With Obelia guiding her, Feril scryed beyond the Kharolis Mountains, after some effort finding another scale next to a totem of bones in the middle of the swamp and another at the edge of a pool of quicksand in a small nearby glade ringed by shaggybarks. Dhamon and Ragh said they were passingly familiar with each of those locations, too. There were several more scales at the edge of a marshy tributary, but they were all broken or cracked. Another two were near a stand of strange stones that Ragh said he might have seen before and thought was located north of the Plains of Dust. One scale was set atop a carved wooden totem and painted with strange symbols that none of them could read. The last scale the spell revealed was in another mountain range that Dhamon said he had traveled. It was in ogre territory to the far east, down the slopes from the city of Bloten.

"Don't forget scales from other overlords," Ragh prompted excitedly. "At least take a look. Let's see if the other overlords have also shed a few."

"The White," Feril said without hesitation. "Frost, who took my home."

A wintry scene filled the calm waters now, and it was a few moments before they could pick out shapes amidst all the whiteness. Frost was there, looking sculpted from ice, and in the lair behind him were more than a dozen frozen carcasses of walrus-men and small whales—his larder. There were a handful of scales scattered on the ground outside Frost's lair. Another white scale rested on an icy peak. A few were bolted to a wall in the Solamnic Keep on the western coast of the island. Another sat at the edge of the large glacial lake, and there were more than a few scattered on the ground in the dragon's lair.

"That cold place is a long way from here," Obelia observed.

Dhamon grunted, and even Ragh had to agree.

The picture shifted again, stirred by the magic running through Feril's fingers. Now they saw a barren land with geysers of steam rising from vents in the ground. In the center of a plateau was a pool of lava. Something drew Feril toward the pool, from whose bottom shone an intense red light.

"Yes, I can see it," Dhamon said eagerly. "There's a scale, large as a kite shield and several smaller ones near it, no doubt shed by Malys."

"Beyond us to retrieve something out of lava," Ragh commented.

"Likely true," Obelia said.

Feril's fingers stirred the water one last time, and a desert stretched for as far as they could see. The color of the sand was the palest brown and contrasted sharply with the brilliant blue sky. Then suddenly Feril focused on a small dune, burrowing deep into it. Far under the sand—though just how far they couldn't say—were buried three blue scales. She sensed others were buried even deeper.

"From the Storm Over Krynn," Ragh pointed out, with a measure of respect. "Those also would appear beyond our ability to obtain."

"Perhaps." Obelia looked thoughtful. "Perhaps not, given the nature-magic my elf-fish commands. In any event, it would take quite a bit of time and luck to find the blue scales, or the red one. The white is far from here. It appears, as I told my elf-fish before, the black overlord is the closest and presents our best opportunity."

"Dhamon can fly," Ragh reminded Obelia. "Nothing is too far when you're on the back of a dragon. I'd rather go far north than tempt Sable's clutches."

Dhamon shook his head. "Sable is closest, Ragh." Narrowed eyes kept the draconian from arguing. "I wasn't planning on flying anyway. Sable's minions would spot me in the air. I can travel more inconspicuously as Feril's shadow."

At her name, Feril sighed and stepped away from the water, swooning slightly from all the exertion. The others stopped arguing and looked at her. "I'll be all right," she said. Hours had gone by. They realized suddenly it was nearly dark. "I think we should try the mountains first, just to be on the safe side."

Ragh puffed himself up and kicked at the water with his foot. "Fine, fine. Whatever you say. I'll get a campfire started."

"I'll see what I can rustle up to eat," Dhamon said mildly, following him.

Feril gestured to Obelia, who retreated into the flask. She carefully stoppered it and spread some clay around the opening to help ensure that no water would leak out. Then she put it back in the satchel and waited for the others to return.

The mountain pass was not difficult to find. Trails led directly to it from the Qualinesti forest. They saw right away that the pass wasn't a natural occurrence. Color bands in the rock had been split by a force that had knocked part of the mountain away. Most of the rockface was smooth, worn away by time and weather, but on jagged sections here and there hawks had built their nests.

"It wasn't magic," Dhamon said, pointing to how the pass had been cut and shaped. "The dwarves carved a path through here a very long time ago."

"To control access to their mountains," Ragh added.

Feril raised a questioning eyebrow.

"They cut only a few passes through the Kharolis so they could watch people going through their mountain range. Easier to keep track of trespassers."

Feril nodded in understanding.

"I watched them at work once, the hill dwarf clans," Ragh continued. "Not cutting this pass, but one that was farther north. Not quite so big as this one—you could fit a wagon and more through it . . . mind you, I didn't watch the whole time. I wasn't that curious, and dwarves aren't that exciting to watch no matter what they're doing. It took hundreds of them with their picks, and at the base of the pass at night they used urkan worms, huge beasts that dwell underground and can't stand the light. Years it took the dwarves, as these mountains are thick. Gave them something to do, I suppose, and it created another route for them to control."

"Kept travelers away from dwarf villages and mines," Feril noted, "except such passes can't keep away the worst brigands and creatures who fly."

"Like we should be flying," Ragh muttered.

"We agreed that it's safer this way," Dhamon rumbled.

"Besides, I'd rather keep my feet on the ground," said Feril.

Dhamon took the lead into the pass. Tucking his wings into his sides, he squeezed through some parts of the pass with inches to spare, followed by Feril and Ragh, the latter making considerably more noise as gravel crunched beneath his scaly feet. Dhamon purposely stepped on sharp rocks as he went, relishing the faint bite of the stone beneath the pads of his claws. His armorlike scales inured him to a great many such things. He could feel pain sometimes, and he could feel a raging storm, the wind whipping around his snout and against his eyes, but the mere touch of a mortal? He couldn't, for example, feel Feril's fingers when she brushed at his scales. He wished he could remember what her touch felt like.

If he were human, all the softer sensations would return.

As he covered ground he could hear the constant chatter and bickering of Feril and Ragh close behind.

"Do you really think the ghost's spell will work?"

"We stand a pretty good chance for success," Feril answered the sivak. "I believe Obelia is . . . was . . . a sorcerer of some merit and . . ."

"Dhamon told me there were quite a few ghosts at the bottom of the lake and that a number of them were not so pleasant and helpful as this Obelia."

"They were mostly Qualinesti elves who stayed behind when the dragon attacked the city, as well as some Knights of Neraka who had fought for Beryl." Feril readjusted the pack on her back. "Oh yes, and there were specters of goblins and horses, all sorts of creatures that were destroyed by the lake when the dragon died."

"How did you manage to coax one of the ghosts to come with you?"

"Obelia wanted to help. He asked to come along."

"Doesn't answer my question." Ragh shuddered. "The dead usually stay where they died, anyone knows that." He was thinking of the chaos wights on the island of Nostar—those undead that had nearly killed him, Dhamon, and Fiona a long time ago. "The dead don't often prefer to mingle with the living."

"Obelia is different. Anyway, I'd mingle with however many ghosts it took to make Dhamon right again. I'd mingle with demons from the Abyss."

"I agree," Ragh conceded, "but that ghost . . ."

"Obelia. The spirit's name is Obelia, and you'll see him again, soon. When I smell water, I'll scry on that scale again, just to make sure we're headed in the right direction, and Obelia will help us determine just how far we are from it."

The mention of water made Dhamon increase his pace. He was thirsty. His stomach was rumbling, causing the ground to vibrate. The bears had satisfied him for a while, but he was growing hungry. His nostrils quivering, he prowled the air for any scent of mountain goats. No such luck. Soon enough, though, they reached a mountain stream that cut parallel to the pass, and Dhamon and the others drank their fill. Feril pulled the flask out of her satchel and released Obelia.

"I'm going to stretch my wings and scout ahead," Dhamon said. He was still hoping for goats and had just picked up a strong odor indicating that there might be a small herd reasonably close by. Feril, Ragh, and the spirit sorcerer could handle the scrying without him. "I won't be gone long." Then he took to the sky and headed upwind of the scent, throwing all of his efforts into suppressing his fear aura so the goats would not smell him coming and scatter.

He closed his eyes for a moment, feeling the wind tease the underside of his wings and the sun warm his face. He understood why Ragh envied flying, and for more than a few minutes he simply relished the glory of flight. It wasn't until his stomach rumbled a little louder than he was reminded of those delicious goats.

He spotted them now. There were nearly two dozen in the herd, one of them an impressive ram with large curling horns. They were perched atop a southern ridge, the ram holding its magnificent head high. Dhamon's mouth watered in anticipation as he dived toward the animals, making sure the wind was blowing in his direction. The goats would be caught unawares.

Obelia, out of the flask, seemed pleased. His gaze lingered on the cloudless sky and the walls of the mountain pass for several minutes before he channeled his magical energy into the Kagonesti, who was kneeling next to the stream.

"Is there a bit of a breeze?" the spirit asked as, gradually, the image of a dragon's scale hove into view. "I can see small ripples on the water."

"A slight breeze," Feril answered. The reflection of the draconian appeared superimposed on the scale's image, as Ragh was peering over her shoulder, trying to get a good look at the scrying magic. "Just a slight stirring is all, Obelia."

"What does it feel like, this slight breeze that ruffles

your hair?" the ghost asked. "It's been so long since I have felt anything like that. I don't remember."

"The breeze gently caresses the back of my neck, and it brings the fragrance of mountain laurel that must be growing nearby, probably on one of the high ledges," Feril replied. "It's a faint, sweet fragrance, and when I breathe deeply, I can taste the sweetness of the flowers on my tongue. The air is cooler here than in the woods, as the walls of the pass shade us from the brunt of the sun. The stream is cool, too, and feels good against my fingers." She went on at some length about other smells and sensations, bringing smiles and sighs of contentment from Obelia, then grumbling from Ragh when she mentioned his acrid scent.

While Feril talked, she also focused on the scale they were scrying.

"I think it's lodged in that crevice," Ragh observed, "lodged deep and tight. It's as though the mountain shifted at some point and is trapping it. I don't see a gap between it and the rock. Probably that's why it's still there and why some passing hill dwarf hasn't grabbed it up and fashioned it into souvenir armor or a shield."

"If it's wedged tight, that is good," Obelia said. "Feril possesses nature magic, and she can shift the stone or turn it to melting liquid if she needs to."

"Dhamon could smash the rock," Ragh offered.

"The stone has a peculiar scent," Feril continued, "clean and dusty at the same time. It smells old, though I doubt there are many who could guess the age, and the dirt on the trail leading up to it . . . I can smell it, too. It's not as old."

"Big deal," Ragh whispered. "So it's old."

He glanced at the Kagonesti, seeing the faint lines around the edges of her eyes and around her lips. She was looking pretty old herself. The sivak wondered if Dhamon had noticed.

As Feril's fingers stirred the image of the scale in the stream, her mind guided the magic. She watched as the view pulled back and the scale grew smaller. Now, at the top, she saw the spiral rock formation of the dwarf lovers entwined forever. At the same time, she spotted living dwarves moving along the pass beyond the ancient formation. They rounded a bend and disappeared from her view.

"Look, there is the formation we seek," Ragh said. He peered toward the east. "I can barely make out the top of it. That means we're not far away—two hours, I'd guess, maybe three. Mere heartbeats if Dhamon flew us there. Those dwarves are probably mining nearby, coming up for some sun and for something to eat."

"The coolness of the water feels good against my arms, Obelia," Feril said, ignoring Ragh. She cupped some water in her hands and drank greedily. "It tastes quite good, sweet, and it refreshes me. I can feel it sliding down my throat."

"Tell me more," the ghost urged. "Tell me everything you feel, my elf-fish."

"Odd, the stone beneath my knees is trembling slightly," Feril continued. "It is not an unpleasant sensation, but still . . ."

Suddenly, Ragh felt the ground shaking, too. The draconian leaped aside as bits of rock broke loose from the walls and rained down, some pieces landing on the trail and others splashing in the stream.

Feril snatched up the flask. Obelia had already jumped safely inside, just as larger chunks started falling. The Kagonesti turned to run, only to fall to her knees again when a more powerful tremor struck. Feril thrust the flask into her pack.

"Should've talked Dhamon into flying," Ragh grumbled as he staggered down the pass, holding his arms over his head to fend off any stray shards. "Earthquakes aren't dangerous if you're up in the air. Elf, stay with me!"

Feril, back on her feet and with the satchel on her back, was rushing past, struggling to keep her balance.

The quake grew in intensity, and large rocks broke free ahead of them, falling and cluttering the trail ahead. The draconian slipped when a chunk careened down and struck him squarely on the back. More pieces followed.

"Elf!" he yelled, struggling to get up from under the onslaught. "Give me some help!"

Feril whirled in time to see more falling rocks pile on Ragh. Before she could take a step to help him, a whole section of the pass broke free, tumbled down, and buried the sivak.

CHAPTER
16

Sable relished the darkness and the cramped confines of the tunnel. The odor of the earth and stone was rich and strong here, laced with the scent of burrowing creatures that had died here long ago. The tunnel lacked the beloved pungency of both thriving and decaying plants, but she would smell that again soon enough. Her sight stifled by the utter blackness, the overlord was forced to rely on her other senses, and these she was stretching magically outward.

It had been a long time since she left her wonderful swamp, years she guessed, though time was an abstract concept to her. Dragons lived for centuries, and the passing of a few years—especially to an overlord—meant nothing. She remembered that the last occasion she had left the swamp had been at Overlord Malys's insistence. At the time, the great red considered herself the most powerful of the massive dragons and ordered around all the others as if they were her servants. Sable raged against Malys's commands, but like the other overlords and all the lesser dragons the Red deigned to speak with, the Black followed most of Malys's orders. The few who spurned her died to her furnace-breath.

Sable recalled that the last significant journey away from her glorious swamp had been to the Window to the Stars portal, where Malys thought she would use all her magical power to ascend to godhood. She was thwarted, in the presence of the other overlords, and Sable inwardly cheered the unexpected turn of events. When Malys was finally slain a few years later, she rejoiced.

As Sable continued to tunnel, she inhaled deeply and thought of the time when she first came to Ansalon and claimed her territory. It was years and years ago in human terms—she was reminded of that just by looking at some of her pitiful subjects in the city of Shrentak. Children they were when she first arrived, old, frail, and beaten down by life now. Human time was a mere heartbeat to her.

Sable had followed Malys here, finding the land ripe for conquest, as the dragons native to Ansalon were not so large or powerful, nor for the most part as devious and brutal. Malys thought the land she took was prime, the best in all of Ansalon. Frost took the island of Southern Ergoth, Beryl the land of the Qualinesti. The only native overlord, the Storm Over Krynn, took the desert to the far north.

Sable had been relegated to a stretch of plains between the ogre country and the Kharolis Mountains.

It was actually the very best land for her purposes, Sable knew instinctively. Relatively flat, it was easier to magically sculpt. It wasn't as populated, so there were fewer humans to challenge her and her minions. What humans there were tended to be clustered in the sparse cities and villages, and they were easy to dominate with her dragonfear and spells. She used them to tend sections of her land and to patrol it; they were useful as puppets, little more than disposable custodians. Few of the humans had the wits to realize they were fortunate to be serving her and to be living in such a sublime paradise.

In the early days she'd spent only a little time patrolling her territory and feasting on the creatures she caught unawares. She spent most of her time shaping the land to fit her foul mood and causing creatures to grow to unnatural size and to mutate bizarrely. She channeled the magic inside of her into the earth and created the greatest of swamps. The ground became marshy beneath her claws. The grass became thicker, the trees—even the smallest ones—stretching high to become giants with dense, woven canopies. Other trees sprouted from nothingness, cypress and black walnuts that wouldn't have otherwise flourished on this soil. The dragon fancied herself an artist, painting trees and ferns, vines, bushes, everything green and dark and tightly coiled together across her land.

She fed some of her magic into a large river, making it wider and swifter and giving it many branches and tributaries. She enhanced three lakes and made sure the waters were populated with bowfin and alligators, the latter of which she mutated into the size of hatchling dragons.

Sable sent her moist breath across the ground, and where it settled swaths of quicksand sprang up. Lizardmen and bakali flocked to the marsh, as did talons of Knights of Neraka, who swore their loyalty to her in exchange for some measure of power and safety. At the same time, she carved out tunnels and fashioned caverns beneath the swamp, though not so far underground that the odors of the marsh couldn't seep down and give her pleasure. She chose some of the tunnels as lairs and began to fill them with treasure collected from the coastal towns and from adventurous souls who foolishly trespassed on her property.

Pleased but discontented with her domain, she began spreading the swamp outward. To the east, the swamp started eating away at ogre lands and eroding the mountains. This was excellent sport for her, watching ogre forces slaughtered by small black dragons and forces of spawn and draconians. She scryed on Blöten and listened to the ogre king and his thickheaded advisors worry over their shrinking land. She sent her spies into the ogre strongholds, while continuing to grow the swamp to the west and the south—and until it could extend no farther north, as it already reached the shores of the New Sea and she had no means to turn the water into land.

The great black never cared much for cities, so until this point in her life she had made a habit of staying away from them. Shrentak intrigued her, especially because the walled city nestled deep in her realm had fallen into such beautiful decay since her arrival, so she defied her nature and settled there, coaxing moisture into every stone and structure, furthering the city's deterioration, but careful not to cause it all to collapse. She enthralled the citizens and wore down their spirits, meagerly rewarding those who became turncoats and spies, betraying their fellows and embracing any ignominious task she assigned.

There were dungeons beneath the foul city, and these she ordered filled with anyone who opposed her. She particularly enjoyed capturing Solamnic Knights and Legion of Steel Knights, as their shining armor and chivalrous natures gave her endless amusement.

She let the shiny pieces rust in her dungeons in front of them and ordered the knights fed from time to time on their own tarnished shields so they would not die too quickly. Their anguish washed like a palpable wave down the corridors and reliably fed her appetite for suffering.

Beneath the dungeons she dug another labyrinth of twisting tunnels, some of them completely filled with brackish water—since she could breathe the foul water as easily as she could breathe air. At the end of the maze was her favorite lair, where the air was heavy and damp, and save for a smooth stretch of rock she enjoyed sleeping on, filled with gold, gems, and choice magical trinkets.

She ought to be there now, coiled in her favorite place, listening to the screams of prisoners being tortured in her dungeon and watching the light from a delicate silver candelabrum make her collection of perfect rubies glimmer. She would be there now, hearing news of trappers who came to Shrentak with fantastic beasts in tow for her nefarious menagerie and watching more paintings, jewelry, and coins being added to her trove, but a courier had arrived to interrupt her routine. It was his news that lured her from the blessed swamp.

"Mistress Sable, ruler of all of grand Shrentak and this glorious swamp . . ."

She remembered the courier's bowing and sniveling.

"Knight Commander Galor Bedell has located the Dhamon-dragon."

She also remembered growling, then watching with disgust as the courier soiled himself in his fear. Sable had sent Commander Bedell on a minor errand intended to insult and punish him for his failure to slay the Dhamon-dragon. Though she was pleased to learn of her foe's whereabouts, she was irritated that Bedell had neglected his assigned task.

"Continue," she hissed, acid spilling over her lip and sizzling against the stone.

"Mistress Sable, ruler of grand Shrentak and this glorious swamp, the Dhamon-dragon heads east toward the Kharolis Mountains. Bedell has been tracking the insolent dragon, and through a chain of messengers he relays this news to your imperious self. He tried to kill the Dhamon-dragon, had powerful poison and . . ."

Sable breathed then, acid spraying in a stream that struck the courier so forcefully that it essentially disintegrated him. She glared at his smoking remains and rumbled for her attendants to come clean up the mess. Some of the acid had also struck a mound of ancient gold coins, and though it did not dissolve the pieces entirely, it ruined some edges and faces, adding to the dragon's ire.

Still, if the courier's news was accurate, the Dhamon-dragon was not terribly, terribly far away, and so might be dealt with now. Sable had considerable forces in the city above and could dispatch them, but she didn't know precisely where her foe was, and it would take a while for her minions to travel on their tiny legs. They would be worn down from the journey, fatigued before they could confront and fight the Dhamon-dragon. The Kharolis Mountains were not very far at all . . . for an overlord who boasted massive wings and a network of tunnels facilitating her movements beneath the swamp. She left the bowels of Shrentak that very night, flying low over the uppermost canopy of her gloomy land and west toward the Kharolis Mountains. Pausing at the foothills, she vowed to succeed where all her lackeys had failed. She would slay the accursed Dhamon-dragon. No creature would again dare to claim even an inch of her precious swamp.

Sable began burrowing, her enormous claws digging into the ground and quickly starting a tunnel that allowed her to slip beneath the first mountain range. If Dhamon had dwelled quietly in her swamp, she likely would have let him be. He wouldn't have vexed her so, but the wretched dragon, who looked like no dragon she had ever seen, insisted on building his own lair and taking some of the treasure due to her and claiming more and more and more land. He had slain the forces she sent to the lowlands . . . forces that were at first just instructed to report about the goings-on in the area. Then he killed those she sent to war against him.

The Dhamon-dragon had cost her land and minions, and now he was traveling through the Kharolis mountains, heading east, no doubt returning to her blessed swamp from Qualinesti lands, bent on vexing her again.

Her thoughts returned to the present. Burrowing into the stone now, angling upward with her tunnel, she used her magic to feel the footfalls on the mountain pass above her. The footsteps were soft and nearly noiseless, and she knew the hated Dhamon-dragon could be as silent as a shadow if he tried. These must be his companions she sensed, the wingless draconian who once served her and whom she could barely remember, and the elf . . . the Dhamon-dragon must be with them.

She roared her excitement, the fury and delight in her voice sending a tremor through the stone. The trembling of the stone gave the overlord an idea. The courier had reported that the Dhamon-dragon was walking, that perhaps his wings had been damaged by Commander

Bedell's goblins so he could not fly. Sable was familiar with the mountains and the pass, with its sheer, high walls that could so easily collapse and trap any creature traveling along the old dwarven trail.

Sable roared louder and louder, flailing with her claws. In response, the quake intensified, the ground shook, and great blocks of stone began to crack. She pictured the pass breaking apart and raining down on the Dhamon-dragon and his sivak friend and the elf that was with them, according to the courier. Odd that an elf would be traveling with the Dhamon-dragon and a draconian.

The ground trembled even more violently, and Sable felt the rocks split and tumble down. She could no longer sense the footfalls of the elf and sivak. The Dhamon-dragon was likely pinned under stone, perhaps dead—she hoped not. Sable wanted to deal the final blow herself. She clawed faster toward the surface.

The goats were nearly enough to sate him, but Dhamon wanted more. He smelled more of the animals over the next rise. He could hear them, their hooves making clicking sounds across the rocks, one of them snorting, probably another ram leading another herd, oblivious to Dhamon's presence . . .

He guessed there to be at least a dozen. Goats were not as delicious as bear, but they were preferable to most of the fare he'd dined on in the swamp, and their meat was reasonably tender. He pivoted toward them, his stomach growling.

Then abruptly he froze, hovering over a peak. The Kharolis Mountains were rumbling below him. A quake was building. At first he thought little of it, hovering only out of curiosity, and when it stopped, he again headed toward the goats, which he could tell were nervously dashing over the rocks now.

The mountain rumbled more violently, enough to send a chunk of rock off the peak directly beneath him. The goats were close, he knew, and would be distracted by the quake. His saliva flowed. He crested the rise and saw the herd, the ram leading them down a trail, but the mountain was still rumbling and rocks were shifting and sliding, giving even the sure-footed goats trouble.

If the goats were having trouble, Dhamon suddenly realized, his companions might be faring worse.

Feril! He beat his wings and turned, climbed over a peak and shot toward the pass where he'd left her and Ragh. Dhamon knew he hadn't been gone very long and that his companions couldn't have made much progress along the trail. The miles melted beneath his wings as the mountain continued to quake.

Streaking over the pass, he spotted the Kagonesti just in time to watch in horror as the southern wall cracked and showered down on the trail in front of her. Feril was agile as a dancer and nimbly avoided the largest of the stones, but some rocks were pelting her nonetheless. He didn't see Ragh at first, but as he dived toward Feril, he spotted a silvery claw reaching up from a mound of rubble.

"Ragh!" Dhamon plummeted toward the sivak, tucking his wings in close, then turning to land lightly on his clawed feet. He grabbed at the largest rocks with his jaws, tossing them right and left while digging at the rocks and trying to free the sivak. Feril sidestepped a shower of rocks as she rushed toward him.

In moments, Dhamon had reached Ragh and plucked him away, holding the unconscious sivak gingerly in his teeth and lowering his head to the still-rumbling earth. Feril sprinted the remaining few yards and leaped onto him, hands closing around one of Dhamon's horns and pulling herself up onto his neck. She sat between shadowy spines and gripped him tightly, heels pressing into him.

Dhamon lumbered forward with rocks falling all around him. He leaped over a pile of rubble and dodged falling chunks. At last the collapsing pass opened wider and Dhamon spread his wings and cleared the top of the crumbling rock walls. Within a heartbeat he was above the Kharolis Mountains and arcing high into the sky. The wind whipped him, a gust nearly unseating the Kagonesti.

Striking out toward the west, he angled down toward the foothills. If he had looked behind him, he would have seen giant black claws thrust up from the earth and bat aside falling rocks. He would have seen an immense snout, wide eyes taking in the carnage but finding no trace of the sivak, the elf, and the Dhamon-dragon.

Sable howled louder than she'd ever howled before. The mountains echoed her fury, and cracks grew wider in the granite all around her. Huge rock slabs fell, stone dust belched up everywhere, and the pass vanished as though it had never existed. Sable climbed to the top of the rubble. The black overlord looked to the sky, but Dhamon had already flown down and was out of her line of sight.

CHAPTER 17

"Down there, Dhamon." Feril held on for dear life and shouted to be heard above a gathering breeze. "Low in the foothills, to the north. See the people? Let's go down there."

Dhamon continued flying—past the foothills and over a thinning forest, happy to be high in the sky on this hot summer day. He didn't slow until she nudged him harder and shouted louder.

"Turn back! Down there! I want to talk to those people down there, Dhamon. We shouldn't leave the mountains. We were so close to that scale. Dhamon! We can't give up!"

He let out a deep breath. He circled, studying the terrain and focusing on the swathe of the foothills that had intrigued Feril. There were shapes moving down there in a single file. At first, licking his lips, he mistook them for goats, but no, they were manlike, and so not very interesting to him. Gnomes or dwarves, perhaps . . .

To the west, he spied stone dust thick as fog, near

where the wide mountain pass had been. The twisting spire from dwarven lore was destroyed. Dhamon stared sadly at the broken remains of the lovers' legend, gone forever from maps.

"Closer to the foothills, Dhamon. Those people. Fly closer!"

Dhamon found a safe landing place on a small plateau a few miles away. Feril was quick to slide off. Ragh, still in a daze, crawled out of Dhamon's mouth. The draconian had regained consciousness, but now he gingerly tested his legs, which had been battered by the falling rocks.

"We were close when the quake hit." Feril spoke quickly, excitedly. "Look, here and here." She pointed high in the mountains. Stone dust billowed everywhere. "Over there, east of the broken spire, things look fairly intact. It's possible the scale isn't completely buried, or at least not buried too deep. There are people over there to the north. I want to speak to them, Dhamon, about dragons in the area, any Knights of Neraka they might have spotted, and . . ."

"Slow down, elf." Ragh sat down wearily. "I want to make sure the mountain's stopped dancing. Been through plenty of quakes in my life. Once I was underground, these very mountains. Knew a draconian who died in one of those quakes. I couldn't get to him in time. I don't want to end up like he did."

"The quake's over," Feril said.

"Don't be so sure," Ragh continued. He rubbed his sore thighs. "Sometimes the ground only pauses, like it's catching its breath before it starts up again."

Feril ran her fingers through her hair and looked back and forth between the sivak and Dhamon. She glanced up, seeing a flock of black birds heading west over the Kharolis peaks and past the ruined spire. The sky was becoming bluer, the stone dust and dirt that had been kicked up finally starting to settle.

"We shouldn't give up on that scale," she said. "We're too close not to look and be sure."

"I agree," Dhamon rumbled softly, not wanting to aggravate the quaking. His eyes were wide, his expression hopeful. "Though it's possible the quake buried it even deeper."

"If it did, we can still dig for it," Feril said. "I saw water down there by those people, a large pond, runoff from the mountain. I can use the water for scrying . . ."

"Hey, look closer—those are not people," Ragh said, pointing across the plateau. "If you crane your neck, you can see them." He gestured to the northeast. "They're dwarves."

Feril brightened. "Dwarves! Wonderful! Experienced travelers in these mountains might be able to help. Wait here for a little while, Dhamon. You don't want to frighten them unnecessarily, and . . ."

He shook his head, closed his eyes, and began folding in upon himself.

"I'm coming—as a shadow."

"That's a good idea, elf. What with all this earth-shaking, we don't need to get separated."

"I don't need you coming along, too, sivak. A draconian's going to scare those dwarves as much as any dragon."

Ragh spat. "I'll keep my distance, Feril. Don't want to set any of their stubby fingers to trembling, but at the first sign of the mountain shaking again, Dhamon had better become a dragon and fly us out of here. Scale or no scale."

Dhamon was already transforming into a pool of

black that flowed toward Feril's shadow and merged with it. The Kagonesti looked at the shadow, admiring Dhamon's handiwork and thinking no one would ever guess that it was him.

"Besides, dwarves and elves don't get along so well," Ragh continued, as he started picking his way down a slope and onto a narrow ledge. "Historically, they just don't get along, suspicious of each other, I understand. They might not be too willing to talk with you. Funny, but you might actually need me."

Agile as a cat, Feril slipped past him, moving effortlessly along a narrowing strip of flat rock, then climbing down what amounted to a natural set of steps. As they progressed, Dhamon's shadow flitted back and forth between her and the sivak.

"I had a dwarf friend some years back," Feril said proudly, "a very good friend."

The sivak looked surprised that the Kagonesti had volunteered personal information.

"His name was Jasper Fireforge, and he was the nephew of the legendary Flint Fireforge. Jasper was one of Goldmoon's most trusted champions. I treasured his friendship and count myself fortunate to have known him. He had a good heart."

"Had?"

Feril paused, picking her way along the rock path carefully. She found a handhold on a small outcropping of sandstone to balance her descent. "Jasper died at the Window to the Stars portal. I assume Dhamon told you something about the events at the Window. Before that time . . . when Malys controlled Dhamon with the scale . . . Dhamon nearly killed Jasper. Of course, Dhamon wasn't *trying* to kill him. He was trying to kill Goldmoon. Oh, it's confusing. That was a long time ago."

Softer and a few feet down, she added, "A very, very long time ago."

"So you like dwarves fine," Ragh said, after he'd climbed down to another ledge.

"Yes, I get along with dwarves." She was following a worn path that had been rutted by heavy rains. "Better than I get along with sivak draconians."

They crested a hill festooned with sizeable chunks of granite and bands of striped slate and obsidian. The odd layering of rock suggested there was volcanic activity here at one time . . . or a lot of earthquakes that shifted things around.

"Tracks," Feril noted, pointing to a patch of dirt cradled in a stony depression. The recent footprints were as wide as they were long. Four or five dwarves, the Kagonesti guessed, only minutes ahead of them.

Feril hurried her pace but stopped momentarily when the dwarves came into view. The dwarves were at the southern edge of a large pool up ahead—she could make out four of them clearly when she crested the next rise.

They were making camp at the narrow end of an egg-shaped basin that brushed up against a steep hill. The pool must have been formed by run-off from the mountains. This side of the Kharolis apparently saw much more rain.

She waved to them until she got their attention, then she rushed forward to greet them. Ragh kept a few yards behind her, his arms out to his sides and hands open, hoping they would take his neutral posture as a gesture of peace. Dhamon was close by Feril, his shadow form overlapping her own shadow.

"Merry afternoon to you, children of Reorx," Feril said in the language of the hill dwarves. She spoke the tongue adequately, having learned it from long afternoons spent in Jasper's company. "May I join your camp for fellowship?"

The four were typical hill dwarves—ruddy skin and bulbous noses, bristly hair, long beards on the three men—but they bore no familial similarities. They were a disparate bunch, probably none of them were related. They might have hailed from different clans.

The one closest to her, who had been rummaging around in a big canvas pack as she approached, was nearly as broad-shouldered as an ogre, though he had none of an ogre's great girth. His hands were large and thickly callused, his arms muscular, his legs were incongruously short and slender. Of middle years, he had wide gray eyes that looked kind and were intently scrutinizing her.

Another was a stocky dwarf with pale brown eyes rimmed in a darker shade. His skin was smooth, showing he was likely just past young adulthood. His fingers were thin and constantly working, twirling around in the ends of a reddish beard that came past his breastbone and flared out. He was standing, shifting his weight back and forth between the balls of his booted feet and looking between his companions and Feril. Likely a Neidar dwarf, she guessed.

The one walking briskly toward her reminded the Kagonesti of a tree stump, his skin dark and as heavily lined as walnut bark. He waddled with a rolling gait as he thrust out a hand in formal greeting. She took his hand, feeling the roughness of his skin with dirt so embedded in the grooves of his palm that it likely never would come out. He had a pick sticking out of a pack on his back, but Feril didn't need to see that to know these dwarves were miners. Their dirty hands and muscular arms told her as much—that and the way they squinted in the sunlight. They were accustomed to working underground most of the time.

The eldest was the only female, and she kept farthest away from the newcomers, taking off her pack and brushing dust off her trousers. Her face was broad and careworn, her hair steel-gray and braided with strips of leather. She was wearing a sleeveless chain mail shirt that was a little too big for her, and a short sword hung in a scabbard from her hip. If the band had a leader, it was the female dwarf, Feril decided. The woman's arms were bare and covered in tattoos. More were on her neck and on the back of her hands. Feril couldn't make them all out at this distance, but she noted emblems of war hammers and battle axes.

"Feldspar Ironbeard," the tree-stump dwarf introduced himself. After vigorous shaking, he finally released Feril's hand. "Odd seeing a wild elf here. Thought forests were more to your liking."

"Ferilleeagh Dawnsprinter. You can call me Feril." She offered a wide smile, reassuring the hill dwarves by her adeptness at their tongue. She pointed to the small ridge behind her. "My companion, you may note, is a sivak draconian. His name is Ragh, and he means no harm."

Feldspar took a step back, setting his fists on his hips. "Odd enough to find an elf here. Odder still that she has a sivak for a companion, and one, I can't help but notice, without wings." His bulbous nose quivered and set his mustache to wiggling.

"She might be a sivak, too." The female dwarf spoke suspiciously. "Them sivaks can paint themselves to look like whatever they just killed."

"No," Feldspar returned mildly. "She smells like an

elf. The draconian . . ." His nose quivered a little more. "That one smells like sulfur. It's a draconian all right. Odd set of travelers for these hills, but I've seen plenty of odd things in my . . ."

The ground began to rumble again as Feril and Ragh quickly braced themselves for the worst. The thin-legged dwarf glanced nervously up at the sheer hillside. Only dirt and bits of stones rained down and splattered in the pool.

". . . long years under the mountains," Feldspar finished, looking around warily in case another, stronger quake was coming along.

Feril nodded to each of the dwarves. "In fact, I do prefer the forest, but often my journeys take me elsewhere. Ragh and I were traveling along a pass through these mountains when that big earthquake struck."

Feldspar chuckled. "Yeah, we don't get many trembles in these mountains nowadays, but it happens. We were in our tunnel, working, when we felt the first tickle of trouble, and of course we headed out immediately." He pointed to a spot above them in the sheer hillside. Feril took a closer look.

About thirty feet above the ground there was a slash in the slope, likely an exit from the dwarves' tunnel. The hillside wasn't exactly a hill, she realized. There was plenty of dirt, but the dirt was clinging to a stone wall. A keep had been carved into this hill a long time ago; the brickwork was smooth from age. It might have been a castle once; she'd heard that dwarves once built immense halls under the hills. She wondered how much of it was intact inside the hill.

"Come quench your thirst with us, Dawnspringer."

"Dawnsprinter," Feril corrected gently.

He pointed toward the narrow end of the basin,

where the other three dwarves were now sitting down and relaxing, leaning back against their packs. "The sivak can come along, too—if it's got a mind to behave itself."

Ragh followed, choosing to sit just outside their circle. His shadow was darker than it should have been, as though Dhamon had merged with his shadow when Feril passed by. None of the dwarves noticed. They were busy passing around a jug and talking loudly. Feril, in their midst, was drinking with them, asking them questions about their mine. She took off her satchel and tucked it protectively beneath her knee as she drank and talked, gazing at the pool. Ragh knew she was thinking of using that water to scry on the scale with Obelia.

"More ale, Dawnspringer?"

She accepted the jug and took her third deep pull. It was a heady and sweet brew, but she was thirsty. She passed it to the female dwarf.

"Grannaluured," the female dwarf said, raising the jug in toast.

It wasn't a Dwarvish word Feril was familiar with, so, after a moment's hesitation, she realized it was the woman's name rather than a toast. This close to her, Feril could observe the intricate craftsmanship of her tattoos. There were images of the constellations and of a hammer suspended above a forge—a tribute to the god Reorx. Just above the dwarf's right elbow was the grinning visage of a one-eyed gargoyle with an outstretched claw. Grannaluured caught Feril staring.

"Eh, admiring my art," the dwarf observed proudly. "That one there . . ." She took a long drink, handed the jug back to Feril, and pointed to the gargoyle. "That one was quite difficult to do, me being right-handed and all. Tough to get all the details right around its eyes and ears using my left hand. Saw the beast perched high in the mountains one night and wanted to record him for posterity."

Feril took another drink and touched the back of Grannaluured's left hand. Etched on it was a fiery sun with a face in the center of the sun. "What does this one represent?" Another drink. The Kagonesti was finding the ale tastier with each swallow. "You spending so much time underground, I wouldn't think you'd see the sun very often, and I notice that the light bothers your eyes." She took another long pull and almost reluctantly passed the jug to Feldspar.

"That's the point of it," Grannaluured said, holding her left hand up for everyone to see. "If I put the sun on my hand I can see it anytime I want—which is usually by torchlight in the tunnels." She waved for the jug and swallowed some more, then sloshed the jug around and scowled to note there wasn't much left. "Feldspar, where's your manners? Get us another!" Softer, she said to Feril, "Maybe the sun wasn't my best idea for a tattoo, but I'd been drinking." She passed the jug back to Feril and chuckled. "Just like now. You can finish that if you want, Dawnsprinter. We got us a couple more jugs of the good stuff. Not going back to the mine today. Want to make sure all the tremblin's done, so we might as well drink up." The dwarf laughed longer and deeper.

Feril tipped her head back and finished the jug, then noticed Ragh staring at her in disapproval. "In the time you spent mining, Granalal, did you happen to find any dragon scales?" The female dwarf winced and Feril scowled, knowing she'd mispronounced her host's name.

"You're good with our hill dwarf words, Dawnsprinter,

but your tongue is clumsy with the nuances. Try Needle, that's my nickname."

"Needle," Feril repeated.

"Much better." The woman shifted against her pack, propping herself up. "Years back," she continued, "I did find me a dragon scale, a pretty bronze one I had made into a shield for my grandson. Found some teeth, too, and strung them on a gold chain. Though I suppose the teeth might not have come from a dragon. There're other big beasts in this world."

"Found me a black scale once," the young dwarf cut in. This, the youngest of the small party, hadn't introduced himself, and Feril raised her eyebrows and nodded in his direction.

"Oh, that's Campfire. Likely you'd have trouble with his real name, too," Grannaluured said. "Nickname's Campfire, on account his hair looks like one and he likes to sit real close to the flames. He's on the cold side." Then she nodded to the broad-shouldered dwarf. "Over there's Churt Ironbeard, Feldspar's uncle once removed."

Feril thought Campfire reminded her a little of Jasper, or rather what Jasper would have looked like so young. "Even among the longest-lived races, life is too short," she murmured distractedly in her own tongue.

"Pardon?" Grannaluured said. "I don't speak Elvish."

"Sorry, I was thinking of old friends." She returned her attention to Grannaluured's tattoos. "You've got an interesting scaled claw here, clutching . . ." Feril turned so she could better see another tattoo, a scepter that wrapped around Grannaluured's forearm.

"You like my tattoos?"

"I used to have a few of my own." There was something regretful in her voice, and Grannaluured picked up on her sadness. "I had them removed, Needle," Feril said with a thin smile, " . . . on a day I hadn't had quite enough to drink."

Grannaluured reached behind her and fumbled in her pack, pulling out a small chest wrapped in black cloth. She faced Feril. "Just means you're all ready for new ones, like your body's a blank page. Want one done by a semi-expert?"

Feril looked across the camp to Ragh. The draconian was pretending to study the scenery, though she knew he had been eavesdropping.

"Would it take very long?"

"Depends what you want exactly, Dawnsprinter."

Feril pulled up the sleeve of her tunic. "How about a dragon's head? Here." She pointed to a spot just below her right shoulder.

"Odd tattoo for an elf," Grannaluured mused, "but then, you're not in the forest, and you're keeping company with a sivak . . . one with no wings. I think it fits the likes of you. I think I'll just have a few more swigs before I start. Funny, I do my best work when I'm drinking just a bit."

Feldspar chuckled. "She does her best mining then, too."

"Loosens up my fingers."

Feril clamped her teeth together as Grannaluured went to work with her dyes and needles. While the dwarf prepared, the Kagonesti told her about the jay feather and the lightning bolt tattoos she used to have emblazoned on her face.

"What color do you want the dragon to be?"

Feril almost said "black," but Dhamon wasn't really a black dragon. "Doesn't matter, Needle," she said matter-of-factly. "Whatever color suits your fancy. I'll trust to the artist."

Grannaluured smiled, reaching for her vial of red dye. "I like lots of color," she said. "I'll put a bit of blue in it, too. I think I've just the shade to match your eyes. Perhaps not very realistic, as far as dragons go, but more colorful. Nice to be able to put some of my work on display—on someone else. My friends here don't care for tattoos, but I figure I'll wear them down eventually. I'd like to put some flames on Campfire's arms."

Feril felt the first sting of pain and let her jaw unclench. "So you haven't been with them long?"

"Not terribly. Only a few months. I fell in with them by accident. They weren't keen on sharing their mining camp, but they were hungry for some good food. You think I'm good with tattoos? I'm even better with a skillet. Wait 'til you see what I do with the cured venison in my pack."

❖

The sun had started to set. Feril had drifted away from the dwarves to the other side of the pool below the hill with the dwarven tunnels. She looked across the water and watched the dwarves talking freely to Ragh, who had moved closer. He was regaling them with some tale of a time when he studied under a Red Robed sorcerer a century ago. They were setting up a campfire and preparing for dinner.

Dhamon's shadow was attached to the sivak, Feril saw. The Kagonesti guessed Dhamon was curious about the dwarves; being the suspicious sort, he was probably also concerned that the dwarves might prove hostile to Ragh and was, therefore, staying close to the draconian in order to protect him, if need be.

"Obelia, help me find the scale again," Feril whispered.

None of the dwarves noticed as she released the spirit from the flask and knelt over the pool, watching an image of the mountain come quickly into view, a sky-high view, as if she were a bird circling above. The ability to scry was coming easier to Feril, and she was quick to move the image around, focusing on different areas. She channeled the energy deeper into the pool, as if burrowing through the stone.

"There," she said, seeing her goal after long minutes of searching. "The scale is there."

"Buried deep, it is," Obelia said. "Real deep, because of the quake, and it looks like it might be damaged, cracked maybe. It won't do you any good if it's broken. The magic in it won't be strong enough, but it seems to be nearby, and if it isn't too much bother, it might be worth some digging to take a look."

Feril leaned closer, her eyes hopeful. "I don't see any damage, Obelia. The crevice is so dark, we can't see clearly enough to tell for sure. We are too close to give up on it. I told Dhamon I won't give up." After several more minutes of scrying, Feril was able to better pinpoint the location of the scale.

All of a sudden, realizing that the scale might be closer than she thought, she stood up, her heart beating fast. "Obelia. I might be able to get to the scale from here, coming up under it instead of burrowing down from the mountain top."

"My elf-fish, I see what you mean. That indeed looks to be a possibility." The spectral face seemed to share her excitement.

Then the ghost disappeared into the flask as Grannaluured looked in Feril's direction. The Kagonesti returned the flask to her satchel, strapping the satchel on her back and heading toward the old wall. She glanced up at the slash in the stonework. There were footfalls behind her. Feldspar was approaching.

"I see what you're thinking, but don't dare go into our tunnel," he said. He held up a small lantern and coaxed the flame in it. "It'll be too dark soon."

"Don't fear. I'm not going to steal any of your ore."

"Ain't worried about that," he returned. "Worried about you. Mountains trembled some today. Rocks comin' down inside. Still ain't safe, Dawnspringer."

Feril didn't correct him on her name. He was likely getting it wrong on purpose as a jab. It was just as Ragh said: some dwarves didn't get along with elves, and this one seemed to regard her with some suspicion. The Kagonesti continued to gaze up at the tunnel entrance. It would be a steep climb.

"Scaling that wall isn't how we get into our tunnels anyway," Feldspar scoffed. "We're not spiders, you know. There's a path. Well, there *was* a path. Some of it's still there. Used it to climb down, and it wasn't easy going. It's around and up the other side. Connects up with the main trail farther back. We're going to have to clean it off some tomorrow." He rubbed at a spot on the glass of the lantern. "I don't see why you're so darn interested."

"I'm not interested in your ore at all," Feril repeated. Then, before he could say anything or stop her, she had moved up to the wall and was wedging her fingers into cracks in the stonework, using the wall as a ladder. The mortar between the stones was old and she could force her fingers and toes into it. The pale, smooth granite—like some she'd seen on the Isle of Cristyne—made for good footing.

As she pressed against the wall, she heard something, and looking over her shoulder, she saw Feldspar, with the lantern handle in his teeth, climbing up behind her. Despite his thick fingers, he was climbing without much trouble. Feril opened her mouth to warn him away, but she decided arguing with a stubborn dwarf was pointless and so climbed the rest of the way up, silently followed by Feldspar.

There was a narrow stretch of dirt just outside the opening, and despite the failing light, Feril could see all the dwarves' bootprints leading inside. The tracks led up a thin trail that looked like it hooked over the top of the hill. The trail might provide an easier way down—but she could make that decision afterwards.

Feldspar was only halfway up, still following her. Feril ducked inside. If she waited for him, he might try to dissuade her, and she didn't want to argue with the dwarf. He would probably just follow her inside anyway.

The tunnel was dwarf-sized—short and only a few feet wide; it forked after several yards, one branch twisting up into the darkness and the other, newer branch angling to the north and sloping down. There was polished stonework on the northern wall, indicating the castle ruins had reached this high and deeper into the hill. The left wall was earthen and might have concealed more stonework. It could have been built centuries ago. At a glance, she could tell that this passage had been dug by picks and shovels; it wasn't naturally formed, and the quake must have brought tons of dirt down from the ceiling. The scale, she thought, was higher up in the mountain, so Feril took the tunnel branch leading higher.

"Dawnspringer . . ."

"I appreciate the concern you are showing for a stranger," she said, turning to spot Feldspar behind her in the entrance. He was holding his lantern up, revealing pieces of stonework along the bottom of the left-hand wall, including one brick engraved with strange runes. "I'm not worried that there will be more tremors. Everything seems to have settled down." Her jaw was set.

"What are you so bent on looking for?"

At first she tried to ignore his question. "I don't intend to wander in your mine for very long, Feldspar." Then she spun around, looking long at him. "I'm looking for something, not gold or silver, nothing like that, but I need to travel through your tunnels in order to find it."

His hairy eyebrows rose. His face was red from the exertion of keeping up with her, climbing the stone wall. "What is it exactly?"

He didn't seem a bad sort; better to trust him. "I'm searching for a lost dragon scale, and I think this tunnel will lead me to one."

He scratched his head with his free hand. "Seen some scales in the mountains before, years back. We were talkin' about that earlier, weren't we?" He trundled closer until he was inches away, setting the lantern on the ground where the tunnel forked. He gestured toward the lantern. "You can do what you want I guess, Dawnspringer. We claim these tunnels for mining, but we don't own the mountains. Reorx gave the mountains to all of us. Take that lantern so you can see better, though, and I'll accept your word that you won't take nothin' that's ours."

Feril turned back to the ascending path. "I won't need your lantern. I see better in the dark than in the sunlight, but thank you, Feldspar."

The dwarf gave a noncommittal grunt. "Me, I wouldn't be wanderin' around just now, Dawnspringer, not until I knew for certain the mountains weren't going to shake any more. And I wouldn't . . ." Feldspar was talking to the air. Feril had disappeared from view. "Daft elf. Gods didn't give 'em any sense." He shuffled to the tunnel opening and shouted down to his companions, "The elf's takin' a walk in our tunnels, looking for something. Couldn't talk her out of it."

The young dwarf gave an angry exclamation and shook his fist. "Feldspar, you get her out of there! She don't need to be poking around our hidden finds!"

Grannaluured was busy putting out her spices, preparing to cook. She tried to calm her companions as she oiled her skillet, scowling as Feldspar retreated back into the crevice. "Churt, Campfire, let's eat first. I had a good talk with that elf. I trust her. I don't know what would interest her in our mine, but . . ."

"Is this some kind of female trick? Bad enough we let you join us and we cut you in for a share. We're not dividing our find again with an elf," Churt said.

"Calm down, everyone. I'll go get her," Ragh said, walking purposefully around the pool as the three remaining dwarves watched him warily. The hill dwarves were making him uncomfortable with all their questions, even before Feril took it in her head to disappear. He glanced over his shoulder, making certain that Dhamon—still a shadow trailing him stealthily—was sticking close.

He froze as the ground rumbled under his feet. A minute later he was swiftly climbing the stone wall then heading into the tunnel opening.

The young dwarf shook his fist at Grannaluured. "Now we got an elf *and* a sivak trespassing on our property, poking around in our tunnel and mine!"

Ragh's keen hearing guaranteed that he could hear everything they said as he climbed higher.

The dwarf woman tried to quiet her companions, but Campfire and Churt were adamant that the newcomers had to be corralled and sent on their way.

"Greedy dwarves, the lot of them." The sivak took a deep breath and entered the tunnel, stooping to keep from hitting his head on the low ceiling.

"Dhamon, your elf friend's pretty headstrong," Ragh said. No reply, and his shadow had vanished in the darkness, but the sivak knew that Dhamon would be listening. "She's too emotional, letting her heart lead her around all the time. I don't like this at all, coming inside the mountain when the earth's still shaking. This could've waited for tomorrow, waited for the dwarves to move on to another part of the foothills. Could've waited for tonight when they were sleeping. No need to alarm and annoy everyone. Could've taken our sweet time and waited to do this."

The draconian stopped where the tunnel forked and stared at the ground. There was dirt, and dwarven prints heading down both passages. "Wonderful," he grumbled. He stooped and looked closer, not seeing Feril's slender footprints obliterated by the heavier dwarven tracks. Then he cocked his head, listening. All he heard was the soft groan of the earth and the continued argument of Grannaluured and the other dwarves below. He sniffed the air for traces of Feril. He could smell dust and the mustiness of the place, and of course the dwaves who had toiled here, but the lighter scent of the elf was difficult to separate.

"Dhamon, in all the levels of the Abyss, this is just marvelous."

With a deep sigh, Ragh stretched out his right hand,

silently rehearsing the words to one of the more practical spells he knew. Within moments, a pale blue globe of light appeared to rest on his palm. Thrusting it ahead, still stoop-shouldered, he took the northern passage that sloped down into the darkness.

CHAPTER 18

In the back of her mind Feril held the scrying image of the black's scale. She knew she couldn't be too far away now. She prayed to Habbakuk that the scale was not damaged. It had to be intact to be of any use to Dhamon.

A slight tremor raced through the ground. She gripped a wooden brace to keep her balance. The tremor persisted for a while, then stopped. She released a nervous breath she'd been holding and continued her ascent. Even without the mountain shaking, mines were dangerous—with their narrow tunnels and vulnerable beams and supports, crevices that threatened to spill the unwary into the bowels of the earth, and musty air that made breathing an unpleasant task.

"Getting closer now, but it's as though the mountain is trying to stop me."

The tunnel widened as she climbed, and she barely squeezed through a niche that had been mined. The soles of her bare feet were thick, but she still felt the sharp shards which littered the ground here. Should slow down, she ordered herself. No, she should hurry up. "Find it and get out," she told herself.

She wished now she had taken the dwarf's lantern. This darkness was unnatural, the gray-brown of rock and earth melding with the thick air.

Light intruded suddenly, a low beam from behind. Feldspar was plodding toward her, holding the lantern so that it highlighted his features from below, throwing shadows against the walls and giving him an eerie appearance.

"Did you feel that big tickle a minute ago?" Feldspar asked. "Told you it's not safe here, not with the mountain still dancin'. C'mon back with me, hear? Don't need you dyin' in our mine, rottin' and stinkin' it up."

Feril shook her head, turning to press on. "It's not much farther."

"This scale you're looking for . . ."

She nodded and coughed. The air was filling with dirt and stone dust.

"Why is it so important, this scale?"

"I need the scale for a spell," she said, before continuing onward, hoping the dwarf would turn back. Though he grunted in surprise, he still followed her, the light from his lantern swaying behind her back. But he was keeping his distance and making a tsk-tsking sound, mumbling, "Fool elf . . . and fool me."

"It's terribly important to me and my friend," she explained as she climbed.

The tsk-tsking was louder. "The sivak?"

Feril opened her mouth to say "no," but said nothing. The dwarves didn't know about Dhamon, who was attached to the sivak as a shadow. Being in the sivak's company was odd enough, they kept saying; best not start explaining about a dragon who used to be a man who was now taking the form of the sivak's shadow.

"Whatever kind of spell are you going to cast with a dragon scale anyway? How can you help that sivak? You trying to get its wings to grow back or something?" Feldspar's feet crunched faster over the gravel as he tried to catch up with the Kagonesti. "You know, I really don't care much for magic."

When she turned, she was taken aback by his narrowed eyes and the light slanted across the underside of his brow, which made him look sinister. She knew from conversations with Jasper that a lot of dwarves were distrustful of magic—save for the healing kind that Jasper practiced.

"I'm not a sorcerer, Feldspar, and the scale's needed for a spell that I don't understand . . . completely . . . yet, but I've no intention of casting this spell anywhere near your mine or your mountain. I just want the scale and then I want to leave." The words tumbled from her lips, slurred a little because of the ale. Just then another tremor struck. Rock shards and dirt rained down and sent her and the dwarf into a coughing fit. It took a few minutes before the air cleared.

"So the scale's valuable? Just what is it worth to you, missy?"

"I can't pay you for it. I have no coins. I just need it for a spell."

"Fool elf," the dwarf said. "Must be some important spell to risk your fool neck. That scale must be worth more than a bit." He stretched his hand out and waggled his fingers, his head bobbing at the same time. "You keep on going, Dawnspringer. There's a chamber up ahead, about a quarter mile or so. Some of our gear's left in it. It's near the main vein we're working. There's a fissure beyond it, and what you're looking for is just past that, I believe. Fissure's too narrow for us. Easier to get at it from the outside. The scale you're looking for is easy to spot . . . from the outside of the mountain, but the quake has buried it deeper, right? That's why you're using our tunnels. To get at it from the inside?"

"Yes, that's why," Feril said.

"Hope it doesn't bury you, too." He shrugged his broad shoulders, waggling his fingers again. "Hurry up. I'll go along with you so you can see where I mean, and so I can watch you, but I ain't helping you—and don't disturb our stuff. You're going to have to pay us somethin' for that scale. Campfire'll insist on it, if I don't. Labor, if nothin' else. That sivak ought to be good for haulin' rocks."

She smiled her acceptance and let him take the lead.

"I want you to be human, too," Ragh said. "I want it every bit as much as Feril does, and as you do. This dragon thing . . . it doesn't suit you." If anyone had been watching, it would appear the sivak was talking to his shadow. "Dhamon, I well know that you're not happy to be a dragon. I envy your wings, but nothing else. You've too lonely a life in that huge body, and I well know about being lonely. You can't even hold your son in your arms. Can't spend a single steel piece of your treasure. Can't be . . . familiar . . . with your elf lady friend."

The light globe in the sivak's hand was fading, as he neglected his concentration. He paused and focused the magic until the light grew bright again.

The tunnel narrowed ahead. He held the globe close to the thick supporting beams on the walls, finding a mix of dirt and granite and the worked stone of a castle wall.

There wasn't a trace of ore, no evidence this area had been mined.

He hunched over and squeezed between a pair of supports. "Wonder how much of a head start the elf has on us? Wonder if I'm headed in the right direction? She might have taken the other tunnel." Ragh sniffed the air, picking out the scent of wood that had started to decay and the strong odor of the dwarves.

"The dwarves have been doing something down here," he said, half to himself, half to Dhamon. "Their smell is strong; the supports are recent, a relatively new tunnel, I'd say." He ran his scaly fingers over one wall. "Probably less than a year old. Maybe as recent as a month or so." He passed under the next set of support beams. "Can't smell the elf. Maybe I ought to go back, try the other tunnel."

He smelled something else intriguing that he couldn't put a name to, so he continued on. He clenched his teeth when the mountain trembled all around him, and he shut his eyes, expecting to be buried under tons of rock. The thick supporting beams held and only a moderate amount of stone dust filtered down.

"Should go back," he said. "Doubt your elf came this way." He wanted to find out what was behind the unknown scent and just what the dwarves had been mining in this tunnel, though. The elf was curious and had keen senses; she might have come this way. His senses were also keen, and he was just as curious.

"Damn," he said, as he noted the tunnel gradually angling downward. "Damn. Damn. Damn. She didn't come this way. This way only goes down."

Ragh turned around to retrace his steps, but then he smelled the unusual smell again; it was slightly stronger heading down, so he thought he might go on just a little farther. Even the faint tremor which he felt didn't give him pause.

"You keep telling me that the elf can take care of herself," he told Dhamon, as he felt the shadow tug in the other direction. "She's probably doing just fine."

The tunnel narrowed further. Ragh pictured the dwarves squeezing through. It would be a tight fit for the one called Churt—he had wide shoulders for a dwarf. It was sure tight for him. The sivak bumped his head on the low ceiling. A long string of curse words came out and faintly echoed back at him.

"Tunnel turns ahead, or maybe there's a chamber," the draconian said, feeling how strange it was to be talking to himself and to keep hearing his own words echo back at him. "Let's see what we've got ahead, then we'll go right back the other way and find Feril. Let's see what's making that smell."

A dozen steps later the tunnel opened into a chamber so small that he imagined that all four dwarves would be hard pressed to fit. He spotted earthen jars stacked three high against one curving wall. He edged forward, crouching under the lowering ceiling. At the far side of the chamber was a small pool of liquid.

"That's what smells." He dropped to his knees and shuffled closer, scraping the satchel on his back and realizing that only the youngest dwarf would be able to stand up in here. Ragh inhaled deep and held his light globe over the surface.

At first he thought he recognized a trace of sulfur coming from the liquid. No, but there was the suggestion of steel or something like steel. It was nothing he was familiar with. It was at the same time a pleasant and disturbing odor, subtle and cloying, rare but memorable. It nagged at his curiosity.

His light revealed that it was a small but deep pool. Welling up from somewhere far below was a liquid metal, glistening brighter than pure silver. He tentatively reached out one finger, finding the liquid cool as a mountain stream and thick as pudding.

The liquid metal clung to his talon, and as minutes passed, he watched it harden.

"By the memory of the Dark Queen, what in all the levels of the Abyss is this?" He scratched on the stone at the rim of the pool, trying to scratch the metal off, but instead digging a line in the rock with its hard edge. "By all of the Dark Queen's glorious heads!" He proceeded to dip each talon of his free hand in the substance, then worked on his other talons. The claws of his feet were next.

"Dragonmetal, Dhamon! This is a pool of dragonmetal." He said these words softly, so softly he wasn't sure that Dhamon even heard. He waited a few minutes as the metal dried. "Dragonmetal is the only thing this could be," he said louder, excitedly. "No wonder they wanted us to stay out of their mountain. People would kill for this. Go to war over this." He glanced at the clay jugs. "They've figured out a way to store it without it hardening up on them. The earth, clay, that's it. Encased in earth it stays liquid. Wonder who they're going to sell it to?"

Ragh was so preoccupied with his discovery that he didn't notice another tremor racing through the stone nor the approaching footfalls of the young red-haired dwarf who had followed him all the way through the tunnel.

"Dragonmetal," the sivak repeated, mesmerized by his discovery. The draconian had lived a very long time and had traveled most of Krynn. He'd never seen dragonmetal, but he'd heard of it from fellow draconians who had witnessed the pool beneath the great Stone Dragon in Foghaven Vale. That was believed to be the only place on Krynn where dragonmetal existed.

"A gift from the gods," Ragh recalled from the legend.

It was said the gods of light bestowed the pool in the Vale, along with the secret of working the metal, to the master armorers of Ansalon. A skilled smith, using the artifacts known as the Silver Arm of Ergoth and the Hammer of Kharan, had forged the dragon-lances from this innately magical metal. It was called dragonmetal because of the dragon statue that loomed over the pool and because of the deadly lances made from it that could slay evil dragons. Solamnic Knights had used it for forging other weapons and armor, but these pieces were generally reserved for members of the order who were particularly distinguished.

"There was said to be only the one pool," Ragh said to his shadow. "That one was under the huge Stone Dragon in Foghaven Vale, but this is also dragonmetal, I'd bet my teeth on it. That makes this absolutely priceless."

"That makes you dead." The young red-haired dwarf stood at the entrance of the small chamber, lantern in one hand and a pick in the other. The pick was tipped with the silvery metal. He hung the lantern from a stone peg on the wall and shook his fist at Ragh. "You sealed your fate when you came down here! I'm going to have to kill you and the meddling elf, too, when I find her."

"Wonderful," Ragh grumbled, turning on his knees to face the fresh menace. With a thought, the globe in his hand grew bright, then he let it fall to the edge of the pool. He crept closer to the dwarf, then stood, stoop-shouldered, his clawed hands held to his sides but at the ready. "Look, I've really no desire to kill you . . .

Campfire, right? That's what's going to happen if you press this fight."

The dwarf chuckled. "Funny, I've every desire to end your pathetic life."

Feril had no trouble keeping up with Feldspar, but she marveled at his deftness and at the speed with which he could travel through the winding tunnel. He was surefooted on the ascending stone, sidestepping patches of loose rock and ducking nimbly under the low support beams. He stopped only once, and this was when the mountain shook and one of the beams shifted and ominously cracked.

"Fool, fool elf . . . and more fool me," he said. Feldspar let out a string of Dwarvish curse words as he shifted the lantern to his other hand. "We're almost there. You better get that scale quick as a rabbit—if you can. Understand?"

"I understand."

"Then you and the sivak are going to pay us something for it. That scale's got to be worth a lot to you, to risk coming here with the world rumblin' so."

At last the tunnel widened considerably, with the ceiling reaching high above them. Feril found herself in a natural cavern, the floor of which was slick in places with guano. There was no sign of any bats, however, and Feril suspected that when the first quake hit they flew out through a crevice above, opening to the sky.

"Is that the crevice you mentioned?" Feril pointed to it.

"Yeah. You're thin enough to slip through it, ain't you? I ain't going to work to make it bigger, don't want to weaken the ceiling anyway." The dwarf held the lantern high, the light barely stretching above, but it was enough to show a black strip wedged near the top of the cavern. "That's the tip of your dragon scale. Looks like it's in there pretty tight, Dawnspringer. Think you've got a way to . . ."

"To get it out of there? You said you planned on watching me, Feldspar. Well, just watch." She crouched and stooped to enter the crevice, then managed to hold the satchel behind her as she found finger- and toeholds. Awkwardly, but making surprisingly easy progress, she climbed the wall. "Obelia, I'm so very close," Feril whispered, hoping the specter could hear her through the flask.

The wall trembled slightly, but she held on and climbed higher, finally reaching the slash in the rocks where the scale was lodged. Only part of it was visible in the faint light provided by Feldspar's upstretched lantern. Feril ran her fingers over the edge of the scale, finding it nearly as sharp as a blade and as hard as metal.

She offered a silent prayer to Habbakuk for guiding them to these dwarves, the basin, and to this tunnel. Then she thrust her arm into the tight gap, trying to feel for the scale. At the same time she closed her eyes and slowed her breathing and forced herself to relax. A tingle raced from her chest and down her arm to her fingers, which were exploring the shield-sized scale and which were somehow molding the stone, cradling it as though the granite were malleable clay.

"I'll get you loose," she vowed. "Might take a few minutes." She pressed and smoothed the stone, while continuing to explore the edges of the scale with her fingers. Her body ached from being wedged so tight, but she pushed the pain aside and focused on the granite and the scale. "That's better. A little more." The rock flowed around her hand and arm as if trying to accommodate her.

"How's it going?" Feldspar asked when he heard Feril's sharp intake of breath. "Are you all right up there, Dawnspringer?"

Feril couldn't be bothered with answering him. Her arm had stretched as far as it could inside the gap in the rocks. Her fingertips had passed over chips and flakes in the scale that might have been caused by battle or by the rocks, and they were now feeling a split in the scale that covered several inches.

"Ruined," she said with dismay. "You were right, Obelia, it is damaged."

"What? Are you all right? Who's Obelia? Mine name's Feldspar!"

"Yes, yes, I'm all right," she said finally, holding back the tears that had settled at the edges of her eyes. "I came so damn close and for nothing."

"It's no good for ya, that scale up there?"

She shook her head and released the spell she'd been concentrating on. She withdrew her hand. The stone hardened again.

"Then let's get out of here, Dawnspringer, the faster, the better. I won't charge you for all the fuss. I bet dinner's on, and I'm as hungry as an urkan worm. You and that sivak are welcome to join us . . . if it doesn't eat too much."

"All for nothing." No, she corrected herself. She'd spotted other black scales when she scryed with Obelia. This particular venture had proved fruitless, but there were additional shed scales to be found and examined in the swamp.

"C'mon, hurry. Shouldn't be in here now, anyway. Not with all the . . ."

Just then a great rumbling resounded through the cavern. The walls shook. Rocks broke loose from the ceiling and clattered to the stone floor. Feril was caught between shifting stone and cried out in pain, the sound of her voice lost in the increased rumbling and the great cracking noise of the ceiling of the cavern.

She heard support beams snapping from the tunnel beyond, more rocks falling everywhere, and the final desperate words of her dwarf companion.

"By Reorx's bushy beard! The mountain's coming down on us! Fool, fool elf!" Feldspar called. "Fool me! Now we'll never get out of . . ."

His light went out. She heard Feldspar scream, his voice trailing off into nothingness. The cavern seemed to explode, huge chunks bursting from the walls and ceilings. She couldn't see anything anymore. Everything was blackest black. The ground beneath her gave way, stone dust enveloping her, so she could barely breathe. She was falling. Feldspar was surely dead, and she would be next.

CHAPTER
19

"Couldn't mind your own business, could you?" The dwarf nicknamed Campfire shook a stubby finger at Ragh. "Couldn't stay out of our tunnels. Couldn't stay away from our property!"

"Look, you little hairy nuisance, you don't own these mountains," Ragh sneered, "and this pool is . . ."

"Priceless, and all ours," Campfire continued.

"It's nothing I'm particularly interested in at the moment," Ragh returned. At the back of his mind the sivak wondered if *Dhamon* might be interested, though. Those ceramic jars filled with dragonmetal would be a prime addition to the lair. "I don't care about your dragonmetal. I'm looking for Feril."

"I don't believe you." Campfire waved his pick menacingly. "This pool, it's not the only little pool of dragonmetal in these mountains. There are two more similar nearby. Nearby and mapped out by us, ready to drain—when we're all done with this one." He thumped the haft of the pick against his callused palm. "We just gotta be getting us some more jars is all, but we've ordered them, and they're coming. See, we have another partner, and he's bringing jars, a wagon and bearers right now. The bearers are for the jars that won't fit on the wagon. Got us a buyer, too. We're going to be richer than anyone could possibly imagine, so much wealth we won't live long enough to spend it all. That's what Feldspar says, and we don't intend to share a bit of it with a sivak and a Kagonesti."

Ragh gauged the dwarf as an easy mark because of his small size and relative youth—likely he was inexperienced with fighting. The sivak knew he could take the dwarf easily, but what about Feril? What was happening to her? Better to stall a little; meanwhile, he could get some more information out of the dwarf, information about the dragonmetal. Because no matter what he told the red-haired dwarf, Ragh was very interested in the dwarves' discovery.

"Tell me this, Campfire. How did you stumble on this great discovery, just plain luck?"

The red-haired dwarf beamed. "Feldspar and Churt, they are the real geniuses. They were mining these mountains elsewhere and found an old, old map. Feldspar's awfully smart, and he managed to translate some of the ancient writing on it. That led us here, to this old, old castle, sunk into the hills. The map said the dragonmetal was hidden in chambers below. It took some looking and digging, but eventually we found it. The map was right."

"So this was once a Solamnic stronghold, is that it?"

Campfire shook his head. His eyes were wild and suspicious, and his knuckles were gripped white against the pick handle. "Nah. Older than the Solamnics, and it's dwarven construction to be sure. Priceless, these pools are, and a secret you won't be sharing with anyone. Dead sivaks can't talk."

He rushed at Ragh. Effortlessly wielding his long-handled pick, the red-haired dwarf darted in and out, chopping at the draconian. One of his first swings struck Ragh, the tip of the pick sinking into the draconian's arm. The sivak cursed. Crouched over, the sivak had a hard time maneuvering in the cramped chamber.

"You filthy stump!" The draconian spat fiercely, edging around. "Dirty little lump of flesh." The pick was hard and sharp and had cut through to bone—a painful wound to be sure. "I didn't want to hurt you, dwarf! Now I got no choice."

"Hurt me, hah! Who's hurting who?"

"No, I had no real reason to before, but I'm going to kill you now!"

The dwarf laughed. "Here's some more reasons!" Young and nimble, Campfire skittered away from Ragh, who was shuffling awkwardly, darting in again, swinging. Again he struck the draconian, this time only grazing Ragh. "I'll be the one who's doing the killing, just like Feldspar is probably busy finishing your elf-friend—wherever they are. There's no way he'll let her live. Can't risk it. Can't share this. Hope he hasn't found her yet, and that he needs my help. I'll enjoy killing the both of you. We'll let your bodies rot in the upper tunnel and keep our secret safe. We're not sharing this precious dragonmetal with anyone."

Ragh growled. "You have no idea what you're playing with, dwarf!" The sivak glanced at his shadow, inky black and shimmering in the light from Ragh's blue globe. The shadow had started to flow away from him. He glanced around the small chamber, knowing that in his dragon form Dhamon couldn't fit inside the small place and wondering what was going to happen. "You've no idea what you've started! Campfire, you have no . . . oh, wonderful. Wonderful timing."

The quaking of the mountain started again, fiercer than before, the rumbling loud. Ragh could hear support beams splintering. There was a horrible scraping of stone against stone as huge slabs of granite shifted and slid around.

"We have to get out of here, you stupid lump!" Ragh screamed at the dwarf.

The single-minded Campfire showed by the set of his jaw that he was intent on slaying the sivak. "Our mine will hold!" he hollered, swinging his pick again and again, ignoring the stone and dust raining down and churning up everywhere. "We've braced it well here. Not even the gods could bring it down!"

"Don't tempt the gods, you stupid dwarf!"

Again the pick sank into Ragh's shoulder, and the sivak cried in genuine pain. "You greedy stump! You'll kill us both by your stupidity." Ragh dropped below the dwarf's next swing, then bolted up and thrust his arms out. His talons coated in dragonmetal were unnaturally sharp and strong, and they dug into Campfire's chest. Ragh tore at the dwarf's flesh and pierced his heart.

"I told you I didn't want to kill you!" Ragh muttered, gasping for air and blinking furiously, trying to wipe the stone dust out of his eyes. His globe of light had been dropped, but miraculously, the dwarf's lantern was still clinging to the trembling wall. "See where greed got you?" he spat as he crawled over the dwarf's body and out into the larger tunnel beyond. His talons were drenched in blood. "It got you dead, you greedy stump. By the Dark Queen's heads!"

Ragh could barely see; the shadows were too thick and the lantern light was clouded with dust, but he could tell some of the support beams had collapsed and part of the tunnel ceiling had caved in. "The gods indeed couldn't bring it down! Well now, how in the levels of the Abyss am I going to get out of here?"

A growl of determination came from deep within Ragh, and he squeezed his eyes shut. His chest felt tight and he willed it to become even tighter and smaller, picturing in his mind the body of the young dwarf that lay bloody and lifeless behind him. The scales receded into his body as the mountain continued to shudder. His long arms and legs shrank while his silvery skin grew tanned, his fingers stubby, filthy, and callused. Hair flowed from his head and face, an unruly red mass that was becoming thick with the stone dust that continued to rain down.

His smaller dwarf form was able to fit under the broken beams and through an opening near the collapsed ceiling. He nearly left the satchel behind, as it would be easier going without it, but the magical baubles inside could help Dhamon—provided Dhamon made it out of the mine alive. Come to think of it, Ragh muttered to himself, nice of Dhamon to wait and worry about his old friend Ragh.

"Dhamon! Wait for me!" Ragh shouted. His Campfire voice sounded coarse and unfamiliarly dwarven. He couldn't see well enough behind him to know if Dhamon's inky form was behind or in front of him. Well, shadow, dragon, or man, Dhamon could take care of himself. "The whole mountain's breaking down on us! You'd better be leaving with me! The mountain's coming down!"

The rumbling grew to deafening proportions. The ground shook and buckled. A chunk of stone struck Ragh squarely on his dwarf shoulders, slamming him down against the floor. The entire tunnel ceiling seemed to give way—just as Dhamon resumed his dragon form and the lantern fell to the floor and died.

Utter blackness coincided with wholesale destruction.

Dhamon's massive body was expanding. He pushed hard against the falling rocks and collapsing walls, praying that the sivak had the wits to hunker down behind him and avoid the deadly rockfall. As he pushed his massive head up to the top of the tunnel, pushing against what remained of the ceiling, he felt his barbels drag across Ragh.

"Ragh! Let's get out of here!" Dhamon shouted, his booming voice adding to the rumbling as his neck bent at a distorted angle against the collapsing ceiling.

He felt the sivak shift beneath him, rising and scrambling forward into the darkness. Ragh felt the hot breath of Dhamon's words against his back.

"Hurry, Ragh!"

Moving his legs required tremendous effort as the weight of the collapsing tunnel threatened to flatten him. Somehow he managed to plod forward a little, and then a little more. He couldn't feel the sivak beneath him any longer.

The world was black. The noise was thunderous, louder than the din of the greatest battle he'd ever fought with the knights, more noxious than any storm he had flown through while mounted on the back of his blue dragon partner Gale. His every small breath was filled with rank, dust-filled air that burned his lungs. Dhamon fought for more air and gained little. He was suffocating.

Not enough air to breathe! his mind screamed. Not enough room to move! Not enough time to break free!

It would be so easy to let the mountain take him, to let his spirit drift with those of Jasper, Fiona, and Rig, but with Feril's whereabouts unknown and the sivak's fate uncertain, he couldn't give up now. He forced himself to take another faltering step, then another, legs bracing against the rocky ceiling that was continuing to break apart, tail lashing behind him, batting away falling rocks.

Got to keep moving! If any part of him hesitated, the falling stones would bury him. The rumbling grew louder but the stony floor suddenly stilled. The center of the quake had moved elsewhere inside the mountain. Grateful, Dhamon moved faster, his claws burrowing through the rocks in front of him as he prayed Feril was all right and that the sivak had managed to escape. Faster!

He heard the scream of stone, the old castle walls laid into the hillside giving way, the thump of rock falling. Faintly, he heard something else. A voice?

It was the draconian calling to him. He threw all his might into straightening his legs, forcing his back up against the sagging ceiling, and moving forward into the blackness that was giving way to bands of gray.

Dhamon didn't know how long he struggled. It felt like forever, and by the time the darkness receded his muscles felt on molten fire. He didn't think he could take another step, until he saw a pale blue glow coming through an opening.

He thrust his snout forward, finding the larger tunnel leading to the mine entrance. In a daze he saw Ragh beckoning him, except that the sivak looked like the dwarf Campfire and was holding a blue globe of light in his hand.

"Dhamon, be quick!" Ragh said in a dwarf voice. "By the memory of the Dark Queen, hurry!"

Dhamon understood, and folding in upon himself

until he was an inky pool, he stretched to become Ragh's shadow. He flowed out of the mine attached to the sivak. Then they were safely coming down the hill, which continued to shake violently.

The stars were just emerging, with the sky a hazy dark blue from the dirt and stone dust that increasingly blanketed this section of the Kharolis Mountains.

"Campfire!" The dwarf woman was frantically waving her arms and motioning Ragh away from the mountain. "Campfire!" The other dwarf named Churt was with her, looking equally frightened but cursing the gods for ruining their mine.

Dhamon was surprised to see Feril lying on the ground at the two dwarves' feet. She looked sorely battered and bruised, and her arm was in a sling, but he could tell at a glance she was breathing. Grannaluured waved a skillet above the Kagonesti menacingly.

"Campfire!" Grannaluured bellowed. "Get over here now!"

"Feldspar's dead," Grannaluured said. She dipped her head for a few moments, perhaps offering a silent prayer. When she raised it, her eyes were watery. "Dawnsprinter told us about it after she crawled down the mountain and we bandaged her arm. She said Feldspar fell into a crevice. Said she couldn't get to him before the ground swallowed him up, as surely as any big beast."

She shook her head, then dropped the skillet on the ground near a smoldering fire. "All for greed. Death's the reward for greed, I tell you. Surprised you aren't dead, too, Campfire, charging in there like that after that damn sivak. You ought to know better. You ought to know to stay out of the mountain when things are shaking like that. No riches are worth your life. Greed kills as surely as any sword, I say."

The dwarf who looked like Campfire didn't reply, just shifted back and forth on his booted heels and tried to look sad. Ragh knew that while he sounded something like the dwarf, he didn't possess all the nuances of the dwarf's speech or his mannerisms. Talking or moving around too much would give him away.

"You're young, Campfire, but if you want to reach my age you're going to have to be more careful. Understand?" Grannaluured sniffed unhappily. "I suppose you'd like some dinner now."

Ragh nodded, his dwarf beard fluttering. The draconian actually was hungry, and whatever Grannaluured had been working on smelled delicious.

Behind Grannaluured's back, Churt was also nodding hungrily, though she couldn't see him. "I sure am hungry, fellows, and we might as well mourn Feldspar on a full stomach rather than an . . . wait a minute, Needle, something's not right." As Churt brushed past Ragh, his nose began to quiver.

Ragh's scent was giving him away.

Churt squared his overly broad shoulders, sniffing the air again and glaring at Ragh. "This one doesn't smell like Campfire, Needle. Doesn't stink of sweat either. Smells a little like sulfur, though." Churt's eyes narrowed. "Got to be the sivak. It killed Campfire and took his body. They do that. Got to be."

"Yeah, I smell it, too." Grannaluured grabbed up her skillet again as Ragh edged back. "I suspect most folks wouldn't notice the sulfur, would think you're Campfire. Tell me you're Campfire! Prove it to me!" Grannaluured shouted.

Ragh said nothing.

"See, I'm a miner, and I've worked in a smithy, so I know what sulfur smells like," Churt said. He reached for a pick on the ground; its tip glimmered silver and Ragh knew it had been dipped in the dragonmetal. "Since you're wearing Campfire's form, that means you're a murderer. I know all about sivaks."

Ragh spread his stubby legs, holding his hands to his sides. "I've no reason to fight you."

"I know *all* about sivaks, and I know they can die."

Ragh tried reasoning with them. "Look, I've truly no wish to fight with you. There's been enough bloodshed today. A fight will only . . ."

"Like Campfire's blood?" Grannaluured said. "Like you didn't want to kill him? We all have been around long enough. We all know about sivaks. You wear the forms of the ones you killed! You did kill Campfire, just like Churt says."

"He didn't give me any choice. He attacked me. Leave this be."

Grannaluured and Churt split to the right and left, angling around the sivak. Behind them both, Ragh saw, Feril was stirring. She lifted her head and stared through Churt's legs to see the dwarf whom at first glance she thought was Campfire. Feril pushed herself to her knees and peered closer to see an inky pool spreading away from Campfire. The dying fire was just enough to illuminate the shadow.

"Dhamon!" Feril murmured. She jumped to her feet just as Ragh let his dwarf form melt away. "Needle, Churt, don't fight them! You can't win!"

"Them?" Churt glanced at her, shrugging his broad shoulders. "I only see one enemy, just one wingless sivak, and soon it's going to be wearing my body. 'Cause if I remember right, sivaks also take on the form of what kills them."

"It'll wear my body! I'll be the one to kill it!" Grannaluured argued.

"Needle, leave them be!" Feril called.

"Them?" Grannaluured echoed mirthlessly. What she saw next made her gasp, however, as the inky shadow that was Dhamon grew into a shimmering dark cloud expanding and contracting behind Ragh. The mass of shadow grew legs and wings and a serpentine neck that stretched above the sivak. "Dragon! A dragon!"

Dhamon released his aura of dragonfear, so Churt whirled and tripped, picked himself up and ran, heading to the south and disappearing into darkness. Grannal-uured froze, trembling, legs locked, the skillet slipping from her fingers. The color drained from her face. Ragh and Feril were affected too, but held their ground.

"The dragon won't hurt you, Needle." Feril stepped behind the dwarf and put her left hand reassuringly on her shoulder. "He's a friend of mine."

"D-d-d-dragon's a f-f-friend?"

"Yes, and I promise that he won't hurt you. I swear!" Feril exchanged looks with Dhamon, who gradually suppressed most of his fear aura. As he did, the elf stepped in front of Grannaluured and walked slowly toward the dragon.

"Feril . . ."

"My arm's broken, Dhamon, but I'm all right." She told him that during the quake her arm had become trapped between shifting rocks. "I got it out. I can make stone move," she explained. "It's how I knew I could get the scale if it was wedged—making the stone flow around it so I could pull it out."

Dhamon nodded. His old friend Maldred was able to perform the same magic with stone. Feril hadn't been so accomplished with her nature magic when he knew her years earlier. He wondered what other surprises she had in store.

"I tried climbing straight down, but everything was shaking so badly. I ended up crawling like a baby to get here. Churt and Needle set my arm."

Cuts crisscrossed her face and arms, and there were welts on her legs from where rocks had pelted her. She was favoring her right side, and Dhamon suspected she might have cracked some ribs. A nasty bruise decorated her cheek.

"I feared you were dead," Dhamon said. Even though he spoke softly, the ground rumbled, and Grannaluured, all but forgotten momentarily, whimpered in fear.

"I wasn't sure I was going to make it, Dhamon. Terribly foolish of me to go in there tonight. Unforgiveably foolish. Feldspar would be alive if I had waited. My curiosity and eagerness be damned. Too much ale, too much . . . Feldspar shouldn't have followed. Now I've blood on my hands." She tilted her head down sorrowfully. "Maybe Campfire would be alive too."

"Doubt it," Ragh said. "Campfire was looking to die." The sivak glanced at his clawed hands, blood still drying on them. Then he looked to the female dwarf, who was still wide-eyed and shaking. "What are we going to do about her, Dhamon?"

Feril raced to Grannaluured's side. "Needle? You're going to do nothing about Needle."

"Got to do something with her," the sivak pressed. "Can't leave her here alone, can we?"

The female dwarf blinked, looking up dully at Feril. "D-d-dragon. We should run." Her legs had stopped shaking, but she was still locked like a statue.

The complicated explanation tumbled from Feril's lips, about how Dhamon was once a man and had been cursed by a shadow dragon to become a dragon. How he could turn himself into a shadow form. How they were in the mountains looking for an overlord's scale that might help make Dhamon human again.

Grannaluured didn't catch everything, and Feril had left plenty out in her effort to explain quickly, but the explanation seemed to be enough to get the dwarf to relax slightly. She took a few tottering steps and breathed deeply.

"Dhamon won't hurt you," Feril repeated. "I promise."

"Churt?" Her words were coming out strangled. "Where's Churt?"

"He ran," Feril said. "The dragonfear took him."

Dhamon nudged Ragh with the tip of his snout, so that the unprepared sivak stumbled forward. "Oh, so I'm elected to go look for the stupid dwarf? Wonderful. Fine, fine. I suppose it's better than staying around here and staring at an old maid dwarf who probably isn't going to serve a decent dinner now." He jogged off into the darkness, in the direction Churt had fled. "Shouldn't be that hard to find him. Dwarves have stubby legs. He can't have gone too far."

Several minutes later Feril was helping Grannaluured stoke the fire. Dhamon stayed nearby, and though the dwarf could see him clearly—and he certainly looked terrifying—gradually she seemed to be calming down.

"D-d-d-didn't see you come out of the mountain with that scale you were looking for, Feril," Grannaluured said. She had seated herself by the fire, back propped up against her pack, eyes glued warily on Dhamon. She twitched each time he moved, but she made no attempt to get away. "Too old to run," she told Feril. "If that dragon's gonna get me, isn't anything I can do about it."

Feril smiled sadly. "We found the scale, but it was cracked, useless. We need one that's undamaged if we're to have any chance to make him human."

"Turning humans into dragons? Turning dragons back into humans? I've seen some odd things in my time, but I don't think that's something I want to be seeing."

Feril put a hand on the dwarf's shoulder, stroking it gently. "I'm hoping to see it. I'll not give up on Dhamon. I'm determined to find another scale."

The nervous Grannaluured tried unsuccessfuly to appear at ease. "Might be more scales in those mountains. If there was the one, why wouldn't there be more? The quakes could have busted them all, I suppose. Yeah, ruined the mine, probably ruined just about everything in this part of the mountains."

Dhamon had been edging closer until his head was directly over the fire. He could feel the warmth on his barbels. He savored the warmth, happy to feel something other than pain. Grannaluured, eyes wide, watched his every move.

"My elf friend Obelia . . ." Feril began. She was going to tell the dwarf about the Qualinesti spirit in the flask in her backpack, but a look from Dhamon warned her against it. Perhaps Dhamon thought the dwarf had dealt with enough this day—a sivak, a dragon, the quake, and the loss of two of her companions. She didn't need to know that a Qualinesti ghost rested a few feet away, swirling his fingerbones around in water taken from Nalis Aren.

"Dhamon, we have little choice," she said. "We have to try the swamp."

Grannaluured spoke before the dragon could. "So interesting the lot of you are. So very, very interesting." The gray strands that had come loose from her braid looked like cobwebs in the firelight. "I think maybe I'd like to be going along with you, Dawnsprinter. Bet you could use a cook . . . though I doubt I could fix enough of anything to fill up that dragon. Yeah, I should come along. The sivak's right. Don't leave me here alone. I might be helpful in a swamp."

Dhamon and Feril exchanged looks. "Maybe," Feril said.

More than an hour passed before Ragh returned, shrugging his shoulders and showing he was empty-handed. "Don't know where he went. Too hard to sniff him out, all this dirt and stone flying. Lost his tracks. Don't have wings to hunt from overhead." He settled close to the fire, ignoring the nervous looks he got from Grannaluured.

Grannaluured was fixing some sort of spiced meat and roots that made the sivak's mouth water. The skillet simmered over the fire. He waited for her nod, then snatched a piece out of the skillet, blew on it, and stuffed it in his mouth. "By the Dark Queen's heads, I'm hungry, and this is very good." Despite herself, Grannaluured beamed at the compliment. The sivak ate several more pieces, noticing she was staring at his dragonmetal-coated talons. "Dhamon, if you want to hunt for that dwarf when the sun comes up, I'll go with you, but I'm done looking tonight. By the Dark Queen's heads, I'm tired. This is very, very good."

Grannaluured nudged Feril, who also took a piece of root mixture and started eating. "Don't worry, Dawnsprinter. Churt'll come back. Eventually. Unless some big critter out there got him," Grannaluured said. "Churt's too greedy to leave the find, an' the mountains are his home after all. Probably won't come back until we're long gone, though. His hair is probably turning white just thinking about that dragon." She paused, pushing aside a stray strand of gray hair. "Just where is it you said we're going to look for a scale?"

"The damnable swamp," Ragh was quick to answer between bites. "Who said you're coming with us?"

Feril gave him a sharp look.

"Like I said," Grannaluured continued, "Churt probably won't show himself until we're long out of sight." She glanced up at Dhamon's snout. "He doesn't know you're not a . . . ahem, bad dragon, and he doesn't care for elves . . . or draconians for that matter. He'll bide his time and pray you're long gone. He'll come back, 'cause he won't easily give up his share of the find."

Ragh chewed on the last piece of meat. "You mean the dragonmetal?"

She put on a sour face. "You found it, I can see that plainly."

Ragh wriggled his fingers for Feril's benefit. His talons gleamed in the firelight. "Campfire had a pick coated in it. Tried to kill me with it." Ragh turned and squared his shoulders, boasting the wound the young dwarf had given him.

Feril shook her head, annoyed with herself that she'd paid no attention to the sivak and hadn't noticed his wound before this. She gingerly stepped toward the draconian, knelt next to him, and prepared her healing magic.

"Don't you think you've got enough to do, healing yourself?" Ragh asked.

"My arm is already feeling better, thanks to Grannaluured, who set it properly. Its healing will continue." The warmth flowed from the fingers of her left hand into his wound. He closed his eyes, allowing himself to enjoy the healing.

"Thanks, Feril." To Grannaluured, Ragh added, in as friendly a tone as he could adopt, "I see you've got a pick dipped in the dragonmetal, too."

She nodded. "Not as good as one forged from it, but good enough. Actually, I've had it dipped a few times. Working on stone, the coating wears off eventually."

"You want to go with us? You don't want to stay with Churt and mine some more of this priceless dragon-metal?" The sivak looked at her meaningfully. "I can't imagine a dwarf giving up on something like that. It's the find of a lifetime."

She laughed, the sound of her laughter craggy and weary. "I'd guess that last quake pretty well buried everything, priceless or no. I'm liking the idea of a new adventure. I don't like mining alone anyway. If you'll have me, I'll go."

Ragh rolled his shoulders, obviously pleased that Feril had taken most of the pain away. "The clay jugs you had stacked up inside are smashed for certain, and the pool you were working is probably covered, but it could be dug out again."

"I'm sure Churt will do just that." Grannaluured started scrubbing at her skillet.

"Campfire said there were more pools."

"Supposedly." Grannaluured chewed thoughtfully on her lower lip. "I came across them three—Churt, Feldspar and Campfire—not long ago, but I already told you that. They needed a cook, or so I convinced them, and I needed the company. Well, I found me some new company today. Oddest company one could come across. I'll keep with you for awhile. Churt can find some new partners."

Ragh still looked skeptical. "You're really not interested in the dragonmetal?"

Another laugh, this one longer and sounding wholly genuine. "Sivak, take a long look at me. I'm an old woman. I figure I don't have too many winters left in me, certainly not enough to spend them digging in the mountains for a fortune I won't likely live long enough to spend. Those other dwarves weren't the best company anyway, truth be told. "

Ragh smiled, showing his jagged teeth. He decided he liked the dwarf. She grinned back at him, shedding her nervousness. He wondered just how old she was.

Finished with her healing spell, Feril headed toward the pool. "I'm going to check on Obelia now, if you don't mind." Dhamon rose to follow her.

Grannaluured cocked her head in the pair's direction. "Obelia. I heard her mention someone called Obelia before. Elf name sounds like. Are we meeting up with him somewhere?"

It was Ragh's turn to chuckle. "You definitely have found yourself in odd company, Needle. You'll probably meet Obelia soon enough, sooner than you'd care to." He coughed. "Ahem, you called yourself an old woman. Just how old are you?"

"Sivak, I'm . . ."

"Ragh. My name is Ragh."

"Ragh, then. I saw my four hundredth birthday some years back. I stopped counting at four hundred."

"That's old for a dwarf. Ancient."

She scowled. "Not so old as you, I'd expect."

"No."

"You're older than the elf."

"I don't know how old Feril is."

"She's got some age to her. I can see it around her eyes. Women are better with age, Ragh. Wiser in all ways, more patient. Should be that way with all the gods' children, I think. Gonna tell me how you fell in with a dragon and an elf?"

"First I fell in with a human . . ." Ragh began. He proceeded to entertain Grannaluured with the long story of Dhamon and the scale while he sorted through the baubles in his satchel, making certain nothing had broken during the quake. He left out parts, embroidered others, and considered that he had done a good job of telling the story—judging by Grannaluured's rapt expression.

"So now you want to make your friend human again." Grannaluured put her skillet back in her pack. "Odd company I've embraced, indeed." She tugged a small pillow out of the pack and laid her head on it as she stretched out on the ground. She smiled at Ragh then, and within minutes she was softly snoring.

The sivak lay down and closed his eyes too, but he didn't go to sleep right away. He was thinking about the reflections Feril and Obelia had conjured up in the mountain stream. He remembered spying a large black scale next to a totem of bones in the swamp. He shuddered—the totem was a collection of dragon skulls, prizes Sable had earned during the fabled dragonpurge. The dread totem was a source of magical power for her, but the draconian had no desire to visit it.

The reflections had shown another scale, at the edge of a pool of quicksand in a small glade ringed by old, moss-covered trees. Ragh thought the glade looked somewhat familiar, and now he decided he should talk them into going there first. The scrying spell had shown others—several more scales, all broken or cracked at the edge of a marshy tributary. Two more were near a stand of strange, ancient stones that Ragh was certain he'd seen before. The stand of stones might be even closer than the glade. The last scale he remembered seeing had been set atop a carved wooden statue and was painted with strange symbols. Maybe it marked bakali lands, because he knew some of the tribes worshiped beings with cryptic names, or the statue could belong to lizard-men, weaker cousins to the bakali.

The last image the sivak recalled was near Dhamon's cavern lair deep in the swamp, with the hoary shaggy-bark nearby, and the king snake that was often wrapped around the base of a thin cypress. That was Dhamon's favorite stretch of water, filled with giant alligators and gar, the one most recently visited by Sable's minions. Not far from it were fetid, stagnant pools and endless swarms of insects.

"Damnable swamp," he muttered, before finally drifting off to sleep.

T his time they flew. Grannaluured sat between Feril and Ragh, thick arms wrapped around one of Dhamon's back spines. The dwarf's stubby legs were clamped as tight as she could, her eyes fixed intensely on Feril's back.

Ragh allowed himself to be slightly cheerful. He'd never fancied the company of dwarves before—though he'd taken the shapes of the dozens of dwarves he'd killed to infiltrate various communities and gain information for Sable. This dwarf was different than most, however. She was thoroughly pragmatic, good-natured and amusing, certainly daring, and above all of that, an excellent cook. He decided he'd get to know her better when they landed.

He felt the air streaking past his ears, the whistling wondrous music that coaxed a few tears down his cheeks. Squeezing his legs to make sure he had a solid perch, he raised his arms to his sides and spread his fingers wide. He dreamed he was flying. He looked down after several minutes. They were well beyond the Kharolis foothills and just south of the ruin of Skullcap, flying low and fast over a stretch of plains that were still green. They passed a farm, and Ragh made out three large wagons being filled with the last of the harvest. He thought he could smell the cut grain, though smelling anything other than the sharp scent of the dwarf and the ghastly odor of Dhamon was likely his imagination. By the Dark Queen's heads, the female dwarf needed a bath and Dhamon needed . . . needed . . . to be a human again!

Hours passed. The sun was straight overhead. Its warmth bathed his shoulders and cut any bite of the wind. The sky was cloudless, a brilliant blue that reminded him of . . . what? The color of Nalis Aren, he decided. He shook the memory of the lake from his mind and continued to daydream as the land slipped by below.

He noticed a herd of what at first glance he thought were horses, but as Dhamon dipped lower, Ragh made them out as centaurs, perhaps a nomad band from the Plains of Dust in search of more hospitable territory and better hunting grounds. Miles later he spotted a smattering of small farms, a village, and a herd of sheep that moved like a wave of white across a pasture when Dhamon flew too close and frightened them.

Hours later, he caught a glimpse of another blue to the north, the shore of the New Sea. As the sun was starting to set, the edge of the swamp came into view. Ragh's heart began to sink.

"Home," Ragh thought he heard the dragon murmur. The draconian shuddered.

Dhamon dived toward the marsh that marked the outer perimeter of Sable's realm. He wasn't a bit tired; he relished the sensation of flying. Years past, when he was a young Dark Knight, he had blond hair and smooth skin not yet scarred by battles. He had been determined and persistent, climbing fast in the ranks and distinguishing himself first as a battlefield medic, then as a commander of men. He was decorated with medals and ribbons, then he was given a far greater honor—he was partnered with a blue dragon. He and the dragon, whose name was Gale, had formed a fast bond and led various campaigns into Solamnic lands.

Yes, he had long blond hair then, he thought, clearly remembering his youthful face and blue eyes. He nearly had died during one campaign, when he was trapped on foot and some distance from Gale. He would have died, too, had not an aging Solamnic Knight taken him in and nursed him back to health, all the while turning his mind away from the precepts of the Dark Knights. Then he met Goldmoon; she had convinced him of right and goodness, and for a time he became her champion. Once again a leader of men, he had guided Feril, Rig, Fiona, and the others against the dragon overlords, and he still had his blond hair.

A scale changed all that; one of Malys's puppets had branded him with it, attaching it to his thigh. At first unbeknownst to him, the scale had controlled him, though it gave him pain and he raged against it. Had it not been for a silver dragon named Silvara and the shadow dragon that cursed him, he likely would have remained under Malys's control until one of them died. Lying in the cave of the shadow dragon, lying in a pool of its black blood, Dhamon's hair had turned black, his eyes also black. His soul started to blacken, too, thanks to the insidious magic the shadow dragon secretly had worked upon him.

The dragons that had manipulated him were responsible for much of the bad fortune that swept across Krynn. Did he really want to be human again and risk running afoul of the dragons? Human, he was powerless against them . . . he knew that truth from his stint as Goldmoon's champion. Oh, you could have minor victories against dragons, but nothing that made a real difference in the world.

Did Dhamon really want to give up all his strength and power? He clenched and unclenched his talons, feeling his leg muscles ripple. He spread his wings and glided down toward the marsh, enjoying the rush of air. He wondered if his passengers, the three riding on his back, were enjoying the flight. Puny as they were, compared to his great size and power, he could barely feel them back there.

Had Gale been able to feel him?

He landed on the soft earth, his clawed feet sinking into the ooze of the marsh. Dhamon stretched his front legs. His tail twitched as he drew a deep breath into his lungs. Myriad scents struck him—the loamy soil, the broad blooms clinging to vines, stagnant water all around. Nothing was truly unpleasant; the complex mix was heady and somehow comforting because it smelled of home.

"Home," he rumbled softly, his voice carrying now to the ears of his companions. Had he actually missed the swamp? Had he come to enjoy its damp and fetid embrace? Dhamon moved forward into a stand of trees as his companions slipped from his back and followed him.

He breathed deep and pulled his wings in close, reached with his neck and rubbed against a thick cypress. As a dragon he could live a very long time, and he was powerful enough that he could claim his own territory, perhaps someday returning to challenge Sable for the swamp. If he became human, he would not live many more years, and he would be trapped in a frail body. If he stayed a dragon, he could build a treasure hoard that would be beyond the dreams of any human.

The Kagonesti came up to his snout, tugging on a barbel. He lowered his head to see her anxious expression. "What's wrong, Dhamon?"

"I don't know if I really want to be a man again, Feril. Maybe it would be better to remain a dragon. I just don't know what I want. I don't know why I brought you here."

"By the grace of Habbakuk, Dhamon, we've gone through so much already on your behalf. I've gone through . . . so much. We're not turning back now."

He stared at her long and hard, ignoring the chatter of Ragh and Grannaluured, who were busy examining their packs to make certain nothing had been lost during the flight. For the first time he noticed the faint lines around Feril's green eyes and at the corners of her mouth. Her hair had white streaks now, too. Had this experience taken its toll? Had something happened to her in the Lake of Death? Had the ghosts cursed her somehow? Was she aging before his eyes?

He knew that the Dark Knights told tales about the dead Qualinesti, and maybe those tales were true after all.

"I need to think and talk things over, Feril. Come talk with me alone."

Dhamon glided deeper into the swamp, Feril following and motioning Ragh and the dwarf to stay put. She left the satchel with Obelia inside in Ragh's care. Her gesture surprised the sivak, as she was showing a new trust in him.

"We'll be all right here," Ragh told Grannaluured. "This is the far border of Sable's land. Not so many beasties out this way. They stick to the heart of the swamp and along the river." He pointed to a dry patch of stunted saw grass that stretched out from the base of a black walnut. "Why don't we wait there for them? Lots of roots and herbs around here, I reckon. Maybe Dhamon will catch us something tasty that you can cook up. I'm hungry again."

"If he doesn't catch something, I have some salted wild pig among my stores. Not a lot, but it'll do, and it should get eaten anyway before it goes bad."

"Yum, salted pig." Ragh grinned. "One of my favorites. Sun's going down, and it gets dark in the swamp early. Let me help you get started. We don't have to wait for those two. Dhamon eats on his own, basically whenever he feels like it, and I don't think that elf in love with nature eats meat."

"Pity."

"Yeah, pity," said Ragh unconvincingly.

"More for us then," she said cheerily. "Maybe I should get dinner started."

Ragh did a bad job of hiding his eagerness. "I'll hurry and get a fire going, Needle. While we're waiting for that meat to cook, you can tell me about some of these pretty pictures." He touched a silvered talon to one of her tattoos.

Grannaluured beamed. "I like to talk about my art," she said. "I could probably give you a tattoo if you want one, Ragh. I've needles that are long and sharp, and they'd probably go through your skin. I'd like to try anyway. Something colorful. A dragon's head like I gave Dawnsprinter, perhaps?"

The sivak growled softly. "Let's get that salted pork going first."

Dhamon and Feril settled down a fair distance away from Ragh and Grannaluured, where the canopy of trees was close and dense, cutting the light. This section of the swamp was low-lying and often flooded. There was a river nearby, sloshing against the banks. Too, they could hear the splashing of otters and the calls of wood ducks. Closer to the swamp's heart, there'd be too many alligators and other predators, and smaller animals knew to stay away.

Low to the ground were dotted clumps of buttonbush, swamp roses, weeping willow seedlings, and patches of smooth alder. It was a world of shadows here, under the weave of branches, but both had keen eyesight.

"Welcome to my home, Feril." Dhamon let his talons sink into the rich, black soil. "My lair is a long way from here, near a lake with a perfect chokeberry bush."

"Your home. It is beautiful. So untouched." Her face bore a wistful expression.

"Untouched by man for the most part, Feril. The villages are far apart, but even they have been corrupted by the Overlord. The forest is unnaturally thick here, just as Beryl twisted and thickened the woods in Qualinesti. It shouldn't be like this."

"Corrupted." Feril looked pensive now. "I have a hard time seeing it like that. It is beautiful to my eyes." She tipped her head back, her fingers caressing the flowers. She looked for the birds that were rustling the leaves far overhead. "What do you want, Dhamon Grimwulf? Do you want this swamp? I couldn't blame you, but I know I still want that treasure you promised. It would go a long way toward helping the refugees and overcrowded villages on the islands."

An awkward silence settled heavily between them. Feril just wanted his treasure, Dhamon thought. She didn't really care about him, didn't care if he became human again, not really. No, he argued with himself, she wanted the treasure because she was an honorable do-gooder. That was one of the things he admired about her. Too bad if she only got a pinch of the treasure, no matter what. She wouldn't know the difference anyway. Do-gooders know so little about treasure. He glanced over at her, fingering flowers. Pathetic? Admirable?

For several minutes the only sounds came from the swamp—the soft splash of the otters, the cry of a hawk, the rustling of leaves. Dhamon listened to the land, smelled it, let the scent of the swamp roses luxuriate in his mouth. He watched Feril, who sat unmoving, head still tipped up and eyes searching for something.

What did she really want? What did he really want?

Feril *and* his treasure, he knew. Impossible to have both, it seemed.

He closed his eyes and tried to recall the Feril of old. She was so light now, his scales so thick, he couldn't even feel her when she touched him. He could faintly smell her and the flowers she clutched. In the back of his mind he saw her from years ago—the proud, strong Feril with long hair and tattoos on her face, and the Feril now. If he was a man, he could feel the softness of her skin again.

What did he want?

Ragh sat against the trunk of a pin oak, fingers interlaced across his stomach. "Needle, tonight, last night, I've not . . ."

"You don't like my cooking?"

"No. I mean, yes, I do. Very much. I was going to say I've not enjoyed cooked food this much for some time."

"Cooking's for civilized folk, Ragh. Never thought of draconians as . . ." She stopped and scowled, half at herself. "Sorry, didn't quite mean it like that. I just sort of . . . used to . . . picture draconians as eating things raw, all the time."

"Like wild animals."

"And more for eating elves than keeping company with them."

Ragh swatted a beetle crawling on his knee. "You'd be picturing us right, for the most part."

"I see now that you're not a typical draconian." Grannaluured was fishing around in her pack, tugging out her pillow and a cloak, then pulling out a drinking flask and tossing it over to the grateful sivak.

"Most of the times I had cooked meals I was wearing someone else's form—a dwarf, an elf, a human . . . they all can stroll inside a tavern and order up the special of the evening. A draconian . . . well, there's not many places we can do that safely, though I'll admit to frequenting a few inns in Shrentak when I worked for Sable." He held up the flask, running his fingers around the lip. "What's this we're drinking tonight?"

"That's real good stuff, Ragh. Dwarven ale made deep under the mountain. Came from a master brewer I spent some time with. You drink it down and it'll lighten the load in my pack. Maybe when that ale fuzzies your brain a little, you'll let me give you a tattoo and tell me the tale of what happened to your wings."

Ragh grimaced. "No to the tattoo. You can give another one to the elf if you want to lighten that pack by getting rid of some of that paint."

"Dye."

"As for the wings . . ." He pulled the cork out of the flask and took a deep pull. "In the memory of the Dark Queen, this is good stuff, Needle."

"As for the wings?"

"I mentioned that I used to serve the overlord Sable. I'm not proud of it, but I've done lots of things I'm not proud of. Anyway, one day she tossed me off to one of her minions . . . or so I've been told. There are some things I don't remember, and losing my wings is one of them." He took another long swig. "I'm glad I don't remember that part, Needle, but I do remember the flying. Wonderful flying . . ." He finished the ale and let the flask fall from his fingers. He leaned his head back against the trunk and closed his eyes.

He didn't open them again until some time had passed. It was deep in the evening; owls were flying overhead. There was no sign of Dhamon or Feril, though that didn't surprise the sivak. He figured they were still talking somewhere. They both liked to talk; they could talk a kender's head off.

What did surprise him was the female dwarf. Enough moonlight had filtered down so that he could see her plainly. She had dragged the satchels under a narrow cedar and was rooting through the one he'd been carrying, pulling out the small magical baubles and holding them up to inspect them, one by one.

Ragh's tongue was thick, and when he made an attempt to shout to her—wanting to warn her to take care—no words came out. He tried to stand and his first attempt met with abject failure. He was dizzier than he'd ever been. True, he'd finished off the flask, and though he recognized potent ale when he drank it, it shouldn't have been enough to make him feel so dumb-headed and weak.

Did you drug me? he mouthed. *Poison me?*

He tried to get up again, this time getting to his knees just as the dwarf pulled out two vials filled with magical elixir. With a harrumph, she dashed them against the tree and dug into the satchel again.

"Hey," Ragh managed. "Stop that!" The words came out all strung together and unintelligible, but his voice was loud and caught her attention.

She whirled around, suddenly agile despite her years, dropped his pack and stepped on it, grinding her heel against its precious contents. "Ragh, you should've stayed sleeping," Grannaluured said as she reached for her pick. Ragh wobbled to his feet. Then she reached for the pack with Obelia inside and put it on her back. "Sleeping, you'd be the innocent, and here I was starting to like you."

The draconian readied himself for her charge, though he was having a hard enough time just standing. Instead, she surprised him one last time, grabbing up the satchel she'd stepped on and dashing away between the trunks of two weeping cedars.

"Damn," he said as he lurched after her, careening into trees and tripping over exposed roots. "Damn it, Needle. I was getting to really like you, too."

Hours had passed, hours of circular talk without any decision. It seemed to Feril that Dhamon was genuinely torn. That maybe he was better off as a dragon.

"I think you like flying, this swamp, everything better as a dragon."

"No. There's one thing that will never be . . . better."

"What is that?"

"I've thought long and long about it, Feril. I want to be with you. I know I frighten you as a dragon. I know that I have a chance with you, if I become human again, so I want to be human, but I fear you'll leave again."

She stood, balancing on his snout, in the darkness finding a trace of her own reflection in his huge shiny eyes. She let the flowers fall from her fingers. "You don't frighten me, Dhamon. Not as a dragon, or human. I won't ever leave."

"Dhamon! Feril!" Ragh stumbled into the clearing. "Needle, she's not the sweetheart we thought her to be. She's stolen the magic trinkets from the lake and fled, and she's got the pack with the Qualinesti spirit in it." He waved his arm, indicating the direction he thought she'd gone in. "It's my fault, I trusted her. By the memory of the Dark Queen's heads, I've no idea where she went."

"Then we're wasting time," Dhamon said. "Let's go."

Dhamon didn't dare fly here; Sable's minions would have passed the alarm, so they crashed through the darkness. Dhamon concentrated on the smell of the dwarf, grateful she'd been working in the mines so long and was rather pungent. He had been taken in by her, too. Perhaps she'd been genuine at first, but their tales about Dhamon, dragon scales, and potent magic artifacts had struck a greedy chord. She had been eyeing their packs and lusting after the magic inside.

It was near dawn when they caught up with her, as the female dwarf had taken a twisting, turning course, at times criss-crossing a sluggish river in an attempt to lose them. Her bootprints here and there were filled with water.

"I'll give her a nod for her courage," Ragh said. "All alone in this swamp, a dwarf. She's gutsy. Even I don't travel through this swamp alone."

The sky was lightening; they could see through the gaps overhead. Dhamon pointed a talon toward small objects that she'd dropped. Feril and Ragh were quick to scoop up all the beads and tiny figurines they could gather.

"She doesn't realize all of this stuff is valuable," Ragh said. "She's not a wizard, so she can't know. She seems to be hoarding the gold and silver bits." He scowled to spot a carved turtle, missing its head, strewn on their path. He dropped the once-magical item, knowing it was useless now. "Maybe she's just so mad at us for losing Feldspar and Campfire that she's trying to punish us."

"Maybe." This from Dhamon, who was stretching his neck between the trunks of bald cypress trees. "It's thick up ahead. I can't go any farther. Ragh!"

Ragh left the collection of figurines and beads and plunged ahead. The intertwining branches blocked most of the light, but Ragh could see the dwarf now.

Grannaluured was hunched over one of the stolen satchels, back to a reed-thin gum, pick raised above the remainder of the magical baubles that were scattered on the ground in front of her. She was muttering to herself. Nutty as a fruitcake, Ragh told himself sadly. In her left hand was a scroll, one that Feril and Obelia had said was necessary for the spell they intended to cast on Dhamon.

"Stop what you're doing, Needle!" Ragh approached slowly now, hands out to his side. "We're sorry about your mining friends. The quake wasn't our fault, either. I know you have grudges against us, but this is not healthy, what you're doing."

"This is not about Campfire, Feldspar, or Churt." Grannaluured said as she turned, glaring at him, an anger in her eyes that gave the sivak pause. "And it's not about losing the dragonmetal or the mine collapsing." She drove the pick down on a tiny glass. Sparks erupted when it shattered. She raised the pick again.

Ragh ran at her, splashing water as his feet pounded across the marshy ground. "That's enough, Needle!"

"Don't hurt her!" Feril cried, close behind. She fast followed the sivak, cradling her broken arm. "Let's talk to her first! See why . . ."

Ragh had already leaped at the dwarf. Grannaluured's pick sliced the air beneath his feet. She had pulled back for another swing when Ragh bowled into her, slamming her back into the tree.

He thought the impact would have stunned her, but she was still active, struggling against him, at first trying to jab him with the pick, then dropping it and kicking furiously at his legs.

"There now, Needle," he said, grunting. "Don't make it worse on yourself." He pinned her arms to the ground, grimacing as she landed a few solid kicks to his stomach.

"Ragh, let her up!" Feril was at his side, tugging him off Grannaluured. "Don't hurt her."

"Because she's old? Because we killed a couple of her friends? Because she just ruined a lot of the magical stuff we needed to make Dhamon human again?" Spittle flew from the sivak's lips as he swiped a claw across her chest. "Don't hurt her because she's a good cook, maybe? That's the only good reason I can think of not to kill her here and now."

The Kagonesti continued to try to pull him off the dwarf. Finally Ragh gave in, stepping back and planting his feet on the pick so the dwarf couldn't grab it again. Grannaluured scrambled up, and Ragh grabbed the other pack off her back. She backed up against the tree. The chainmail shirt she wore was shredded in the front by the dragonmetal-tipped claws of the sivak. Where he had cut through the chain-metal, no flesh was revealed. Instead, a black scale gleamed on her body.

Ragh gasped in horror, pointing for Feril's benefit. "Look! She's an agent of Sable! Dhamon," he shouted for the dragon's benefit, "she wears the Black's scale. Just like you wore Malys's scale!"

The scale was black as midnight, covering Grannaluured's chest and abdomen. The scale was bigger than the one that had been branded against Dhamon's human leg, and it was solid, not streaked with silver as Dhamon's had been.

"It had to have come from Sable," Ragh hissed. "No other dragon on Krynn could have . . ."

"We don't know where it came from or why she's cursed with it," Feril cut in. She stepped close to Grannaluured, gently touching the top of the dwarf's head, sticky with blood from Ragh's blows. "I need to heal her."

"No!" Dhamon bellowed, his head thrust above the canopy, his rumbling word shaking the ground and rustling the trees. "Ragh is right. She is one of Sable's evil minions. Feril, remember Malys's scale? This is the same kind."

Feril shook her head as she fussed over Grannaluured. "It's not her fault, any more than it was yours. Don't worry, I'll not let them hurt you, I promise Needle."

Dhamon snorted in contempt, letting out a breath that stirred the trees and undergrowth all the way down to the saw grass. He exchanged a hard look with the sivak. "*Admirable* of you, Feril. Keep your eye on the dwarf, Ragh."

"My pleasure." The draconian bent and grabbed up Grannaluured's pick and tossed it several feet away. "All makes sense now, Dhamon. When I watched Feril and Obelia scry in the water, looking for Sable's scales, we saw faces of men and dwarves. By the Dark Queen's head, I swear now one of them was Needle's mug. Thought nothing of it at the time, but I bet there were scales on all those puppets of Sable. Had to be. Bet ol' Campfire, Churt, and Feldspar had scales, too. Bet their client for the dragonmetal was old Sable herself. Damnable dragon!"

Dhamon's eyes were cloudy. "All the pain I felt from that scale. The dwarves surely have felt the same." He glanced at Feril, busy with her healing efforts.

Ragh shot a question at Grannaluured. "Hey, how long has Sable been inside your head?" He poked her with a talon, drawing an irate look from Feril.

Grannaluured didn't answer for several moments, as Feril continued to treat the wound on her head and prod her elsewhere to make sure she was all right.

"Yes, I serve the mistress of the swamp," Grannaluured answered at last. "For more than two decades I have been blessed to wear her scale."

Dhamon's eyes widened in horror. "Needle . . ." His voice was a whisper, but it rumbled easily to her. "Does Sable see through your eyes?"

Pride filled Grannaluured's face. "Yes, through my eyes," she echoed. "She sees what I see, hears what I hear, feels the wind that washes across me. I am an extension of the mistress of the swamp. Glorious Sable has blessed me. She sees you . . . filthy, disgusting dragon-who-is-not-a-dragon. Stinking, hideous beast! She sees you!"

"She's mad, is what I think," Ragh said. "Driven mad by the damnable Black." He stared at Feril, busy healing, then glanced again at Grannaluured, who was wildly casting her eyes around and muttering to herself. "Elf, she's a lost soul, you must realize that. The dragon's been inside her so long she hasn't got any willpower left."

"Feril knows," Dhamon said sadly. He closed his great eyes, digging his talons into the wet ground. "And Sable knows we're after one of her scales. The dwarf's been stringing us along, hindering us, while Sable waits and watches."

Ragh stabbed a finger at the dwarf. "We can use her scale! Rip it off her traitorous chest and use it for the spell!"

"Yes," Dhamon said.

"No," Feril interjected sharply, "It would kill her."

"So what?" said Ragh. "She's better off dead than having Sable in her head! Dhamon knows that! He prayed for death when he wore Malys's scale."

Feril pushed Ragh's hand away. "Can't use that scale anyway. The magic in it won't be strong enough—it's been siphoned into the dwarf for too long."

"Dhamon, I should kill her."

"Yes, you should," said the dragon. Ragh and Feril both tensed. "Let her be for now, Ragh."

Grannaluured's eyes grew wide. Her voice was even, unsettling. "It doesn't matter what you do to me, silly sivak and stupid Dhamon. Mistress Sable hates you, Dhamon-dragon. She will stop your plans and crush you. She'll make certain you're never human again. She'll make certain you're dead."

Dhamon pulled back from the trees, leaving Ragh and Feril to the dwarf. He moved silently away, listening to their continued heated discussion.

"The other dwarves, Needle . . . were they Sable's spies, too?" Ragh demanded.

The dwarf didn't answer.

"We can't just leave Needle here," Feril said. "She's old and still injured a little."

"She's a needle all right. A needle in our hearts. A needle for Sable, her eyes stabbing us." Ragh snarled at the dwarf. "Sable can watch over her here, if she's a mind to, heal her the rest of the way or let her rot." The draconian squatted and began putting the few undamaged baubles back in the satchel. "You better pray you haven't ruined Dhamon's chances, Needle. If you've broken so much that the spell's beyond us, I'll hunt you down and kill you myself, Sable or no Sable!" To Feril, he added fiercely, "Needle—and Sable—don't know where we're going next. We can still make this work. Oh, she'll be looking for us, and if we don't hurry, some of her other 'eyes' will find us. Let's get moving."

Feril cautiously backed away from Grannaluured, picking up one magical trinket Ragh had missed. She passed him the scroll she had taken away from the dwarf. He carefully put it in the satchel.

"Dhamon's right. I should kill her now," Ragh said. "For her sake and ours."

"He also told you to leave her be."

"I should kill her first and leave her be afterwards. C'mon, let's find Dhamon."

Ragh left first. Feril followed after a few moments, catching up with him and handing him one more figurine that had escaped his notice.

"You can't really feel sorry for Needle," Ragh said.

Feril ruefully touched the tattoo the dwarf had etched on her arm. "There's not enough 'sorry' in this world for what the dragons have wrought," the Kagonesti said.

CHAPTER

23

Dhamon stomped ahead, his tail swiping at small trees and his heavy footfalls crushing the undergrowth. He was so angry he forgot all stealth. He lurched against a golden python wrapped around the trunk of a tree. The beautiful but deadly snake fell limp to the ground, and when Feril hurried by, trying hard to keep up with Dhamon and Ragh, the Kagonesti stared at it sadly.

The dragon paused to feast on a giant-sized crocodile he managed to pin beneath a claw, crunching it quickly, then growling when a second crocodile eluded him. He brushed against the mossy trunk of a shaggybark, coating his side with foul-smelling lichen. Then he stomped through a thick swath of mud and stagnant water, which altered his scent so that he reeked all the worse.

Eventually they reached a spot where the trees grew closer together, and in a pique Dhamon began to swat at them. The trees splintered, bent, and some were uprooted entirely, with their avian occupants taking to the sky, shrieking.

"Dhamon!" Feril screamed to be heard. "Stop this!"

A dozen trees later, he did stop. He turned to regard her, the blood from his crocodile feast still dripping from his mouth. A glimmer of remorse flickered in his dark eyes, then he folded in on himself and became a shadow, never saying anything. For a long time then, he drifted back and forth between Ragh and Feril as they wended their way toward the very heart of Sable's swamp.

Ragh claimed to know the safest route, one that would keep them away from bakali villages and the numerous nests of spawn and abomination that were absolutely loyal to the overlord. This route was also the slowest and involved skirting quicksand bogs that stretched as far across as a lake and cutting through sections of mangrove that boasted treacherous animals. The presence of a dragon would be unusual, so Feril and Ragh urged Dhamon to keep his shadow form.

They stopped near a stagnant pond and Feril called Obelia out of his flask. The ghost was paler than before, his voice weaker, and his eyes empty sockets.

"Elf-fish. I've not seen you for days. I heard such a ruckus."

Feril and Ragh huddled close to the image to hear his weak voice. Indeed, the Qualinesti spirit looked sickly. Their faces showed their concern.

"Yes, I fade," he informed them. "I knew I would, eventually, this far away from Beryl's corpse. I knew as much from the beginning, though I did not care to tell you. Believe me, I did not know it would happen so fast, my elf-fish. I had hoped to help you, then see my sister again, so we could be united. I wanted to tell her that she was right. In life, I never conceded anything to her. I never treated her as lovingly as I should. I wanted her to know she was right about Qualinost, that everyone should have fled. I wanted to say that to her before I faded."

"I'm sure she must realize your good intentions," Feril told the specter, "but it can happen still—you and I will find your sister. We near our goal for Dhamon, and when we are finished with that, all of us will look for Elalage."

Ragh kept quiet, turning his attention to the surface of the pond, which was swirling, more slowly than previous times, with the Qualinesti ghost's magic.

"You'll see," the Kagonesti continued. "We will find your sister together. We'll use our magic to search for her, just like we've searched for the scales. We'll find Qualinesti elves who fled the forest and pinpoint where she might be."

Obelia's image seemed to brighten, then it flickered and wavered. "My magic is ready now. Use it, my elf-fish. Let's help your friend Dhamon."

Together, they concentrated on images of discarded dragon scales. Ragh watched the scrying intently. Curiously, there seemed to be more scales than when they'd scryed this area before—Sable was moving recklessly through her realm, no doubt, and shedding a few. Ragh noted one not far from Dhamon's lair.

"Damn Sable has found our hiding place," Ragh muttered to himself. "Well, fine, fine. It was inevitable. Probably plundered our hoard already. Probably had her damnable bakali haul out every last piece of steel. All that work, all our dreams of treasure, all our pain and risk—all for nothing."

"The air is different here than in the mountains," Feril was telling Obelia, soothing the anxious Qualinesti spirit. "It is heavy and wet and brings so many smells to me. Flowers mostly, so much sweeter than the ones in the forest, but there is also a musky smell underneath everything, of plants rotting and of the earth. It is not . . . unpleasant, but it cuts the sweetness. Too, I can smell wild boar. One passed this way not long ago. Something else I can smell, but cannot name, stalks the boar. This land teems with life. This land is glorious."

Feril was a talker. Ragh yawned. The draconian took the opportunity of taking out one of the magic scrolls and carefully unrolling it. He could speak far more languages than he could read, but he was able to make out most of these words—an old Elvish dialect from before the time of the War of the Lance. He'd studied under wizards a long time ago, long before he'd come under Sable's command. This particular spell didn't look terribly complicated, as it was meant to break magic, not create some spectacular effect or cause any destruction.

"Hmmm," said Ragh, half to himself, as he continued reading. "I think I'm beginning to understand what your ghost friend has in mind. The combination of spells, along with the dragon scale—it might work. It might actually work."

Feril and Obelia weren't paying any attention to him. The elf was continuing to tell Obelia about the swamp, how the rich earth felt between her toes, how unpleasant the pool smelled when she leaned close. "Something rots nearby," she said. "Something small, recently dead. I love this teeming land."

"Perhaps you are right and we will indeed find my sister," Obelia said in a soft voice, "but I am so tired, elf-fish. I did not know specters could grow weary." He weakly retreated into the flask as the image on the water's surface faded.

"Feril . . ." Ragh finally commanded her attention. "That ghost is worse than tired. He isn't looking too healthy . . . I mean, for a dead elf."

She glared at him.

He softened his tone. "Do you think there's anything for us . . . after this?"

"After what?"

"This. After this life. I've heard there are places where spirits dwell, a place beyond Krynn yet close enough that we can almost touch our old haunts. When Obelia's spirit is finally freed, will he go there? Or will he fade to nothingness, as though he never existed? Do you think there really is a place for the dead?"

"Or is this all there is?" she mused sadly. "I wish I knew, Ragh."

He raised a scaly eyebrow. It was the first time she'd called him by his name.

"Maybe there is nothing after this life," she said. "Maybe this . . . what we have here and now . . . is all there ever really is, but does it really matter?"

Ragh got to his feet, putting the pack on his back. He had transferred everything to the one satchel; there was plenty of room for all the items, considering that Grannaluured had destroyed so many of the magic artifacts.

"If this is all there ever is, if when we die, we die forever . . . what's the point . . . of all our struggles, of all the . . ."

"Maybe it's all pointless." Feril walked away from the pond, stopping and staring at a massive black walnut with tangled roots. "Sometimes I wonder."

Ragh hadn't expected that. Such talk, coming from the Kagonesti, really worried the sivak. "Hey, don't get downhearted," the sivak said clumsily. "We're doing our best. We're doing it for Dhamon, right? If this life is all he has, he should have the chance to live it as a human—if that's what he really wants." Ragh took a last look at the stagnant pond. "Even if Sable has found all our treasure," he added with forced cheerfulness, "Dhamon and I can always get more."

Feril looked up, caught his eye, and offered a nod that said more than any words.

It was late afternoon by the time they approached the largest river in the swamp. "The blood of the swamp," Ragh remembered Sable calling the water. He could hear the foul water sloshing and the buzz of the insects that perpetually made life unbearable around the river. "I hate this damnable, stinking swamp."

Feril tilted her head back and stretched a hand up to touch a hanging vine. "I find it beautiful, and I find you puzzling. From what Dhamon's told me, you and he fared well here. Since leaving the swamp and searching for me, you have been tortured by goblins, attacked by dwarves, and nearly squashed by a mountain quake. I'd think you'd be happy to be back in this glorious place. It seems safe by comparison."

Ragh swatted at a cloud of gnats that had found him. He glowered at her. "In case you didn't hear me the first hundred times, I don't like this place, Feril. I don't like the black dragon that made it, and I don't like the foul creatures that crawl across the swamp's earthy bosom." He touched her on the shoulder and pointed south, past a black willow and to a tributary of the river.

Following his fingerpoint, she saw an unnaturally large alligator sunning itself. The beast had six legs and a double tail. Four eyes were perched at the top of its snout. Two other alligators lay near it, these smaller and looking normal.

"Sable likes strange plants and animals," he said. "When the overlords discovered the secret of making spawn—creatures like draconians, but not quite so powerful—Sable instead tried to corrupt ordinary creatures. Oh, she made some of her own spawn all right. I saw dozens of them each day in Shrentak, but she favored ones with arms so long that the creatures' fingers dragged across the ground, wings too short for flying, heads so massive they needed thick collars to keep them upright. Takhisis, the greatest dragon of all, made me. She made all draconians by corrupting eggs. What right do dragons have to interfere so?"

"Never figured a sivak for a philosopher," Feril said, half kidding, but now the elf stared in horror at the mutated alligator. "There is not enough sorry in this world," she repeated. Then she moved ahead, threading her way through another mangrove and not making a sound when thorns slashed at her exposed arms.

It was nearly sunset, and the sivak called for her to stop and rest.

"I'm worn down," he explained. "My feet ache. It'll be dark soon, and maybe Dhamon can fly us a little then. It's not much farther down to that scale somewhere near the river. I think we're getting very close to it, in fact."

She nodded. "The terrain looks familiar from my scrying, but we should be able to make it there on foot before nightfall . . . if we hurry. I want to keep going until it's dark. Then, you're right, perhaps Dhamon can fly us the rest of the way."

He rubbed at his sore legs, marveling at her stamina. "All right. Fine, fine. Keep going, and I'll keep following." As he spoke, her shadow began to separate and expand. Within minutes, Dhamon had joined the discussion.

"I don't like it here," Dhamon said. "It's too quiet."

Ragh's ears pricked up. "You're right. I hadn't noticed. Been talking to Feril too much. Let myself get distracted." His narrowed eyes peered into the foliage all around them. "Don't see anything. Maybe it's a predator of some sort."

The flowered vines hung down so thick everywhere that they formed a curtain. Only shadows could be glimpsed through them. Moss grew dark on the vines.

"Yes, I agree," Feril said. "Something is out there. Maybe it's a predator. Maybe it's something else. I don't care to find out. That's why we should keep moving."

Dhamon took the lead now, passing by rows of cypress and other hardwoods that were tolerant of the steamy temperature and watery soil. A few oddities caught his attention—a water snake with two heads and an unusual scale pattern, an unusually big caiman with knobs on its back that made it look like a fallen tree. Some of the plants were aberrant, too—ferns with woody stems taller than Feril, blades of saw grass towering above the cattails, lianas and strips of moss hanging so thick from branches as to completely cover their host trees.

He stopped at a hedge of buttonwoods, cedar, and willow birch stretching more than forty feet high. A bird cried shrilly, then another. In the distance a large cat snarled. More sounds put Dhamon at ease. He could have sworn he'd been this way before, but he didn't remember it being so lush and overgrown.

Ragh was looking at the high plant wall too, scratching his head. "Short way is through it," the draconian said. "Easy way is around it. The best way is over it, but there is still too much light and we don't need you spotted."

Dhamon shoved his head through the hedge, pushing

over the trunk of a buttonbush and flattening it beneath his massive body. "I vote for the short way."

"The short, *noisy* way," the sivak muttered as he gestured with an arm for Feril to follow first.

The hedge was another of Sable's unnatural creations, they soon discovered. It was part of an ever-changing maze, the trees and bushes growing and shifting in front of their eyes. Feril was captivated, twisting her fingers in the supple branches of a shadberry and seemingly talking to the trees they passed. Rath rolled his eyes in exasperation as Dhamon continued to lead the way.

Soon they were surrounded by the green maze. Ragh felt disoriented. Dhamon grew frustrated and tossed his head back and forth, snapping trees and slashing at vines and trampling grass patches that tried to entangle him.

"Don't hurt the plant life, Dhamon." Feril had come up near one of his legs and was stretching up and tugging on a dewclaw. "Stop killing everything. The trees don't threaten us. I was wrong. We can wait . . . wait until it's dark and we can fly over this. When it's dark, it will be harder for Sable's eyes to see you."

Dhamon twisted his head to look in her eyes. His expression was no longer angry. "It will all grow back, Feril. Don't worry. Any damage I do today will be repaired by tomorrow. The swamp is as strong and magical as the overlord."

That seemed to satisfy Feril, and indeed she began to aid their progress. She stretched out with her senses, intensely feeling the warmth and dampness of the ground beneath her feet, the roots that raced everywhere, the tangled trunks and branches, the clotted leaves. When she twirled her fingers, the branches in front of Dhamon parted. Even Ragh grinned to see that. Feril lost herself in the rhapsody of the magic. Like a musical conductor, she directed the plants and trees to bend out of their way, then spring back into place after they passed by.

This went on for some time. Dhamon happily allowed Feril to lead. Ragh fell behind the two and watched the pair with some envy.

"Legs are really tired, though," Ragh muttered to himself. "Walking through this muck isn't easy. Won't need to walk through this much longer, I trust. Find that scale and get out of here. That's my intention." His voice dropped lower. "He's going to have to hire some bearers to go to his lair, get all the treasure. We have to sell all those gems and jewels and buy us a mansion."

They came upon piles of bones, colored a bright pearly white, probably because the swamp's denizens had picked them so clean they gleamed. Feril stopped at the first pile, her fingers fluttering over a bone longer than herself.

"This was once a young green dragon," she pronounced. "An innocent victim—it was flying over this swamp to reach its home in the Qualinesti forest." At her gesture, the vines ebbed away from the bones so she could inspect them better.

"You can tell all that how?" Dhamon's head loomed over her. Saliva threaded its way over his lower lip and spilled onto her tunic, instantly staining it. She coughed awkwardly and moved out from under him. He instantly edged away, knowing he had upset her.

"Somehow," the Kagonesti said gently, "I can picture the dragon, and I can see Sable flying up toward it. I see Sable's jaws opening then closing on the young green's neck. I sense that it happened quite some time ago."

"During the Dragon Purge."

"Likely, Dhamon. This bone over here is from a different green, a little larger. It was another dragon that met the same fate."

She rose, her magic still controlling the bushes and trees in the maze and urging them to part. They found more and more bones along the way.

"This came from a blue," Feril said, pointing, as she passed another large bone. "Over there, that came from a bronze that presented more of a threat. Sable had some difficulty besting the bronze, and she still bears a scar from that fight. The scar gives her pride but it also displeases her."

A little farther, deeper into the maze, she pointed to other bones. "Those came from a small gold. Sable was especially pleased with this kill. The gold was agile, and its hide was thick."

"Stop." Ragh stared at the last pile of bones. "I keep noticing something, something that makes me want to be somewhere else. There are no skulls. Leg bones, ribs, thin bones from wings—plenty of all those. Not a single head."

"No," Feril admitted. "I don't see any."

Ragh ground the ball of his foot against the mud. "Well, that's bad news. That tells me we're not headed in the right direction. Yeah, this place is familiar to me, but bad familiar. I thought we were on a path toward the river."

"Aren't we?" Dhamon asked. "I can certainly smell the water."

"So can I," Feril said, "and it smells close. It has smelled close for quite some time, though. Come to think of it, the water smells unusually . . ."

"Bad," Ragh finished. "Stale. Not fresh and moving like river water." Ragh smacked his fist against his palm. "Dhamon, let's fly! I don't care how much light there is! Let's make sure of this place, find out where we are. 'Cause I don't think we're near the river at all. I think we've gotten turned around somehow in this damn maze, and it's gotten all quiet again. Notice it? Way too quiet."

Feril tipped her head, listening. "It is quiet again," she agreed, "but not unduly so. I hear cranes in the distance." A moment passed, and she nodded when she heard wings overhead. "I disagree, Ragh. We're close— too close to stop."

Dhamon shrugged, plunging ahead in the same direction, deeper into the maze. All discussion ended. A few minutes later, so did the maze.

Stretching before them was a large lake ringed by tall plants. In the distance to the north, they could see where the river or a large tributary fed into the lake. The surface was calm, a dark blue color speckled with gold from the setting sun. The water was stagnant along the banks and coated with a viscous slime.

"Yes, this place is familiar," Dhamon said. "I realize now I was here years ago, with Rig and Fiona." He looked to the south shore and saw a monstrous totem of skulls. Faint lights shone from the eye sockets—green, blue, red, gold, and more, all the colors the dragons had been in life. At the base of the statue, nearly obscured by the grass that grew tall around it, rested a black dragon scale.

"This was the last place I wanted to come looking for a scale," Ragh grumbled. "Wonderful. And I led us here. What was I thinking?"

"You were thinking you wanted to help your friend," Feril said. She was heading straight toward the totem, eyes fixed on the scale. "There it is."

Ragh followed, glancing over his shoulder and noticing that Dhamon hadn't budged. Dhamon was staring at the lake, which was nearly as large as Nalis Aren. Feril was already at the scale, kneeling in front of it and motioning to Ragh.

"I'll need your help," Feril called to him.

"I suppose you do. I've got the dead Qualinesti, after all," Ragh said, adjusting the satchel on his back, "and all the magical baubles that Needle didn't destroy." He paused, adding for Dhamon's benefit, "Dhamon, I hope with my heart this works. I hope we'll be strolling into a tavern somewhere . . . some place accepting of me . . . and buying tall tankards of ale, the two of us. We even got some clothes in here for you. Feril got 'em in Nalis Aren. They've had a while to dry out."

Dhamon said nothing, just kept staring at his reflection in the lake.

"Ragh!" Feril called, motioning. The sivak loped toward her, handing the satchel to her.

"I hope you can do this fast," Ragh said. "This place sends shivers down my spine."

Feril smoothed the grass away from the scale. It was large, mirror-slick, and shiny; her own expression stared back at her. This scale was loose, just waiting for them—simply shed by Sable and left here, forgotten.

Without a word, Feril began sorting through the trinkets, separating the metal beads from the carved figurines and setting aside the scroll. There were two vials of potions that Grannaluured hadn't smashed, and these Feril snatched up and opened. She poured the contents on the ground, then tossed the vials away.

"Hey, are you supposed to do it that way . . ."

Before the sivak could say anything else, Feril clutched the scale with both hands, lifted it up and brought the tip of it down on one of the figurines, shattering it. She raised the scale and brought it down on another.

"What about Obelia . . . don't you think you should call out the ghost of Obelia and ask for his advice? After all, he's the sorcerer."

She smashed a third trinket, then, to Ragh's astonishment, raised the shield above the flask that held the Qualinesti ghost, bringing it down hard and cracking the flask. A wisp spiraled up as the water and fingerbones from Nalis Aren spilled out.

"Feril! I don't understand . . ."

The Kagonesti whirled on Ragh. Her eyes were black and shiny and filled with an anger and emptiness that was uncharacteristic. She swung Sable's scale at the sivak and he dodged at the last moment, realization dawning on his craggy face.

"By the memory of the Dark Queen, Feril . . . when did Sable take you?" He jumped out of her way again, noticing she wasn't as agile as before, but then Feril wasn't the one doing these things, Ragh knew. It was the overlord. Feril wouldn't have destroyed the magical trinkets. Feril would have called out Obelia.

The Kagonesti's upper lip curled back in a snarl. "In the mountains," she said, her voice strange and hollow and flat. "When the mountain was crashing down I found her, struggling with one of my scales wedged in a crevice. I knew her as a companion of the Dhamon-dragon, so I took her as my eyes. She is my puppet."

It was Sable's voice. The black was speaking through Feril.

"Feril . . . where's the scale, Feril?" Ragh edged away, keeping his eyes fixed on the elf, gesturing wildly to Dhamon. "Sable can't possess you entirely. Tell me, where is the scale that the Black is using to control you?"

Feril obliged with a gloating grin, tugging up her tunic to display a black scale on her stomach. As she dropped the tunic back in place she kicked at the assortment of magical trinkets, scattering them in the tall grass and pools of water.

Ragh felt sick and weak and defeated. "Sable, you foul beast! You could have let him become a human! What does it matter to you? You could have let this magic work. As a human, Dhamon Grimwulf wouldn't have challenged you, would have left this damnable swamp far behind. You would have won!"

"I'll still win," Feril said in the flat, hollow, and eerie voice of Sable, "and the victory will be all the more rewarding. The Dhamon-dragon will be utterly defeated, and his love will have helped destroy him, but I . . . I will deal the killing blow. I will feel his blood pulse over my talons and down my throat."

Feril rushed at Ragh, just as the sivak heard Dhamon's roar from behind him.

CHAPTER

24

The great black dragon had risen from the lake, with at first only her huge eyes visible, like an alligator surfacing slowly in search of prey. Then the entire head, massive and midnight black, scales liquid, overlapping, and gleaming in the pale light of the waning sun, burst from the water. When Sable's eyes locked onto Dhamon's, they sparkled with malevolence. The black overlord snorted in derision at her hated foe, the water around her snout bubbling and hissing.

Then she breathed a gout of acid that raced across the surface of the lake toward the shore. Steam rose from the water. The lake surged as the water boiled furiously and a heavy stench like rotten eggs cascaded through the air.

Sable rose higher, revealing her back spines and serpentine tail. She breathed again, the acid creating a wall of steam that all but obscured her. The incredible stench made all of them choke and gag, even Dhamon.

Sable swam effortlessly toward him, spewing acid into the lake until the surface was like a fiery cauldron.

She reached the shallows and stood, regally revealing her full size. Sable dwarfed Dhamon, easily three times larger than him.

Her legs were as thick and tall as the giant swamp trees. Her muscles rippled and her tail twitched with nervous energy. She clacked her jaws and stretched her neck forward, the breath from her cavernous nostrils blasting the smaller trees into scorched earth and withering leaves, branches, and plant life.

The great dragon was larger and more sinister than ever, Ragh thought, gazing at Sable in horror. The dragon-fear that pulsed outward from her made his knees shake. He glanced at Dhamon, who also appeared to be affected; he was bracing himself, however, for the coming fight. Not Ragh, who struggled to flee, though his legs were rooted. "Run, damn you," the sivak urged himself. "Run. Run. Run."

Behind him Feril threw back her head and laughed hideously with a cackle that belonged to Sable. The Kagonesti dropped the scale and twirled her fingers in the air, and in response, the grass spiraled up to ensnare the sivak's legs.

"You'll die in good time, sivak," Feril said in Sable's voice, "slowly and with great pain, but first she will kill the Dhamon-dragon. I will bathe in his black blood, and we will bless you, sivak. We will let you watch."

Ragh struggled against the plants as vines whipped down from the trees and twisted tightly around his arms. He barely could see anything now as the vines were starting to cover his face. What little he saw made the situation look hopeless. Dhamon had reared back on his hind legs and was beating his wings to buffet Sable. The force of his wings sent tree limbs and water flying, but the overlord's acid breath shot back and caused a noxious cloud to blanket them all. The draconian, choking and gasping, closed his eyes and waited for the end.

Dhamon roared his anger, the sound deafening. "Monster!" he bellowed at Sable. "I have long wanted this battle! I want to feel my teeth sink into your flesh!"

Dhamon lashed out with talons as he let loose with his own formidable breath. It was a stream of gray lace shooting through the noxious cloud. Up and toward Sable's snout it arrowed, hanging momentarily suspended there before striking.

Sable flinched. Gagging and retching, the black overlord lurched back toward deeper water. She whipped her head, her barbels striking the water and sending out a spray in all directions. Acid dribbled from her mouth, causing great billows of steam. The entire lakeshore was drenched in heat and moisture.

Rearing up on her hind legs, the Overlord retaliated, breathing a gout of acid that flew across the water to batter at Dhamon's legs. Again the water roiled, the steam and the foul stench exploded everywhere. The scales on Dhamon's legs burned. He howled in pain. He plowed forward into the water, which bubbled furiously from the acid dribbling from the overlord's mouth. She opened her maw wide, showing teeth as long as pillars, stark white against her black insides, her tongue lolling out, lips curling up, acid shooting forth and hitting Dhamon squarely on his snout.

He didn't howl this time; he gritted his teeth and, as much as he feared water, dived under the steaming lake. He swam toward Sable, feeling as though he was being boiled alive, opened his mouth underwater, and let loose. His poisonous breath lanced into her, and propelling himself with his tail, he slammed into her, his teeth closing on the scales of her abdomen, biting down with all his strength.

Her scales cracked as he sank his teeth into tough flesh. He felt the warmth of blood in his mouth, the taste vile and acidic, scorching his tongue and throat.

Sable gave a great roar, more in surprise than in pain. She spread her wings and beat them furiously, rising above the lake with Dhamon clamped onto her for a brief moment before he fell back into the water and vanished below the surface. She shot up high in the sky, trailing blood and scales, still roaring. Then she turned in midair, angled her head steeply down, and breathed her worst acid breath.

Dhamon was just emerging from the depths, obscured by billowing steam. He ducked under again to escape the worst of the poisonous wind, while all around him hundreds of dead fish floated up and washed against the shore.

The reek of sulfur was so thick that Ragh felt he was suffocating. Even the Kagonesti covered her mouth with her hands and blinked her eyes, trying to clear them.

The draconian had doubled over, entangled by vines. He couldn't speak; his mouth was parched and filled with the deadly stink of Sable, but the black overlord wanted him to watch Dhamon's death. A vine wrapped around his waist and brought him around just as Dhamon came out of the water again, bursting up through the steam and flying like a missile straight toward the overlord.

Scales were slipping off Dhamon, and Ragh could see gaping sores on his friend's head and neck where Sable's acid breath had taken its toll.

Run, Ragh tried to say. Fly away from here. Get away and live.

Now Dhamon met Sable in midair, lunging at the overlord, maneuvering under, then dropping down to stay out of the reach of her deadly claws as he swept back up and behind her. She twisted to breathe more acid at him, showering the sky with her deadly poison, bursting into steam as it struck the lake.

"I lured you here," Feril taunted Ragh in Sable's voice.

Ragh worked up some saliva. "Go ahead . . . gloat."

"I hate you, but that is nothing compared to how much I hate the Dhamon-dragon. I . . ." Feril paused, glancing up with a rapt face to watch Sable wheel around and attack Dhamon, using her tail like a whip. The black overlord cut a gash in Dhamon's right wing, sending him off balance and careening down toward the lake. "He took too much of my land, so he will die for it—die horribly."

Dhamon tucked in his wings as he plunged into the lake. The waters heaved and pitched as more dead fish and alligators bobbed to the surface. After a heartbeat, Dhamon burst up out of the water, streaking impossibly fast toward Sable. More scales fell off Dhamon, but the black dragon was also wounded and losing scales. Sable's tail had begun to twitch uncontrollably.

"You'll die, Dhamon-dragon!" Sable screamed as birds screeched off in every direction. Then she spun in the sky, still surprisingly nimble despite her great bulk and her nagging injuries. Her snout and talons were aimed against Dhamon, rear legs kicking him away and into the uppermost canopy of the trees. Branches broke as he collapsed into the weave, and Sable howled in pleasure.

"No one challenges me," Feril taunted Ragh. "I lured you here using the pathetic ghost from Beryl's lake. This elf body is useful, sivak, and I expect to be Sable's greatest puppet ever." Feril brushed past Ragh, gazing up reverentially at Sable.

The entwined plants continued to hold the draconian captive no matter how much he struggled, yet between thin vines he could watch the battle and Feril.

"I tried to kill you all in the Kharolis Mountain pass," Feril said over her shoulder, in Sable's voice. "I tried to bring the walls down on all of you, but you eluded me. Then in the mines, I tried a different tactic. I took the elf's body and used her to bring you here . . . to this spot. Fitting that I should kill the Dhamon-dragon right here in my own realm, in the place I first landed when I came to Krynn. The swamp will record his death and ensure that no other creature challenges me! No one ever again will challenge my rule. No one will . . ."

Dhamon had disentangled himself from the canopy and was back aloft, streaking toward Sable again. He came at her hard, lashing out with his tail, catching hers and holding it fast as he buffeted the Overlord with his huge wings.

"You can't win, Dhamon," Ragh whispered. "Become a shadow and run from here. Nothing can beat such a foe, my friend. You can't do it alone, not by yourself."

"True. It took a cunning trick and an entire army in the Qualinesti forest of Wayreth to take down the Green Peril." This voice was thin, lacking strength. The sivak was surprised to hear it again, coming from behind him. "No, your friend cannot beat the overlord. I fear the Black is even more formidable than Beryl was."

"Obelia? So you are still here. Well, you'll soon die, me too," Ragh told Obelia. "Dhamon can't save himself, so he certainly can't save us."

The ghost drifted past the draconian's shoulder, lingering there as he gazed at Feril, her attention still riveted on the battle in the sky.

"Did you know about Feril?" Ragh asked Obelia. "Feril and Sable?"

"Ah, my poor, poor elf-fish," murmured Obelia distractedly, addressing Feril and not answering the draconican directly. "This should not be your fate. I thought you were destined for greater things than serving a vile dragon."

Feril inhaled sharply, barely glancing at Obelia. "This elf body," she sneered in Sable's voice, "is destined to serve me for as long as she is useful! That is her great destiny. What is yours, dead one?" Her back rigid and her arms held out straight, she splayed her fingers and aimed at the trees on the far side of the lake.

Sable and Dhamon were locked in struggle above the canopy. The overlord's weight slowly bore Dhamon down toward the trees. Suddenly, the branches whipped and unfurled, grabbing at his limbs and wings. Vines wrapped around him. Dhamon was caught, and Sable's talons flashed in the light of the setting sun.

"Poor, poor elf-fish," Obelia repeated as he stared in dismay. Ragh saw that the specter was barely visible now; he was more like a vague shimmering disturbance in the air. His form inched slowly forward until he stood just behind the unsuspecting Kagonesti, then Obelia put his arms around the elf and embraced her, merging with the elf's body. Feril shuddered. Her lips trembled as Ragh saw Obelia's ghostly fingers reach deep into the elf's heart.

"Be quick, Ragh! There is little, so very little left of me."

Momentarily, Ragh felt the vines relax around him. He tugged at them until he was free.

"The scale," Obelia whispered. "Get the scale."

Not entirely certain what Obelia meant, Ragh rushed toward the skull totem and snatched up the scale Feril had used to shatter some of the magical baubles. He grabbed the scroll tube and pulled the stopper off with his teeth, then raced back to the Kagonesti. He could see the wispy Obelia, inside Feril, gesturing.

"Break the magic of the scale," Obelia whispered, his voice softer than ever.

"How? What do I . . ." Ragh's eyes widened. He understood. The sivak cursed in an ancient language and quickly began to read from the scroll he had flattened on the grass. Obelia appeared over his shoulder, floating, and reading the same words along with him. Feril, Ragh saw at a glance, was in a kind of trance.

Ragh tried to bend Sable's scale. He threw all his strength at it, straining his muscles from the effort. He was enveloped by incredible noise—Sable cursing through Feril's lips, Sable howling in triumph during her battle with Dhamon, trees snapping, the air filled with dragon breath and beating wings.

Finally he heard a loud snap as the scale in his hands cracked. That was followed by a keening wail coming from Feril and from Sable across the lake.

Ragh looked up to see the Kagonesti fall to her knees, hands holding her stomach, her head pitched forward. Looking around, he couldn't see Obelia.

"Feril?" Ragh sucked in air. "Obelia? Feril!"

Slowly she raised her head, tears streaming from her sweat-streaked face. Her breathing was ragged, her palms were red with her blood where she'd gouged herself. She struggled to stand as Ragh edged warily away.

Then he saw her familiar blue eyes, flecked with bits of gold and green; all the harshness and severity had left her face.

"Ragh ... by Habbakuk's grace ... forgive me, I meant to kill you. I used the trees to trap. I couldn't help myself, I ..." She turned to stare across the lake.

Dhamon and Sable were high above the canopy, twisting in air, locked in a death embrace. The last of the sun's rays caught scales from both of them, falling from the sky. Sable was raking Dhamon with her claws. He hung limply in her grasp.

"She's killing him," Feril cried. "By all the gods, she's killing him!"

A determined Ragh picked up the scroll again, seeing that the words were faint but still legible. He hurried to the lakeshore, wading in, dead fish swirling all around him, reaching and searching for something. "There!" Cradling the scroll under his right arm, he pulled out a scale the size of a small shield. "Hope this is one of Sable's," he said to Feril, who had rushed to join him. "Don't have time to be sure."

Then he was out of the water and rushing to the base of the skull totem where he scooped up a few trinkets Feril hadn't destroyed. He spread them on the scale and said a quick prayer to any god that would listen. Then, reading from the scroll, remembering everything Obelia had whispered to him before, he held the scale.

Feril knelt at his side. "Do you know what you are doing, Ragh? If he becomes human now, she'll kill him instantly. Is that what you ..."

Ragh shook his head, reading faster. Feril took Obelia's part, adding her voice to his and directing all of her inner magic into the shield-shaped scale.

All around them the swamp roiled and shook. Sable and Dhamon plunged into the canopy then rose again. The ground shuddered. The creatures of Sable's territory—the natural and the perversely transformed—wailed their panic.

"Now," Ragh said, whispering urgently.

Together, he and Feril, with an effort that depleted all their remaining strength, smashed at the scale, breaking it. They looked skyward.

Dhamon slammed into Sable, giving her a jolt that sent her tumbling end over end toward the lake. She opened her wings in the last instant and hovered. Dhamon, bleeding from dozens of wounds, struck her again, diving forcefully into her from above, with all his weight slamming her down under the water.

The water exploded, steam blasted forth, and the air filled with sulfur. All the remaining creatures of the lake popped, floating and bloated, to the surface. The grass that rimmed the bank receded and turned brown, and the trees lining the shore died.

Ragh and Feril backed away from the lake as a great bubble formed, then erupted, with Dhamon and Sable soaring skyward one last time. Blood and scales dripped from the two dragons. The sky turned the color of dark blood.

It may have been hours or minutes that the two dragons fought on. Sable was the larger, but now seemingly the weaker. Her movements had become slow and jerky, and she had to exert herself merely to stay aloft.

Once, it appeared to Ragh and Feril, she tried to slip away, but Dhamon clamped his jaws on her throat and slashed at her underbelly. His tail twisted around hers to grip her tightly as his wings beat furiously to keep both of them in the air. His wings looked like battered sails, shredded in places. Still, he fought on.

Blood and scales rained down. The world was filled with horrible noise and the poisoned breath and hideous screams of dragons. Sable hissed and spat, twisting and contorting, trying every means of staving off Dhamon.

Feril clutched Ragh's hand. "They are killing each other."

"Pray," Ragh answered. "We can only watch and pray."

Lunitari and Nuitari were starting to rise above the canopy.

Sable screamed deafeningly, lashing out one last desperate time. Then she and Dhamon, clutching each other violently, plummeted into the lake. They fell into the shallows, with the overlord's body cushioning Dhamon's fall.

Ragh and Feril stumbled toward the two dragons as they twitched slowly, almost automatically unraveling from each other. The Overlord bore hundreds of slash marks that glistened with blood in the moonlight. The draconian and the Kagonesti waded out into the water to meet the one crawling wearily onto the bank.

"Dead," Dhamon pronounced, his eyes dazed. "Sable will corrupt nothing again." Blood dripped from his teeth and jaws. His lower lip hung loose and a great gash across the side of his head spilled thick blood into the water.

Feril climbed onto his snout and peered with concern into his massive eyes. "Dhamon, you are magnificent. A dragon like no other. Ragh and I know how to work the spell now! With scales from Sable we can make you human!"

He shook his head, nearly unseating her.

"No!" she wailed, her trembling fingers moving over the small scales around his eyes.

Ragh saw in the same instant that his friend was mortally wounded. His black blood continued to spill into the lake, his breathing growing shallower.

"I can heal you!" Feril searched for the spark inside. Quickly the warmth rushed from her chest and down her arms, into her fingers. "Be strong. Be well. . . ."

Dhamon looked long and hard at her. She briefly caught an image in his huge eyes. It was a face she well remembered from long ago—all angular and handsome with wheat-blond hair and sparkling eyes. Then the great dragon eyes closed as a last wisp of gray lacy breath escaped from his nostrils.

"By all the gods, no!" Feril cried in anguish and anger. "No! By Habbakuk's grace, no!"

Ragh tugged her down and held her, his own tears streaming down his face and onto her shoulder.

CHAPTER

25

They left Sable's corpse to rot in the shallows of the lake. By dawn, the giant alligators that had survived the dragons' battle had returned to feast on the slain overlord.

"Dhamon knew it would take his life, going against Sable," Ragh said ruefully. "There was nothing you or I could have done to save him once it had begun. He didn't fear dying that way. Better than living, cursed as a dragon."

Feril was pale and weak from weeping. Her chest ached as she knelt on the marshy loam and spoke to the land, coaxing it into creating a deep depression and swallowing up the dragon that had been Dhamon Grimwulf. His grave was far from the Overlord's carcass, yet still in sight of the foul water. Not Dhamon's favorite place, but it would have to do.

Another Lake of Death for Krynn, Feril told herself.

The sun would touch the grave in the morning, but the trees that rose above it would shade it and keep it cool during the hottest days. Fitting, Ragh thought, that most of the time Dhamon's grave would lie in shadow.

"If I hadn't been Sable's puppet . . ." Feril began.

"It wouldn't have mattered," Ragh interrupted her. "Sable would have found another way to slay Dhamon. It was fate. He understood that. Nobody can blame you. I was little help to him in the end, too."

Ragh helped tamp down the ground, then stood back as Feril urged the vines to rise up and shroud the massive grave. The sivak bowed his head for several minutes, then went off alone into the trees. When he returned some time later, Feril was sitting on the grave, fingers deep in the earth, her lips still moving.

He waited for her to finish whatever spell or prayer she was invoking. His own throat was dry, his chest tight with anguish. He'd never had a true friend before, so the loss was profound for him. Even breathing seemed an effort.

When she looked up and their eyes met, he held up what he'd found. It was a small chokeberry bush, the kind Dhamon had always favored, and now, with Feril's help, he planted it at the head of his friend's grave. Feril used her magic to strengthen its roots.

"I loved him," the elf said simply, feeling surprised at her own words. "I don't know if I ever told him that."

"You didn't have to. He knew," the sivak answered, equally surprised that the elf was confiding in him, "and he loved you with all of his being. You were the one thing he left the swamp for; you were always in his mind."

"He'll always be here," she said, pointing at her heart and then her head.

The sivak nodded. "A good man, my friend Dhamon."

They stayed at the grave until the sun set and the two moons rose over the lake. They spoke little, only a few sad words. They left when the night birds took flight and the great horned owls went off in search of prey.

"Where are you headed?" Feril asked tentatively. "Do you want to come along with me?"

"What, looking for those Qualinesti elves who left the forest?"

She nodded. "Looking for an old elf woman named Elalage. I need to tell her about her brother Obelia. He, too, was a friend of Dhamon's, to the end." She stared up at Ragh, her eyes still misty. "Who knows? We might stick together. I'm sure you've got some stories to tell that'll pass the time, and I've got some to tell you about Dhamon in the old days, too."

The War of Souls is at an end, but the tales of Krynn continue...

THE SEARCH FOR POWER:
DRAGONS FROM THE WAR OF SOULS

Edited by Margaret Weis

After the War of Souls, dragons are much harder to find, but they should still be avoided. They come in all hues and sizes and can be just as charming and mischievous as they are evil and deadly. The best-known DRAGONLANCE® authors spin tales of these greatest of beasts, in all their variety and splendor.

PRISONER OF HAVEN
The Age of Mortals

Nancy Varian Berberick

Usha and Dezra Majere find that a visit to the city of Haven might make them permanent residents. The two must fight both the forces of the evil dragon overlord and one another in their attempts to free the city—and themselves.

WIZARDS' CONCLAVE
The Age of Mortals

Douglas Niles

The gods have returned to Krynn, but their power is far from secure. Dalamar the Dark, together with the Red Mistress, Jenna of Palanthas, must gather the forces of traditional magic for a momentous battle that will determine the future of sorcery in the world.

THE LAKE OF DEATH
The Age of Mortals

Jean Rabe

Dhamon, a former Dark Knight cursed to roam in dragon form, prays that something left behind in the submerged city of Qualinost has the magical power to make him human again. But gaining such a relic could come at a terrible price: his honor, or the lives of his companions.

October 2004

Follow Mina from the War of Souls into the chaos of post-war Krynn.

AMBER AND ASHES
The Dark Disciple, Volume I
Margaret Weis

With Paladine and Takhisis gone, the lesser gods vie for primacy over Krynn. Recruited to a new faith by a god of evil, Mina leads a religion of the dead, and kender and a holy monk are all that stand in the way of the dark stain spreading across Ansalon.

First in a new series from *New York Times* best-selling author Margaret Weis.

August 2004

Long before the War of the Lance, other heroes made their mark upon Ansalon.

Revisit these classic tales, including the *New York Times*
best-seller *The Legend of Huma*,
in these brand new editions!

THE LEGEND OF HUMA
Heroes, Volume One
Richard A. Knaak

STORMBLADE
Heroes, Volume Two
Nancy Varian Berberick

WEASEL'S LUCK
Heroes, Volume Three
Michael Williams

KAZ THE MINOTAUR
Heroes, Volume Four
Richard A. Knaak

THE GATES OF THORBARDIN
Heroes, Volume Five
Dan Parkinson

GALEN BENIGHTED
Heroes, Volume Six
Michael Williams
November 2004

Strife and warfare tear at the land of Ansalon

FLIGHT OF THE FALLEN
The Linsha Trilogy, Volume Two
Mary H. Herbert

As the Plains of Dust are torn asunder by invading barbarian forces, Rose Knight Linsha Majere is torn between two vows— her pledge to the Knighthood, and her pledge to guard the eggs of the dragon overlord Iyesta. To keep her honor, Linsha will have to make the ultimate sacrifice.

CITY OF THE LOST
The Linsha Trilogy, Volume One
Available Now!

LORD OF THE ROSE
Rise of Solamnia, Volume One
Douglas Niles

In the wake of the War of Souls, the realms of Solamnia are wracked by strife and internecine warfare, and dire external threats lurk on its borders. A young lord, marked by courage and fateful flaws, emerges from the hinterlands. His vow: he will unite the fractious reaches of the ancient knighthood— or die in the attempt.

November 2004

The Ergoth Trilogy

Paul B. Thompson & Tonya C. Cook

Explore the history of the ancient DRAGONLANCE® world!

THE WIZARD'S FATE
Volume Two

The old Emperor is dead, sending shock
waves throughout the Ergoth Empire. Dark
forces gather as two brothers vie bitterly for the
throne. Key to the struggle for succession are
the rogue sorcerer Mandes and peasant general
Lord Tolandruth—sworn enemies of one
another—and the noble lady Tol loves, whose
first loyalty is to her husband, the Crown Prince.

A HERO'S JUSTICE
Volume Three

The Ergoth Empire has been invaded on two
fronts, and the teeming horde streaming across
the plain is no human army. As the warriors
of Ergoth reel back, defeated and broken, the
cry goes up far and wide, "Where is Lord
Tolandruth?!" Banished by Emperor Ackal V, no
one had seen Tol in more than six years. To save
Ergoth, Egrin Raemel's son rides forth to find Tol
and forge an alliance between a kender queen,
an aging beauty, and a lost and brilliant general.

December 2004

A WARRIOR'S JOURNEY
Volume One
Available Now

The Minotaur Wars

Richard A. Knaak

A new trilogy featuring the minotaur race that
continues the story from the *New York Times*
best-selling War of Souls trilogy!

Now available in paperback!
NIGHT OF BLOOD
Volume One

As the War of Souls spreads, a terrible, bloody
coup led by the ambitious General Hotak and
his wife, the High Priestess Nephera, over-
takes the minotaur empire. With legions of
soldiers and the unearthly magic of the Fore-
runners at his command, the new emperor
turns his sights towards Ansalon. But not all
his enemies lie dead...

New in hardcover!
TIDES OF BLOOD
Volume Two

Making a bold pact with the ogres, and with
the assurances of the mysterious warrior-
woman Mina sweetly ringing in his ears, the
minotaur emperor Hotak decides to invade
Ansalon. But betrayal comes from the least
expected quarters, and an escaped slave
called Faros, the last of the blood of the lawful
emperor, stirs up a fresh, vengeance-driven
rebellion.

Legends Trilogy

Margaret Weis & Tracy Hickman

Each volume available for the first time ever in hardcover!

TIME OF THE TWINS
Volume I

Caramon Majere vows to protect Crysania, a
devout cleric, in her quest to save Raistlin from
himself. But both are soon caught in the dark
mage's deadly designs, and their one hope is a
frivolous kender.

WAR OF THE TWINS
Volume II

Catapulted through time by Raistlin's dark
magics, Caramon and Crysania are forced to aid
the mage in his quest to defeat the
Queen of Darkness.

TEST OF THE TWINS
Volume III

As Raistlin's plans come to fruition, Caramon
comes face to face with his destiny. Old friends
and strange allies come to aid him, but Caramon
must take the final step alone.

November 2004

The Elven Nations Trilogy is back in print in all-new editions!

FIRSTBORN
Volume One

Paul B. Thompson & Tonya C. Cook

In moments, the fate of two leaders is decided. Sithas, firstborn son of the elf monarch Sithel, is destined to inherit the crown and kingdom from his father. His twin brother Kith-Kanan, born just a few heartbeats later, must make his own destiny. Together—and apart—the princes will see their world torn asunder for the sake of power, freedom, and love.

New edition in October 2004

THE KINSLAYER WAR
Volume Two

Douglas Niles

Timeless and elegant, the elven realm seems unchanging. But when the dynamic human nation of Ergoth presses on the frontiers of the Silvanesti realm, the elves must awaken—and unite—to turn back the tide of human conquest. Prince Kith-Kanan, returned from exile, holds the key to victory.

New edition in November 2004

THE QUALINESTI
Volume Three

Paul B. Thompson & Tonya C. Cook

Wars done, the weary nations of Krynn turn to rebuilding their exhausted lands. In the mountains, a city devoted to peace, Pax Tharkas, is carved from living stone by elf and dwarf hands. In the new nation of Qualinesti, corruption seeks to undermine this new beginning. A new generation of elves and humans must band together if the noble experiment of Kith-Kanan is to be preserved.

New edition in December 2004

THE NEW ADVENTURES

JOIN A GROUP OF FRIENDS AS THEY UNLOCK MYSTERIES OF THE DRAGONLANCE® WORLD!

TEMPLE OF THE DRAGONSLAYER
Tim Waggoner

Nearra has lost all memory of who she is. With newfound friends, she ventures to an ancient temple where she may uncover her past. Visions of magic haunt her thoughts. And someone is watching.

July 2004

THE DYING KINGDOM
Stephen D. Sullivan

In a near-forgotten kingdom, an ancient evil lurks. As Nearra's dark visions grow stronger, her friends must fight for their lives.

July 2004

THE DRAGON WELL
Dan Willis

Battling a group of bandits, the heroes unleash the mystic power of a dragon well. And none of them will ever be the same.

September 2004

RETURN OF THE SORCERESS
Tim Waggoner

When Nearra and her friends confront the wizard who stole her memory, their faith in each other is put to the ultimate test.

November 2004

For ages 10 and up